CHRISTOPHER BUSH

THE CASE OF THE SEVEN BELLS

With an introduction
by Curtis Evans

DEAN STREET PRESS

Published by Dean Street Press 2019

Copyright © 1949 Christopher Bush

Introduction copyright © 2019 Curtis Evans

First published in 1949 by MacDonald & Co.

Cover by DSP

ISBN 978 1 913054 05 2

www.deanstreetpress.co.uk

CHRISTOPHER BUSH
THE CASE OF THE SEVEN BELLS

CHRISTOPHER BUSH was born Charlie Christmas Bush in Norfolk in 1885. His father was a farm labourer and his mother a milliner. In the early years of his childhood he lived with his aunt and uncle in London before returning to Norfolk aged seven, later winning a scholarship to Thetford Grammar School.

As an adult, Bush worked as a schoolmaster for 27 years, pausing only to fight in World War One, until retiring aged 46 in 1931 to be a full-time novelist. His first novel featuring the eccentric Ludovic Travers was published in 1926, and was followed by 62 additional Travers mysteries. These are all to be republished by Dean Street Press.

Christopher Bush fought again in World War Two, and was elected a member of the prestigious Detection Club. He died in 1973.

INTRODUCTION

Labouring under Suspicion
Christopher Bush's Crime Fiction in the Postwar Years, 1946-1952

Seven years after the end of the Second World War, Christopher Bush published, under his "Michael Home" pseudonym, *The Brackenford Story* (1952), a mainstream novel in which a onetime country house boots boy, having risen for some time now to the lofty position of butler, laments the passing of traditional English rural life in the new postwar order, as signified by the years in which the left-wing Labour party held sway in the United Kingdom (1945-51). The jacket description of the American edition of *The Brackenford Story* reads, in part:

> *The Brackenford Story* is the story of a changing England. William saw the political enemies of the Hall gradually successful, whittling away the privilege it stood for. He saw squire begin to sell his land, the taxes increase, the great Hall sold, the beautiful trees along the drive cut down. And then with a Second World War, nationalization, rationing, pre-fabricated houses and queuing. William recalled with gratitude the kindness of his masters and their sense of responsibility for others. He saw that the bad old days of Toryism were not so bad after all. And he never lost his sense of outrage at the loss of something he felt was worthy of preservation.

A few years earlier, in July 1949, Anthony Boucher, the postwar dean of American crime fiction reviewers and a highly socially conscious liberal (small "l"), wrote with genial bemusement of the conservatism of British crime writers like Christopher Bush, in his review of Bush's latest crime opus, *The Case of the Housekeeper's Hair* (1948), making topical mention of a certain anti-Utopian novel penned by a distinguished dying tubercular English writer, which had just been published in June. "However much George Orwell, in *Nineteen Eighty-Four*, may foresee the forcible suppression of 'crimethink' under 'Ingsoc,' English socialism in 1949 takes pleasure in exporting mystery novels which disapprove of the Government and everything about it," Boucher observed with wry irony. "Like most of his colleagues, Christopher Bush is tartly critical of the regime; and an understanding of his unreconstructed Tory attitude is necessary if you're to hope to understand the motivations of this novel."

In both the detective novels and mainstream fiction which Christopher Bush published between 1946 and 1952, Bush, like many other distinguished mystery writers of the Golden Age generation (including Agatha Christie, Dorothy L. Sayers, Georgette Heyer, John Dickson Carr, Edmund Crispin, E.R. Punshon, Henry Wade and John Street), indeed was critical of the Labor government and increasingly nostalgic about a past that grew ever more golden in blissful, if perhaps partially chimerical, remembrance. Yet keeping Bush's distinct anti-left bias in mind, fans of classic crime fiction will find between the covers of the author's crime novels from these years--*The Case of the Second Chance* (1946), *The Case of the Curious Client* (1947), *The Case of the Haven Hotel* (1948), *The Case of the Housekeeper's Hair* (1948), *The Case of the Seven Bells* (1949), *The Case of the Purloined Picture* (1949), *The Case of the Happy Warrior* (1950), *The Case of the Corner Cottage* (1951), *The Case of the Fourth Detective* (1951) and *The Case of the Happy Medium* (1952)--fascinating observation of postwar social malaise in the age of British imperial decay and domestic austerity, as well as details about the rise of rationing, restriction and regulation, the burgeoning black market and, withal, that ubiquitous flashily-dressed criminal figure from Forties and Fifties Britain: the spiv (dealer in illicit goods).

Puzzle-minded mystery readers also will find some corking good no-nonsense "fair play" mysteries. "Few writers can equal Christopher Bush in handling a complicated plot while giving the reader a fair chance to solve the riddle himself," avowed the American blurb to *The Case of the Corner Cottage*, while Anthony Boucher applauded Bush's belated return to the American fiction lists after the Second World War, declaring: "It's good to have Mr. Bush back after too long an absence . . . he presents the simon-pure jigsaw-puzzle detective story with unobtrusive competence." Concurrently in the United Kingdom, author Rupert Croft-Cooke, who himself wrote fine detective fiction as "Leo Bruce," pointedly praised Bush's "urbane and intelligent way of dealing with mystery which makes his work much more attractive than the stampeding sensationalism of some of his rivals."

In the pages which follow this introduction by all means attempt, dear readers, to match your keen wits against those of that ever-percipient gentleman sleuth, Ludovic Travers. Frequently in tandem with his old friend Superintendent George Wharton and with occasional input from his smart and sophisticated wife Bernice Haire, the former classical dancer, Ludo continues to hunt, in his capacity as a sort of special consultant to Scotland Yard (or "unofficial expert," as he puts it), more not-quite-canny-enough crooks. Additionally Ludo, a confirmed fan of American crime films like *The Blue Dahlia* (1946) and *Call Northside 777* (1948), comes to find himself in ownership of the Broad Street Detective Agency, perhaps the finest firm of private inquiry agents in London. In these old and new capacities in the postwar world Ludo confronts his greatest cornucopia of daring and dastardly crimes yet.

THE CASE OF THE SEVEN BELLS

Now I had been in the Seven Bells it seemed incredible that there could be such things as razor-slashing, and spivs who laid plans in eating houses, and frightened barmaids.

Ludovic Travers, *The Case of the Seven Bells*

The detective fiction of Christopher Bush's Detection Club contemporary Cecil John Charles Street is characterized by its engaging grounding in solidly "English" settings, particularly the great institution of the British public house, which John Street, like noted authors G.K. Chesterton and H.G. Wells before him (see respectively *The Flying Inn*, 1914, and *The History of Mr. Polly*, 1910), romanticized as a locus of all that was good in his native land. "[N]ever neglect the pub," series policeman Superintendent Hanslet fervently advises a local police inspector in Street's "John Rhode" detective novel *Dead Men at the Folly* (1932). "If the landlord keeps his ears open, he can hear more of what's going on than the squire, the parson, the schoolmaster and the policeman put together. And I'll go so far as to say that if he's a decent, right-minded man, he can do more good in a little place than any of them." In his own detective fiction Christopher Bush employed the pub setting with much less frequency than John Street. When he did do so in *The Case of the Seven Bells* (1949), however, it is significant that it was during the postwar years, a time when many British mystery writers felt that traditional standards were under assault by an iconoclastic Labour government and the disruptive social forces which it and the Second World War had loosed upon the land. In the novel it appears that the sacred precincts of the eponymous public house, the Seven Bells, have been invaded by spivs—those flashy, nasty criminal traffickers in black market goods who were the scourge of British postwar crime fiction.

The Case of the Seven Bells, Christopher Bush's 35th Ludovic Travers detective novel, opens with amateur sleuth Ludo Travers hanging round the premises of Bill Ellice's Broad Street Detective Agency (which, Bush fans should know by now, Ludo hopes to buy and run with his old friend, Superintendent George Wharton, when the "Old General," as he is known, finally retires from Scotland Yard). Loyal Agency secretary Bertha Munney ushers a barmaid, Maud Ethel Brown, into Bill Ellice's office and Ludo's presence. "She was a Londoner, there wasn't a doubt of that, and not common so much as showy," assesses Ludo of "Maudie," as she is known, before the barmaid proceeds to tell her tale of woe. Next door to the Seven Bells, at a café called Porelli's, Maudie explains, she overheard a couple of "flash boys or spivs" planning a robbery at some place called The Grange—and the spivs know she overheard them. Since then these villains have strolled insolently into the Seven Bells and in Maudie's very presence pulled out razors and bantered menacingly and meaningly of foolish women who blabbed to the police when they should not have and of the nasty messes that resultantly had to be made of their formerly pretty faces. Inclined to discount Maudie's story as so much melodrama, Bill Ellice promises to help the petrified barmaid if he can, but before he and Travers have done much to speak of, Maudie Brown has vanished and George Wharton is asking Ludo to help him investigate a murder at a bungalow in Carr's Hill. ("Quiet little part of North London, that. Almost an oasis.") The victim is not Maudie Brown, however, but rather a "resting" actress who goes by the stage name of Audrey Grange! Now Audrey will be forever resting and poor Maudie seems to have been vindicated—but have the bells tolled for Maudie too?

Into another baffling murder case is Ludo Travers thus drawn, along with his investigative allies George Wharton and Bill Ellice and their assorted satellites. Suspects in the case are numerous and the clues queer indeed. Are Harry Quarren and his truculent wife, Maudie's employers at the Seven Bells, holding out information about their missing barmaid? What about Audrey Grange's actor husband, the startlingly handsome Harlan Wyster, star of the hit play *Round Square*—was his and Audrey's marriage on the rocks? What does rival actress Merril Holme, who also stars in *Round Square*, know about the affair, not to mention her brother James? Or Audrey's seemingly doting stepfather and mother, Frank and Clara Merlin? What about that Nosey Parker neighbor of Audrey Grange, Mrs. Ganton, who insists that she heard a baby crying in the bungalow on the night of the murder, though no evidence of any baby has been found. ("What do people do with babies that aren't wanted," askes Mrs. Ganton nastily.) What is the meaning of the photo Audrey had of the popular comic stage performer named Bobinot? And how does the German V2 rocket attack at a Woolworth's department store in Lewisham, South London that took place on November 25, 1944, killing 168 people in the worst V2 attack on England during the war, fit into this cloudy picture? (In this last instance *The Case of the Seven Bells* bears a certain resemblance to an Agatha Christie novel published the previous year.)

All the world's a stage, recall, so read on to see Ludo Travers take yet another of his masterful star turns at detection, once again upstaging a conniving and callous killer in an outstandingly dramatic final act. Curtain. Applause.

Curtis Evans

Chapter I
MAUDIE BROWN

It is not usual perhaps before a problem actually begins to present the reader with a first-class and essential clue, but in that problem which I am calling the Case of the Seven Bells there seems no reason why the reader should not at the very outset be in possession of facts which were well enough known to Bill Ellice, and especially to myself.

As a general statement it is not wrong to say that where a clever murderer has planned exceptionally well, it can be only by some curious slip or circumstance beyond all possibility of anticipation that that murderer comes after all into the hands of the law. But in the Case of the Seven Bells the murderer was clever enough for anything and the planning was perfect. There was apparently nothing that had been overlooked and nothing that didn't go according to plan. There was, in fact, nothing that could be called a slip. Why then was the murderer caught?

This is the reason and this is the clue with which I am about to present you. I don't say the murderer would never have been caught if the weather had been other than it was, for something might ultimately have turned up and given us a vital clue. But there it was. We discovered a murderer for one reason only—that the day on which the Case really opened was remarkably fine and that the next few days were much cooler and generally wet.

So there is the clue and its relevance lies, as I said, in the first day and the first hour in which the Case began. That was on the morning when I listened to the story of Maudie Brown.

I was in Bill Ellice's Detective Agency in Broad Street and it was about ten o'clock on a glorious September morning. In the intervals when there was nothing doing for me at the Yard I dropped in most mornings to lend Bill a chance hand or hear how things were going. Bill wasn't in so I made free of his office as usual and sat at the small table writing a letter to my wife who was with friends in Scotland. I had hardly begun it when Bill came in, and Bill was not in the room a couple of minutes when Bertha Munney—the receptionist-secretary—rang through to say a possible client was waiting.

"Do you know what she wants?" Bill asked.

"She won't say," Bertha told him. "She looks in a bit of a dither."

"Did you tell her we don't do divorce stuff?"

"She says it isn't that."

"Well, what's she look like?"

"A bit common."

"So do I," Bill said with an arch reproval. "Send her in and we'll have a look at her."

Bertha announced her as Miss Brown. Bill shook hands, or rather took the hand she mawkishly held out, and was going to place a chair, but she took the chair I had just hurriedly vacated. And she was certainly in a bit of a dither, as Bertha had put it, for she was looking apprehensively round the room and it was almost a scared look that she gave my harmless self.

"Mr. Travers is my partner," Bill told her unblushingly. "Anything you tell me, Miss Brown, will be regarded as highly confidential. Exactly as it would be with your doctor."

Bill looks rather like a doctor himself. His bedside manner is marvellous—it has to be in his job—and he's as straight as they make them. That's why his Agency has the reputation of being as good as any in town.

"And now what's your trouble, Miss Brown?"

"Well"—she gave a nervous titter—"now I'm here I'm almost ashamed . . . I mean I hardly like to say."

She was a Londoner, there wasn't a doubt of that, and not common so much as showy. The face was lavishly and almost crudely made up. Lipstick had made an unnatural Cupid's bow of what might have been a pretty mouth; rouge and powder gave an artificiality to the cheeks, and under the eyes the skin was darkened, though whether or not that were natural I couldn't tell. Her age seemed about thirty-five. Her hair—as much as could be seen beneath the showily flowered hat—was almost black. In the room was already the scent of some cheap perfume. Her height was just about normal but while her figure gave an impression of slimness, she had a prominent bust. One would have expected to find the legs bulky but they weren't, unless it was the sheen of the cheap silk stockings that gave them a false slimness.

"Suppose you tell me in any case," Bill said quietly. "No harm will be done and it won't cost you anything."

She gave me another quick look, and why I don't know, unless it was part of a general nervousness. Or it might have been that I didn't look like a partner in a detective agency. Bill, for instance, had a quiet blue suit and a soft shirt, while I was wearing a rather natty tussore and a sports tie. Then there was the unusual sight of my vast horn-rims, and my six-foot three of leanness, but whatever it was she even seemed to shy from what I imagined to be a gentle, reassuring smile.

"You just tell me what it's all about," Bill said coaxingly. "We're here to help you. That's our job. What's your Christian name, by the way?"

"Maud. Maud Ethel Brown. Maudie, I'm generally called."

"And the address?" Bill said as he wrote that much down.

"Well, it's the Seven Bells, really. It's at the corner of Hoad Street and Witney Street."

"I know it," Bill said. "And you're employed there, Miss Brown?"

"That's right. In the saloon bar most of the time. This is my day off and as I was coming by I suddenly thought I'd pop in. I mean, I'd seen the name before, only I was feeling worried so I thought I'd come in."

"The very best thing you could have done," Bill told her. "And what is it that's worrying you?"

When George—Superintendent to you—Wharton and I are on a Case and questioning is being done, it's George who does the talking while I watch reactions. There was never a thought of anything serious in my mind that morning, but that's just how things went with Bill and me. He asked the questions and elicited answers and I merely sat and looked and listened. Not that I saw much beyond what I've already told, except that though Maudie Brown had calmed down sufficiently to become almost fluent at times, there was nevertheless an underlying nervousness, and it betrayed itself by the way her fingers fidgeted round the cheap bag which she had placed by her on the table. Now and again the fingers strayed beyond the bag and groped among the papers on which it stood, and all the time she was unaware of what her fingers were doing.

Her story, as I edit it, was this. She was a barmaid at the Seven Bells, of which a Mr. Arthur Quarren was the landlord, and sometimes just before the bar opened in the morning she would slip into Porelli's Café—almost next door—for a quick coffee and what she called a change of air. She could have had something in the pub itself but it was the change of atmosphere more than the coffee that made the difference. On the Tuesday then, she had slipped into Porelli's.

Now Porelli's is one of the old-fashioned type of eating-houses with high-backed seats that make each table for four a kind of separate compartment. Maudie Brown went to the far end near the urn and just after she'd received her coffee and biscuits, she heard two people settling themselves in the compartment that backed on her own. When she saw them later they looked like a couple of flash boys or spivs, one about twenty and the other a bit older. She heard them order coffee.

Now she was leaning back with her head against the partition and soon she was hearing fragments of conversation. A word that sounded like *grange* was repeated more than once, and there was a mention of a car and jewellery, and soon she was realising that the two were planning some sort of robbery. That was what she was to be sure of later, in fact, as a result of what subsequently happened.

"Probably at some place or other called The Grange," Bill said. "And what happened next, Miss Brown?"

"Well, it was as I came out. They heard me moving and they was staring like anything. Just as if they was scared I'd heard what they'd been saying."

Obviously they'd thought the compartment beyond them was empty. Maudie paid her small account and scurried back to the Seven Bells, but when she turned the corner to Hoad Street she looked back. There were the two men just coming out of Porelli's and looking each way to see, as she thought, where she'd gone. That scared her rather badly, but it was nothing to what was to happen the following night—the Wednesday.

At about nine o'clock the two men came into the saloon bar of the Seven Bells. One—the younger spiv—ordered two doubles from Harry Eagles, who was helping that night in the saloon, and took them to a corner table. In a few minutes a third man joined them. He was older—about thirty-five she thought—and with spiv written all over him. Asked what she meant by that, she said she knew the type—smartly dressed, moustache trimmed to a thin line, and tough-looking in a flashy sort of way. All sorts of questionable characters used the Seven Bells and customers in the know would whisper who they were, and naturally she couldn't help hearing.

In a moment or two she was aware that the two men had spotted her as the woman who had been in Porelli's. The elder came to the bar—and to her instead of Harry—and ordered three doubles.

"Haven't I seen you before somewhere, Miss?"

Maudie plucked up a false courage and told him pertly that maybe he had. Every night except Thursdays she was to be seen where she then was.

"You remind me of someone I used to know," he told her, and gangster-fashion out of the corner of his mouth. "Poor girl! She had a bit of bad luck. Went blabbing to the police about something she'd heard. Then the gang got on to her. Nasty mess they made of her. Carved her face up something shocking."

As if to add a vividness to that brief history he suddenly began trimming his nails with what looked like a safety-razor blade fitted in a short handle. When he took the drinks his look was chill and menacing.

"Funny you should remind me of her," he said as he put the safety-razor blade away. "You don't look the sort who'd open your mouth too wide."

He took the drinks over to the corner where his two pals were sitting and in a few minutes the three left the bar, and on the way out the one who had spoken deliberately waited till he caught her eye again. She was shaking like a leaf, and even when the pub closed that night she hadn't got over it.

"You didn't think of going to the police?" Bill asked.

"Not the police!" she told him quickly, and the scared look in her eyes was for that razor blade.

"What about Mr. Quarren? You didn't mention it to him?"

"I daren't," she said. "Not to a soul."

Her tongue went nervously along the thick red of her lips. "Besides, I didn't know what he'd think."

"What do you mean?"

"Well, I can't really say. Only sometimes I think he's in with some queer sorts himself, the way they go through to the back room and—" A new alarm was on her face. "I oughtn't to have said that. If he ever got to know . . . Besides, it mayn't be right. I mean they might be all right. I mean they might be just ordinary friends of his, or something like that."

"Now don't you start to worry," Bill told her. "Nothing that's said in this room ever gets out."

Then he was wanting to know if there was anything she could suggest. Would she like protection for a few days? But she didn't know what she did want. All she did know, she said, was that she was feeling ever so much better now she'd told someone just what had happened. Then she was opening her handbag as if to pay.

"Just a minute, Miss Brown," Bill said. "I admit I don't see what I can do for you—not until something else happens. One thing you could do if you thought it necessary. Here's my telephone number and we're open day and night. Give me a ring and we'll be at your service at once."

For some reason or other that seemed to scare her again, and Bill sheered tactfully off. And there, in fact, was where the interview virtually ended, and all he could do was use the old convenient phrase about keeping him informed about developments.

"Nothing at all," he told her when she asked how much she owed him. "We haven't done anything for you yet. Personally I don't think we shall have to do anything. In any case I'm sure you needn't worry."

He had pushed the buzzer and Bertha appeared to show her out. She gave Bill a nervous little simper of thanks and that was the last I saw of her, though long after she had gone that scent of hers haunted the room. Bill's bulk hid her at the door and then the door closed. I hastily retrieved my unfinished letter, though it was plain that I'd have to begin all over again, for the paper was crumpled and there were red marks from the cheap polish that had adorned the flashy nails.

"Well, what do you make of everything?" Bill asked me with a sigh.

"Melodramatic," I said, "but I imagine perfectly true."

"Not so melodramatic if you knew the Seven Bells area," Bill said. "Plenty of smart boys in that locality. And what did you think of Maudie?"

I said I hardly knew. Probably she had a heart of gold, but I hadn't seen enough of her to try the acid test. She'd certainly had a scaring.

"Yes," Bill said heavily. "And I'm damned if I can see what we can do for her."

"Why worry about that?" I said. "She won't let you approach the police or her boss, which are the only sensible things to do. But my own idea is that you won't have to do anything. She's been warned to keep her mouth shut, and if she does then she'll come to no harm. All that razor-blade business was bluff and just to ensure that she keeps quiet. If they think she was wise to what they were planning, then they'll have turned the whole thing down. There's only one small point that rather worries me."

"And what's that?"

"Why did they go to the Seven Bells and warn her? If they thought she knew too much, they'd only to keep well away from the locality."

"Plenty of reasons," Bill said. "They might live near the Bells. And it rather struck me that when they went into the Bells last night they were extremely surprised to find that she was the woman in Porelli's. That's why they acted quick."

He slumped into the chair at his desk and had a look at the paper on which he'd noted her name and address.

"Maudie Brown," he said, and frowned. "There was something about her that wasn't quite right and I'm damned if I can think what."

Then he was saying that maybe it was because she was just a bit too showy. Barmaids weren't that type nowadays. And whereas that heavy make-up might be right for the bar of the Seven Bells in artificial light, it didn't seem right for broad daylight and a barmaid's day off.

"Maybe she has acne," I said. George Wharton always says I can theorise at a second's notice. "That make-up was a sort of covering. Besides, it takes all sorts to make a world. Maybe she's the kind that likes plenty of colour."

Bill frowned but said nothing. I asked what he was going to do about her—if at all.

"Not a thing," he said. "She doesn't look as if she could afford to pay for protection. The best thing is to lie low and see if she comes again, or telephones. One thing I would like to know, though—if in the course of the next day or two there's a robbery in the Home Counties at any place that calls itself The Grange."

"There must be almost hundreds of them," I told him. "Besides, she wasn't any too sure that the word she heard was actually *grange*."

Bill waved a dismissive hand.

"I don't like it a bit. Here's a woman who's been threatened in a dirty back-handed way by a cheap crook, and the crook's going to get away with it. That's what hurts."

But, as we agreed, there was nothing we could do. Maudie Brown wasn't a client in actual fact for she'd paid no fee or retainer and yet it would have been a gross breach of confidence to have approached the police against her express wish. All I could say was that I'd have a look at that Seven Bells area, not that that was likely to help.

It was about a ten-minute walk at the leisurely pace at which I went. Had it been a dull morning I might have hurried, but that September sun veneered the drabness of dingy streets and coloured the catacomb-like foundations of the bombed spaces and their gaudy wild flowers. As I neared the Seven Bells there was a shopping centre that swarmed with people. Barrows were along the kerbs and there was a blaring of jazz from a couple of amusement arcades, and a raucous jamming of traffic and the stenches from car exhausts and a pickle factory, and the smell of beer from an open tap-room door. I'm no authority on what are now called spivs, but Hoad Street seemed to me a likely spiritual home.

Porelli's had a good sprinkling of customers, but I found an empty compartment and ordered a coffee. Everything that Maudie Brown had said about overhearing conversations was dead right, for with my head against the partition I could hear almost every word that two women were saying, first about the dubious character of a mutual acquaintance and then about rations. The coffee was incredibly bad but I wasn't forced to drink it, and when I'd paid the necessary threepence I made for the Seven Bells at the corner of Witney Street.

The pub was doing a roaring trade, but the saloon was much less crowded than the public bar and the landlord himself seemed to be in charge since it was Maudie's day off. At the table to which I took my glass of bitter a man confirmed it.

"Yes, that's Arthur Quarren," he said, and then gave me a look. "Haven't seen you in here before, have I?"

I said I'd only been in once before, just over a week ago. And if I'd remembered rightly there'd been a barmaid named—now what was her name?

"Maudie, I expect," the elderly gentleman told me. He was the quiet, philosophic type and evidently an habitué. "She hasn't been here all that long. Knows how to stick up for herself, though."

"I expect that's necessary in this locality."

"Well, you know how it is," he told me mildly. "Loose talk and all that, you know. Some of them think it's clever. No real harm, though, especially when a girl can look after herself."

"Would you call it a rough neighbourhood?"

"All sorts," he said. "You can't go by looks. Decent enough people most of them. Some of the other sort as well. Like everywhere else."

"Plenty of spivs and clever boys?"

"Plenty of *them*," he said. "All posh and pimples. You don't often see them in this bar though."

"I suppose they're capable of some pretty nasty work?"

"Not them," he said. "Black-marketing and sneak-thieving— that's their line. Mind you, though, we have had one or two of the top-notchers in here before now. There was that couple that nearly did that copper in at Hampstead when they were cornered. They were in here the night before it happened. But you can't tell, if you know what I mean. Them as do the big jobs, it don't pay them to be flashy—not as a rule. And this is a well-conducted house. Arthur don't stand for no nonsense. He's got his licence to consider."

He refused a drink from me and got up to go. I had a good look at Quarren who was the very spit of an ex-heavyweight. And there was a certain flashiness about him too. The white, rolled-up shirt sleeves were held up by shining clips; the greyish hair was too closely smarmed down and the quiff too elegantly turned up, and a flashy stone sparkled when he waved his hand. His waistcoat was the old-fashioned double-breasted kind and an old-fashioned gold ring held the loops of his tie in place. But there was nothing showy in his manner as he attended to customers, and he looked the very man for the place and the job.

I made for Aldgate Station when I left the pub and, as far as I was concerned, that seemed all for that day in the matter of Maudie Brown. I did think for a moment of dropping in at the Yard and having a highly confidential word with a certain Chief-Inspector, and then I changed my mind. Bill had introduced me as his partner and, as far as the client went, I *was* a partner, and the same reasons that kept Bill from private action demanded secrecy for myself, and any other argument would have been sheer sophistry. But I was still sure that nothing more would be heard of the matter. Now I had been in the Seven Bells it seemed incredible that there could be such things as razor-slashing, and spivs who laid plans in eating-houses, and frightened barmaids.

I was to be very much wrong. Purely by chance I went straight to my flat at St. Martin's Chambers, and I hadn't been there ten minutes before the telephone bell went. It was Bill Ellice.

"I hoped I might get you," he said. "It's about that Maudie business. You hadn't been gone long before she rang up."

She'd been so agitated that he hadn't been able to get much out of her, but what he did get was this. Almost as soon as she left the office she became aware that she was being followed by that same young tough who'd covertly threatened her in the bar of the Seven Bells. At a corner she had turned and run and when she looked round there was no sign of him. Where she was telephoning from was Liverpool Street Station for she was going on to Chingford to spend the day with a friend. All Bill could tell her to do was not to worry and then the line went dead.

"What are you doing about it?" I wanted to know.

"Precious little I can do," he said. "But I've just sent Hallows round to the Seven Bells to see if he can pick up anything likely. A pretty forlorn hope."

I said I should be in and I'd be glad if he'd give me a ring if there was any more news. And I too didn't see what good Hallows, even if he was Bill's best operative, could do at the Seven Bells. I didn't see what any of us could do except to wait for what next might turn up when Maudie went on duty in the morning. But more than ever I was wishing that we didn't have to be so punctilious. Here was a clear case for action by the police. At the best a woman was being annoyed by a set of cheap toughs and it was galling to think of swine like that swaggering around and threatening with razor-blades and getting away with it.

And something else struck me. Why should it be necessary to threaten Maudie Brown again? Had that crime been committed, the planning of which she had overheard? Had there been more serious consequences than had been anticipated and was it more than ever necessary to ensure that she kept her mouth shut? I didn't know, but the more I thought about it the less I liked it, and it was rather trying work waiting till Bill rang again, and that was not till three o'clock.

Hallows had done good work. He had discovered, for instance, that Maudie Brown slept out. Posing as a cousin who'd just heard where she was working, he had obtained her private address; a necessary thing, for it was there that she might possibly be molested or once more threatened. That address was 37, Welman Street, about a couple of hundred yards north-west of the Elephant and Castle. But when Hallows got there he found it to be a tobacconist's and stationer's—one of those places, in fact, that are used for an accommodation address.

That, as Bill said, complicated matters, though even there I had a theory to account for things. Maudie Brown might have excellent reasons for not wanting the Seven Bells to know her real address. There might be things about herself she didn't want found out. Though she hadn't worn a wedding ring in the office I had noticed on her ungloved hand a mark where a ring had been. Possibly then she was married and didn't want Quarren to know it. There might in fact be a dozen things to account for that use of an accommodation address.

"Hallows could wait near the Seven Bells and pick her up when she arrives in the morning," was all I could suggest.

"And what if she doesn't turn up?"

"What are you implying?"

"Well, she was warned to keep her mouth shut, and she didn't. That fellow who picked her up must have followed her here. He saw her enter and leave a detective agency. What would he think of that? It doesn't look good to me. In fact I'm worried."

"Whatever happens is no responsibility of yours," I told him. "She wouldn't let you do what you wanted to do, and that's that. But why not wait till the morning? Have Hallows waiting as I suggested."

"Wait a minute," he said. "If she was followed to this office, where was she followed from? She didn't sleep at the Bells last night. And she didn't go there this morning. Hallows found that out. That can only mean she was followed from her home. From wherever she slept."

"I don't think so, Bill," I said. "Everything points the other way. But let's leave it. Wait till the morning and for the Lord's sake stop worrying. I'll be along bright and early."

Chapter II
STRANGE SEQUEL

AT NINE O'CLOCK the next morning I was in Bill's office, and outside the rain was coming steadily down. Bill was out, and probably with Hallows. Bertha Munney had just arrived and had taken over from the man on night duty.

"Is anything the matter with the boss, Mr. Travers?" she asked me.

I asked what she meant and she said Bill had been all over the place the previous afternoon and evening. Once he had snapped her head off, and that was pretty rare with him.

Now there's little that Bertha doesn't know about Bill's business so I made no bones about telling her what I thought the trouble was. Besides, in a case dealing with a woman it can do no harm to hear another woman's point of view.

"That's the trouble with Mr. Ellice," she said. "He's too conscientious. What's he worrying himself for? She wasn't a client. There isn't even anything filed."

I said it was a border-line case. She'd consulted Bill and she'd rung him up, and if business was done, then both those would be considered in the matter of payment.

"Well, I didn't like her," Bertha said. "I know I didn't see her for more than a minute or so, but I think she was a bit crackers."

My eyebrows lifted enquiringly.

"All that scared act she put on," Bertha said. "When people are scared they're just quiet and tense, if you know what I mean. They don't act all jittery, not in a private office like this. And look how she was made up. Anyone'd think she had some skin disease."

"She probably had," I said. "And different people react to fear in different ways."

"But what had she got to be frightened about? She'd only to go to the police. She could have had protection and everything else."

Bill came in then and he didn't seem at all nervy. Hallows had both entrances to the Seven Bells under observation, and once he'd seen Maudie Brown enter the pub, he'd merely have to report.

"I've been thinking all this business out," I said, "and there're a couple of things that don't quite fit in."

"You mean that accommodation address?"

"Oh no," I said. "She didn't mention any address. She didn't consciously let us assume that she was living at the Seven Bells. In other words she told us nothing that was actually at variance with her story. You get me so far?"

He thought so.

"Then let's consider her story as a kind of jigsaw. Everything she told us fitted nicely. I went along to Porelli's and the Seven Bells and everything fitted perfectly. Nothing was out of keeping and nothing actually contradicted what she told us. Except in two instances. Two pieces, if you like, didn't quite fit. Probably they could be made to fit with a bit of squeezing, but that isn't the way jigsaws should go. The first is about her being scared. *When* was she scared?"

"When she left Porelli's and saw how the two spivs looked at her."

"Exactly! She overhears something so vague that she *thinks* they're planning a job. She can't tell us what she heard except that it was to do with a grange, and a car and jewellery. Why then should she have been scared when she left Porelli's, even if the two spivs did look a bit startled? They didn't threaten her then. They didn't reach out and grab her arm and ask her what she'd heard. Instead of being scared, she ought to have been the other way. *She* had the whip hand. If they were up to no good, she knew it. What was there to be scared about? She was only a few yards from the pub. Police weren't miles away. In fact there was probably one at the very corner—there was yesterday. All her acquaintances in the pub were round her."

"Yes," said Bill, and frowned. "But she definitely *was* scared the next night when she was threatened with the razor-blade. You think she sort of ornamented the story by putting the fear back a bit. Kidding herself she was scared from the start."

"I don't know why she did it," I said. "I only know that when I thought things over, what I've mentioned didn't strike me as absolutely true. The piece didn't fit exactly in. And the second thing's this. She led us to assume that she'd often seen this place as she passed and knew it was a detective agency. Yours is still the only one that advertises in the principal papers and she might admittedly have seen the name there, but that isn't what she said. She gave us to believe that she'd seen it when she passed. Now when did she pass?"

"On her way to work."

"Quite so. Then if she lives somewhere along the prolongation of a line drawn roughly from the Seven Bells to here, why did she have an accommodation address in the opposite direction? On the other side of the river, in fact, and completely out of her way?"

"Don't know," Bill said. "But as you say, it doesn't fit in. It might fit in if we knew all the answers."

"You mean the answer to why she had an accommodation address, for instance? That could be explained in a dozen ways, as I said. But to go back to what we assume her real address to be. According to her statement about passing here on the way to the pub, it's somewhere north-east of here. And that makes a third piece that doesn't quite fit in. Where was she spending her free day yesterday?"

"At Chingford. Taking a train from Liverpool Street."

"There we are then. She left her home to go to Liverpool Street. But you can't make her home, this office and Liverpool Street anything else but a triangle. Wherever her home is, she couldn't conceivably have had to pass this office to get to Liverpool Street. Her way was simply along one side of the triangle. If she came to Liverpool Street via Broad Street, then she deliberately went round two sides of the triangle. And if you remember, she distinctly said she *happened to be passing*. Why did she happen to be passing this office? She couldn't have been. She must have come here deliberately. And if so, why didn't she say so?"

"Yes," Bill said, and frowned again. "But you can't always find explanations for the things women do. We handle plenty of them here, as you know, and, my God! sometimes they drive you nearly crazy."

"Let's forget it," I said. "What about going out for a coffee?"

It was a quarter-past ten when we got back and almost at once Hallows rang to say that Maudie had not yet turned up, though she was due at ten. Bill told him to stick around till opening time. I suggested I might relieve Hallows and go into the pub myself. It would be easier for me than Hallows, after his posing as Maudie's cousin.

Five minutes after the Seven Bells opened, I was in the saloon bar. My acquaintance of the previous day wasn't there, but when I took my half-tankard from the middle-aged barman, I made for the same corner. There were only three of us in that bar and then a fourth came in.

"Morning, Harry," he said, and then, "What're you doing here? Where's Maudie?"

"She haven't turned up," Harry told him. "First time that have happened. Maudie's always on the dot."

"She'll be along, I reckon."

He took a seat at the bar and had a swig at his usual.

"Nice girl, Maudie. No nonsense about her."

"Maudie's all right," Harry said. "Coming along very nicely, she is."

"How long's she been here now," the other asked. "About three weeks isn't it?"

"Just about," Harry told him. "She used to be at the Old Bear in Kennington before it was blitzed. A different kind of trade to this, though. It took her a day or two to get the hang of things."

"A bit different from that one you had here before her. I couldn't stand her at any price. I don't know why Arthur kept her as long as he did."

"You can't get 'em," Harry said. "Real good barmaids are like diamonds these days."

More customers drifted in and that was all I heard. But it was easy to tell the casuals from the regulars, or so I flattered myself. The casuals would order a drink and then remark on the change of weather and the vagaries of temperature. Some said it was two overcoats colder than the day before, and opinions varied about the rain. Some said it was a hell of a day and others that a drop of rain wouldn't do any harm. Those, I guessed, would be the ones who owned gardens. And so much for the casuals.

The regulars were different. They ordered what they called 'the usual' and expressed surprise at the absence of Maudie. There was a definite relief that Maudie hadn't left and that her absence was only temporary. Maudie, in fact, seemed both popular and respected. And that was something that once more set me off thinking—that the Maudie of Bill's office and the Maudie of the saloon bar didn't fit so snugly into the puzzle as they had done before I entered that bar that morning.

Divest Maudie of the uneasiness at being in a strange office under strange circumstance, and divest her of her fright, and what remained? Not a person, as far as I could see, who could inspire what seemed almost the affection of the regulars of the Seven Bells. I had seen nothing in her to inspire any affection. I hadn't even felt any sympathy, now I came to assess just what I had felt, even while she had told us her tale. What I had felt was an indignation that she should have been so crudely and brutally threatened, but for the woman herself, the Maudie Brown whom I could have touched if I had leaned forward, there had been no particular feeling at all. To me she had been sexless and somehow curious as a specimen, and precious little more.

Just as I was going out, my acquaintance of the previous day came in. I heard his enquiry about Maudie, and then I had a look in the public bar. That was full, and Quarren and a young barman seemed up to the eyes. Then I rang Bill and told him what had happened so far and said I'd get some lunch and then look in at the pub again.

About a quarter of an hour before closing time I took a quick look in the saloon bar. It was fairly full but Harry was coping well enough with the trade. Bill was out when I rang—I knew he was pretty busy—but I left a message with Bertha that I'd be in the Bells again in the course of the evening and then report again. I also said there'd be no need for Hallows to keep the place under observation.

It was still raining steadily that afternoon when I got off the bus at the Elephant and Castle. Welman Street was a kind of tapering off of the main shopping centre and there were few people about. The tobacconist was alone in the shop. He was an elderly, disillusioned-looking man with a mournful moustache and the shop itself had a frowstiness. His only response to an inspection of my Warrant Card was a lifting of the eyebrows. I said my visit was semi-official—which indeed it had to be—and didn't concern him or his shop. What I wanted was information about a Miss Maud Brown.

From under the counter he produced an ancient, dog-eared kind of ledger.

"One letter," he told me. "Received on the 3rd. and called for same day. Nothing since."

"Just over a fortnight ago," I said. "And what was she like? I mean, how did she strike you?"

He did a bit of thinking before he answered that, and then had very little to tell. She had dropped in on the 30th of August and asked if she could have letters sent there, and she paid a sixpenny preliminary fee and that was all. With a grimy finger he showed me the entry in the book.

"Did she seem nervous at all?"

"Most of them are," he told me. "Generally they have some particular reason for using an address and it isn't a reason they'd like made public. But that's no business of mine, if you know what I mean."

I described her appearance and he thought he remembered her. When I said she was a barmaid, he said that might fit her.

Then I wanted to know how people knew they could use the shop as an accommodation address, and he said there was a card in the window, and when I looked, there it was, and a reasonably prominent one at that.

And that was all the information I could get. And if you want to know why I should have taken the trouble to go there at all, I can only say it was the triumph of hope over boredom. I was at a loose end that afternoon, and also I am the possessor of an incredible curiosity. An unsolved problem gnaws at me like an aching tooth, and for me—however unreasonable that may appear to you—Maudie Brown had become very much of a problem. If she hadn't, I should never have risked that scarcely justifiable display of a Warrant Card, for my only excuse might have to be that I'd suspected something suspicious and was prepared to take a risk.

That evening I had an early meal and at half-past seven I was in the saloon bar of the Seven Bells again. It was the fullest I'd seen it—maybe because it was still raining—and with Harry at the bar was a woman of about fifty with a full face and bust and a head of fluffy peroxide hair. It was from her that I ordered my drink and she seemed a bit short-tempered, for she almost snapped at me when I thought she'd forgotten my change.

I stood at the bar for a minute or two for I'd caught sight of that acquaintance of the previous morning. Then a couple sitting by him rose to go and I made my way across. He gave me a nod of recognition.

We mentioned the change in the weather and then I asked who the new barmaid was.

"That's Mrs. Quarren," he told me. "You don't often see her in the bar nowadays. I reckon it's because Friday's always a busy night, and Maudie's not here. Didn't turn up today, so Harry told me."

"Doesn't she sleep in?" I asked guilelessly.

"Between you and me, Mrs. Q. doesn't like them sleeping in," he told me. "There's not a lot of accommodation in any case. Most barmaids sleep out nowadays. It sort of gives them more time to themselves. When you sleep in you never know when you've finished."

"I only saw Maudie once," I said, "but I liked the look of her."

"Maudie's all right," he said. "Likes a joke, mind you, but don't let it get too far. Everyone likes Maudie."

I left it at that, for I didn't want to make questioning obtrusive, and then a friend of his appeared and I shifted up to make room for him. They had a drink with me and then I had one with them, and as it was getting on for nine o'clock I got up to go. And there had been nothing unusual that I'd seen or heard. The occupants of the saloon bar—both the men and their womenfolk—had all seemed decent citizens and never a one of them was my idea of a tough or spiv.

The bar was really crowded now with a terrific fug of tobacco smoke, and a smell that was a mixture of beer, scent, wet clothes and humanity. At the bar Mrs. Quarren was looking hot and bothered, forehead damp and hair wispy. Something suddenly told me to ask her about Maudie.

I edged through to the bar and a man was still just in front.

"Pint of bitter, Ma, please."

"Not so much of the Ma," she told him tartly, and was pretty tight-lipped as she filled the tankard. I edged aside to let him through.

"What's yours?" she asked me.

"Any news about Maudie?" I said.

"Maudie?" she said, and her eyes narrowed. "What's Maudie got to do with you?"

"Just a friendly enquiry," I said mildly. "I wondered if you'd heard when she was coming back."

"I haven't," she told me curtly. "And what's more I don't care if she never comes back."

A man was pushing in alongside me.

"What's yours?" she asked him, and I was left standing there looking like the fool I felt. So I sidled back and made my way out to the cool of the street. The rain was now little more than a damping drizzle.

I went back to the flat before I rang Bill's office and again I had to leave a message. Maudie hadn't turned up, I said, and perhaps Hallows might be on watch again in the morning. I'd be round at the office early. But there I was to be wrong. Very early the next morning the telephone was to ring, and it wouldn't be Bill who was ringing. I'd no idea of that, or that less than an hour later I would get one of the biggest surprises of my life.

It was just before seven o'clock and I was sound asleep when the ringing of the bell woke me. I hooked on my glasses, without which I'm blinder than a mole, and made my way to the telephone. I knew it was Bill Ellice ringing and I guessed he must have some important news.

"Travers speaking," I said.

"This is George Wharton. Are you free at the moment, or not?"

"Free enough, George," I said. "What's up?"

"Tell you later," he told me. "Can you be opposite the Garrick in twenty minutes' time?"

"I'll be there," I said, and then he rang off.

I stood there blinking for a moment and with a feeling of blankness. Everything had been so sudden, and very much of an anti-climax. There was I, all keyed up about Maudie Brown, and Wharton's voice coming out of nowhere and suggesting heaven knew what and heaven knew where. Then I realised I'd precious little time to lose. In fact, by the time I'd shaved and dressed and rung Bill's office to say I'd been called away but would try to ring him later, I had about a minute in which to slip through the short cut to the Garrick. Luckily Wharton was a bit late.

It was a cold, damp morning, more like November than September, and I wished I'd had time for a spot of breakfast. But I had only a couple of minutes to wait. I saw the police car coming and almost as soon as it slowed at the kerb I was in the back with George. His greeting was a bit of a grunt.

"Where're we making for?" I asked him, and had a good look at him as I settled in my corner seat. I hadn't seen him for a month, not that George ever changes. The same old weeping-willow moustache went forward like an opening umbrella as he pursed his lips.

"Carr's Hill."

He gave the information as if it hurt. But one mustn't be impatient with George, who hates his left hand knowing there's also a right. I've worked for best part of twenty years with George, and he still treats me like an apprentice, and if not it's for some guileful reason of his own.

That morning he had on his ancient bowler and the blue overcoat with the worn velvet collar. In the breast pocket of his brown suit would be another stage property that helped to make him look like a mild and henpecked father of a family— the antiquated spectacles in the even more antiquated case. At the moment his massive shoulders were hunched well into the collar as if he was none too warm, and I wasn't exactly perspiring myself.

"Carr's Hill," I said. "Quiet little part of North London, that. Almost an oasis. Good golf course there too. But what's the actual job? A murder case?"

I passed my cigarettes and held the lighter for him. That brought the first thawing out.

"You know almost as much as I do," he told me. "A woman's dead there in a bungalow. A side road that runs alongside the fourth hole. The name seems to be Wyster. A Mrs. Wyster. Shot at close range and no gun."

The streets were clear of traffic and already we were turning left at Finsbury Park. As if afraid to commit himself, George let out a little more, and by the time we were through Enfield, I think I really knew all there was to know. And that was that a constable had been on his usual patrol just before dawn and had heard an unusual noise. Then he saw the garage was open and the car gone. A nearer inspection showed the front door closed but not locked. A holler brought no reply and so he looked inside and there was the woman lying dead in a passage-way. There had been a robbery and the telephone wire was cut. He'd got in touch with his station from the nearest bungalow, and his Detective-Inspector had got in touch with the Yard.

I may be wrong but the country seems to lie much nearer to the North of London than the South. In the outer suburbs there are oases of open country and areas of woodland that have escaped the clutches of the builder. In the case of the land and woods that were separated from the first half of the golf course by Hurst Avenue, the reason was simple, for the golf course itself owned all the land and had originally intended to make on it a subsidiary course.

Our car seemed to be in open country with an extraordinary suddenness. We turned beneath the railway bridge and there we suddenly were in Hurst Avenue and on our left was the golf course, parched and yellow after the long drought. We were going uphill and one bungalow was passed. There was another—a superior brick structure like the last—just short of the crest of the hill. Another hundred yards down the hill and just beyond a tiny wood was a third bungalow. It was called The Croft and it was there that we drew up. Two other cars were drawn in on the grass verge just ahead.

I liked the look of the bungalow. It was well pre-war and a good bit of money had been spent on it, even if it was far from large. But it looked good and its small front garden was nicely laid out and terraced in the uphill slope. Brick steps led up to a roomy porch that had oak seats let in at the sides. A dining-room-lounge had the up-to-date kitchen with a hatchway behind it; on the other side—the nearer to town—were two bedrooms and a handsome bathroom. All that, of course, I was to see later, not that it was important. I mention it to give you an idea of the character of the place, which was one that I'd certainly have liked to have myself. The garage was brick, and spacious too, and approached from the far side by a gravelled stretch, and between garage and bungalow was a path that led to the kitchen door. Just short of the door and parallel to the road was a brick-built shed, the near end used for tools and oddments and the other for fuel. From the porch one had a grand view of the golf course with the clubhouse about half a mile away. To the right of it, in the same fold of ground, was what I guessed to be Carr's Hill Station, and it was there that Hurst Avenue would end. Between The Croft and the railway station was only one more bungalow.

Here I should add that the curtains in every room of the Croft had been closely drawn, to facilitate the search that the burglars had made. The one exception was the kitchen.

Just inside the door to the right was a hall-cloak-room but the passage led on through to give access to the other rooms. The dead woman lay face downwards with her feet just inside the lounge and her body in that wide passage.

"Looks as if she was making for the telephone in the hall there," Wharton said, almost as soon as he saw her, and the Detective-Inspector—Glass was his name—said that was how it had struck him too.

She was quite a young woman and wearing what I should call an evening frock of a rather bright red. But I couldn't see much of her for old Ousten, the police-surgeon, was in the way and then Wharton got down on one knee as well.

"Tip her over gently," Wharton said. "That's it. Just keep her there a minute."

He gave a grunt and got to his feet again. Ousten let the body down.

"Clean through the heart," Wharton said. "The bullet still there. Point-blank range."

I eased my way behind and through to the lounge. Everything was in the devil of a confusion. The drawers of the long sideboard were open and some of its contents and two of its small drawers were on the floor. A desk had its drawers open and its contents scattered around. The tall bookcase in the near recess by the chimney had its bottom open and music sheets and gramophone records were on the oak surround, and the books were all askew on the top shelves. In the corresponding recess a radiogram had its doors open too. Wharton's voice came from behind me and I turned back.

"Belongs to a June Harboard," he was saying. "And who's she when she's at home?"

"She's a film actress," Glass told him. "Now in America, I believe. I think she must have rented it or let it to this Mrs. Wyster. I haven't had time, sir, to—"

"All right, all right. I know you've had no time," Wharton told him testily. "I'm not grumbling. I'm trying to find things out. How did you know, for instance, that her name was Wyster?"

"I saw the milkman," Glass said. "He used to leave the milk outside there in the shed. Mrs. Wyster wasn't an early riser."

"Good," Wharton said, and pursed his lips reflectively. "Wonder just why she was living here. Whose golf bag is that in the hall?"

"Hers, sir," Glass said. "At least it's got A.W. on it." The telephone wire had already been repaired. Above the telephone was a card with a long list of numbers. Wharton consulted it and then did some dialling.

"That the Carr's Hill Clubhouse? . . . I want some information, steward. The name's Wharton. Superintendent Wharton of Scotland Yard . . . That's right. It's about a lady who's at present occupying a bungalow called The Croft in Hurst Avenue. A Mrs. Wyster . . . Really? . . . That's excellent . . . Fine! I may be along to see you, or the secretary . . . Right. Goodbye."

He hung up and took out his notebook and made an entry or two. Then he had a look at us over the tops of his spectacles.

"The steward knows her well. She used to play here quite a lot. She's an actress too, by the way. Her husband's name is Wyster. Her stage name's Grange. Audrey Grange."

CHAPTER III
WHARTON DISAGREES

I COULD hardly believe my ears. I knew well enough that actress's name, but it was that word *Grange* and in that particular context, that knocked me all of a heap. Then I thought it might be a coincidence. Then, and all as it were in the flash of a second, I thought somehow the moment not the right one for telling Wharton what would be a long-winded story. Besides, far better wait till ten o'clock and find out if Maudie Brown had turned up at the Seven Bells.

It is a nervous trick of mine and one of which I have never been able to cure myself, that at any unexpected happening or idea my fingers go to my glasses, and sometimes I find myself giving them an instinctive polish. I was doing that then and George, who knows the habit well enough, was quick to spot it.

"What's up?" he said. "Do you know her?"

"I know the name," I said. "Mind if I have a good look at her?"

The body was stiff but Ousten knelt and gave the head a sideways tilt. It was Audrey Grange, there was never a doubt about that.

"It's Audrey Grange," I said. "You ought to recognise her, George."

"I?" he said, and gave me a glare.

"Didn't you go with Bernice and me"—Bernice is my wife—"to see *Three Angels*? Now do you remember her?"

George hesitated. Maybe he was considering if it was derogatory to his dignity to own up in front of Glass to anything so frivolous as going to the pictures. Then he gave a grunt which seemed to be an assent.

"I saw her in *The Longest Road*," Glass said.

"So did I," I said. "I thought she was about the best of the younger school of English screen actresses. She must have made a packet these last few years. And she had a tremendous future."

"Well, she hasn't got it now," George said, and cut the rhapsodies short. "What about her husband? There must be a Wyster somewhere."

"He must be Harlan Wyster, the actor," I said. "Anybody got a newspaper?"

One of the cameramen produced a *Telegraph* and I had a look at the theatre announcements. I found what I wanted straightaway and perhaps because I had an idea what it was. When one has a wife who's mad about things theatrical, something's bound to stick in the memory.

ORPHEUM. (Ger. 7707) Evgs 7. Thurs. Sats. 2.30.
ROUND SQUARE with Harlan Wyster. Merril Holme.

"There you are," I said. "Playing in *Round Square* at the Orpheum. There's a matinée today so if we want to see him it may have to be this morning."

Wharton went to the telephone. I had another look at the woman who lay across that passageway. What I had expected I don't quite know but to me she was now no more than a woman who lay dead. But perhaps I'd better explain that pictures for me are a kind of soporific in advance. I generally lie for a long time on the borderland of sleep and I need something to push me over the edge, and for that there is nothing like the remembering or recalling of a first-class picture. *Strange Encounter*—and its nostalgic background of Rachmaninoff—so haunted me that for days it bridged and closed the gap between bed and sleep. And *Three Angels* had been such a picture. That woman who lay there had dominated it, and not by thrustfulness or over-acting but by some subtle insinuation that slowly gripped and remorselessly held. I thought her superb, and yet as I sent my mind back and began a quick recalling of that picture—

"Wyster ought to be here in about an hour," George was telling me, and that brought me back to Hurst Avenue. And it was at that very moment that I recalled something else.

"About that picture—*Three Angels*—George. You remember the three women?"

"More or less," George said grudgingly.

"Remember their names? Not that it may be of any importance, but one was Audrey Grange. She was the younger daughter. The mother was June Harboard who owns this bungalow apparently, and the hard-bitten daughter was the Merril Holme who's now playing with Harlan Wyster in *Round Square*."

"All one big happy family," George said. "But where's it get us?"

"I can't say—yet," I said, and then George was asking Ousten how long she'd been dead.

"I don't know that I can say, offhand," Ousten told him. "I might put it roughly at thirty-six hours."

"Round about midnight on Thursday?"

"Somewhere about that. I'll probably narrow it later. If we knew anything about her meals we might get quite a lot from stomach content."

"I'll have a look round," George told him. "You won't be able to get her away till the husband's seen her. That shouldn't be too long."

He made another note or two in his book and then seemed to be aware of Glass again. There was almost an unctuousness in his smile and I thought he was going to clap him on the shoulder.

"I suppose you don't know if there was a daily woman in the house?"

"I don't, sir. But I could find out." He gave a dry smile. "There's a very nosey party lives at the last bungalow you passed before this—the other side of the hill. She'd be bound to know."

"A tall, scraggy woman, is she?"

Glass said she was and Wharton said that in spite of the rain she'd been at her gate peering down the road as our car went by.

"The thing is this, Inspector," Wharton said as if confidentially. "We're finger-printing the place and we want the prints of anyone who had a lawful reason for being here. You might find out about a gardener too. And drop in at the golf course and find out who she played with last, and how much she played. She must have done something with her time. Use your own men and give me a ring when you've found anything out."

"That's thinned things out a bit," Wharton told me when we were in the kitchen. "You try those dresser drawers and I'll look round for signs of a meal."

That kitchen was a housewife's dream—electric cooker, sink fitment, refrigerator, electric iron, washer and toaster, white-tiled floors and walls, and wide windows that gave all the view one could want. I had a look in the drawers of the cream enamelled dresser, and I had a bit of luck. The ration book was there and in it an Emergency Card issued by the Finsbury Park Food Office. I showed it to George.

"Issued for three weeks," he said. "Then she was only intending to stay here three weeks." Then he was giving me a look. "The three weeks is just up!"

"Yes," I said. "It's either remarkably bad luck or else there's something in it."

A moment or two and I found something else—a diary of the usual New Year presentation kind that had been used for scribbled notes about rations and shopping. The front page had the usual personal details list, and some had been filled in. Among them was the number of her car, and that was something we'd been wanting. Wharton told me to get it through to the Yard at once.

When I came back he'd had a find or two. Inside a bottom cupboard of the sink fitment was an airtight refuse bin, and in it he'd found an egg-shell. There were also some stones from plums that had almost certainly been recently stewed. Half a brown loaf was in the bread bin and there was butter in the refrigerator. Ousten didn't seem too excited. Maybe that was her last meal, as he said, but everything depended on when she'd had it.

"The kitchen was spotless so she had time to clean up," Wharton said, and then we sheered off into the dead woman's bedroom, for what with the flash-light and finger-print men everyone seemed in everyone else's way, not that it wouldn't soon sort itself out.

Hers was the front bedroom overlooking the Avenue and the golf course, and it too looked a bit of a wreck. Every drawer had been crudely searched and the contents of the wardrobe were strewn about the floor. Books from a stand on the side-table were on the floor too, and even the clothes had been pulled off the largish single bed. Something caught George's eye and he was making a careful way among the debris towards the dressing-table. What looked like a photograph was tucked into an upper corner of the mirror.

"A damn funny sort of pin-up boy?"

It certainly was. It was a cutting from a newspaper—about six by four—of what looked like a clown, and this clown was seated at a piano with his left hand on the keys and his body and face were turned towards the camera. On the face was a look of the most humorous astonishment. Beneath was the caption:

BOBINOT whose screamingly funny act in SKIP AND JUMP at the Palliceum is drawing all the town.

Wharton removed it with his gloved fingers, had a look at both back and front and handed it to me. It was evidently cut from one of the Sunday pictorials; which, we could soon find out. With my gloved fingers I put it gently back.

"Reckon it was the comical face that appealed to her," George said.

"He might be a friend," was my opinion. "Everyone in his and her profession seems to know everyone else."

"You know him, this Bobinot?"

"I don't," I said. "I admit I'd made up my mind to go to the Palliceum show because I'd heard he was extraordinarily good."

We left the pin-up clown and hunted round generally. If she had had any jewellery, there wasn't a sign of it. And, as George said, there'd been ring marks on her fingers but never a ring, or a bracelet or watch. There was never even a sign of a handbag. I glanced at my own wrist-watch. It was about a quarter to ten, and suddenly I came to a decision.

I never saw George react so curiously as he did to that story I told him—the story of Maudie Brown and the three spivs. There was hardly an interruption for one thing, except to have some point explained, and when I'd finished there was only a slightly pained look by way of upbraiding me for not having told that story the moment I'd heard the woman's name. But the really curious thing was that after he'd shown a startled interest, that interest petered out and it was almost perfunctorily that he listened to that part about the telephoning from Liverpool Street.

"But surely there's a connection," I said. "It couldn't be coincidence. A robbery and a car and presumably jewellery missing, and someone of the name of Grange."

"Everything hinges on who the three men were," he told me. "She said they were spivs. I say they weren't. Spivs don't do a job like this. And they wouldn't shoot to kill. Black-market stuff's their speciality. Even if they had got in here, what would they have been after? Valuable rugs here, aren't there? A couple of good clocks, silver-ware and no end of stuff. That's what they'd have packed the car with, and why? Because it's easy to get rid of.

"And another thing," he went on, with a quick wave of the hand to check an interruption. "They weren't spivs—not that that matters. They were a house-breaking gang. Very well then. What you've said shows they had this place under observation. Therefore they knew the woman would be here when she *was* here. They'd anticipated that, and all they had to do was gag her and tie her up. She couldn't put up a fight. She isn't a hefty great virago. She's a slim-built, ordinary woman. Then why did they have to shoot?"

"Lord knows," I said. "Unless she heard them enter. One lost his head and shot and then they did the ransacking later."

He gave me a look of the most pitying contempt.

"What's happened to your brains nowadays? If you've got any, for God's sake use them! What if she did disturb them? Why should they shoot? Why not collar her? Crack her on the head? Anything—but not shoot. Shooting's a hanging matter. Shooting makes a noise. Cracking on the head doesn't."

I ventured to say the bungalow wasn't near enough to its neighbours for a shot to be heard. Besides, everyone would be asleep.

"That remains to be proved," he told me curtly. "But there's another thing. The light in the passage must have been on. You don't shoot anyone plumb through the heart in the dark or by the light of a torch. That wasn't a chance shot."

"You seem to be suspicious of the whole thing," I had to expostulate.

"Of course I'm suspicious," he told me annoyedly. "But what's the good of talking? I'll find out from Ellice if that barmaid's back on the job."

I stayed there, and I was thinking that maybe I had been a bit obtuse. Everything George had said had been shrewdly to the point. Not that it seemed to me to matter whether or not Maudie Brown had been right in her estimation of the three as spivs. The crux of the matter was just why it had been necessary to shoot.

I made my way towards the passage and as I passed the bed I moved the pillows. I don't know why but after the disorder of the room and the bed itself, maybe it seemed curious that the two pillows should be in place. And there beneath the bottom pillow was a book, still in its gaudy jacket.

Number Thirty was the title and the author a Matthew Riche, and I knew all about it because my wife had read it. It had been a phenomenal seller, and Bernice had raved about it. I had been pestered to read it but had somehow had no time, and then her copy had been taken back to the library. As far as I remembered from her brief synopsis, it was about a cheap apartment house that was number thirty: one of those novels of London life in which one is given a cross-section of the humbler classes by means of the various residents at such a house.

That was all the interest that book now held for me. Audrey Grange had been reading a best-seller. She had kept it under her pillow which showed that she was none too good a sleeper. Maybe she read it by the light of the bed-side lamp in order to get to sleep, just as my mind would run over an interesting film, and if she woke in the night, then the book would bring sleep again. So I replaced it and went on to the passage. Wharton was coming back.

"Ellice says that woman hasn't turned up," he told me, and he was looking a bit serious. "Looks as if we shall have to drop in at the Seven Bells some time later."

Then he was saying that Glass had rung up to say there hadn't been any woman employed at the bungalow for at least a couple of years. Miss Harboard used it only at weekends and when she came down it was usually with a crowd of friends, and presumably everybody turned to and had a dust round and did what jobs there were to do. Lunch and tea could be had at the clubhouse.

There had been a jobbing gardener who came, so Glass thought, two days a week, and he was just on the way to question him.

There was the sound of a car drawing up in the Avenue. Ousten had a look out.

"Looks like the husband," he told us, and Harlan Wyster it was.

Wharton met him at the door, and as soon as he entered I recognised him, for I had seen him several times in various shows in town. He looked about forty and I don't think I've ever seen a more handsome man. He was fairly tall and had a good figure, and his clean-shaven face was of the Attic, patrician type—the kind of face one sees sometimes among clerics or lawyers. He was wearing a heavy overcoat with the collar turned up, and I knew that it must be raining again for he shook the moisture from his bowler hat as he came through the door.

"This is Mr. Ludovic Travers, my colleague," Wharton said gravely. He can be both dignified and impressive when the occasion demands it, just as he can be most other things.

Wyster gave me a quiet smile and a how-do-you-do. He had a beautiful voice, something like Ainley's, but I was noticing that his eyes were never on mine after that briefest necessary second. The eyes were along the passage, as if he had somehow known where the body would be. But it was not there now. The other bedroom had been cleared up and Audrey Grange was lying there on the stretcher, ready for the ambulance.

"A bad business," Wharton said heavily. "And a great shock to you, Mr. Wyster. You'd like to see her before she's taken away?"

Wyster bit his lip. He nodded, as if afraid to trust himself to speak. Wharton gave a backward nod and led the way. Inside the room Ousten drew back the sheet, and Wyster stood there looking down. He bit his lip again, and in spite of that the lip was quivering. Wharton gave me a nudge and Ousten a look and we backed quietly from the room.

Two or three minutes and he came out to the passageway. His voice was now steady.

"I'm sorry, gentlemen, to have . . ."

"That's all right, sir," Wharton told him. "It was a tremendous shock. Perhaps you wouldn't mind coming through to the kitchen. It's the one place where we can have a bit of quiet. That is if you feel like being able to answer one or two essential questions."

"I'll be glad to answer anything," Wyster told him, and all at once his hand rose and the knuckles of the clenched fist were white. "I want the one who did it. That's what I want."

"So do we," Wharton told him sadly. "And I've no doubt we'll get him—or them."

"Them?"

Wharton explained about the robbery, and he placed one of the kitchen chairs. My long legs adapted themselves to the fitment and then Wyster was asking if he might smoke.

There was a general exchange with his taking one of my cigarettes and I one of his and George lighting a pipe. Everything suddenly had less tension and it looked as if we should soon have most of the answers.

"Your wife didn't smoke?" Wharton began.

"No," Wyster said, "and she very rarely drank."

"That's why there was nothing of the sort in the house," Wharton told me with a deliberate touch of the obvious. "But about her being here. I wonder if you'd explain it to us in your own time and way."

Wyster frowned. It was a roundabout sort of story, he said. Audrey—he called her that throughout—had apparently asked June Harboard if she might have the use of the bungalow for a short time as June was going to Hollywood. June had put it into the hands of an agency to let, being terrified that squatters might move in if it were unoccupied, but she was glad to ask the agents to hold it back for a month.

"Your wife wanted a quiet holiday or something?" Wharton asked.

Wyster hesitated. He looked at the tip of his cigarette and frowned. Then he seemed to make up his mind.

"I take it you want me to tell you the absolute truth?"

"I'm sure you'll tell us the absolute truth," countered Wharton gallantly.

"It's going to be difficult," Wyster said, and let out a breath. "But the plain truth is that I didn't know—wasn't supposed to know, rather—where my wife was. But June Harboard—she's a much older woman than my wife and a very dear friend—happened to ring me just before she left and she told me what I've just told you. My wife had merely told me that she was taking a holiday to study a new part." He shrugged his shoulders. "So that was that. I didn't let on to Audrey that I knew where she was going. I had my pride."

"Yes," said Wharton. "Naturally you had."

I could see him hunting for a lead. Then he turned to me.

"You and I lead quite different lives from people like Mr. Wyster. Their hours seem so unnatural for one thing."

I didn't see his drift, but it brought something from Wyster.

"I don't think so," he said. "I mean about us being different in any way. Plenty of husbands and wives live more or less apart. My wife had her work; in fact she lived for nothing but her work. Nothing else counted, at least for the last year or two. And I had my work. It is true we lived at the same flat even if with different bedrooms, but that was about all."

"But you weren't on bad terms?"

"We weren't on any particular terms at all," Wyster said, and without the least bitterness. "Pardon my frankness—but I imagine it's what you want—"

"Of course it's what we want."

"Then I'll say that only in the first year or two of our marriage—that was eight years ago—was my wife at all normal or natural in what you might call our married life. She'd made up her mind to get into pictures and to the top of the tree. More than once I thought she'd married me because I might be a help, and when she found I wasn't—well . . ." He shrugged his shoulders. "But she did realise her ambition. She was a big name, as I know you'll agree. What it cost her I don't know, except perhaps that it sapped her vitality. We never quarrelled, mind you. Brawling is just vulgarity, if you'll pardon anything so trite. We merely slipped gradually into our separate ways, not unlike a brother and sister. I'm pretty sure there was no other man in her life, just as there was no particular other woman in mine."

"I'm grateful for your frankness," Wharton said, "and you may be sure all these confidences will be respected. But how did your wife manage here all alone?"

"She was thoroughly domesticated," Wyster said, and his smile was suddenly warm. "Her mother saw to that. For one thing she was a really excellent cook."

"The mother's still living?"

"Oh, yes. She's a Clara Merlin of 2, Greenwood Street. That's just off Mornington Crescent. The father—stepfather, I should say—is Frank Merlin of the same address."

Wharton took notes while Wyster gave details. Clara Grange's husband had been killed in the last war when Audrey was quite a tiny girl. Two years later Clara married Frank Merlin who was then acting as musical adviser to the Blenheim group of companies touring in Gilbert and Sullivan and grand opera.

"Frank Merlin," I said. "He was a very well known person at one time. Didn't he write a bit too?"

"He did," Wyster said. "Light music, but very good of its kind. His trouble was the usual—swollen-headedness and lifting the elbow. It cost him his job. In fact, he slipped so far down the ladder that he was reduced to taking music pupils, and Clara took in lodgers."

"All the more credit to your wife," I said. "I mean for getting on as she did. She must have been brought up in a pretty hard school."

"Well, the house was Clara's," Wyster said. He was talking quietly and reminiscently but he seemed glad to be talking at all. Maybe there were other things of which he didn't wish to think too much. "It was a tragedy of course—about Frank—but don't mistake me. He was a good husband but for his failing and he absolutely worshipped Audrey. The two were always very close together, maybe because Clara always hated the stage and everything connected with it. She had good cause, of course. Frank was naturally the other way. The theatre was in his blood just as somehow or other it was in Audrey's. Probably it was Frank who gave her her first ideas."

"And how are things there now?" I asked.

"On quite a different footing," he told us, and smiled. "Clara came in for what I believe was quite a nice legacy, and Audrey of course has been very generous. Frank drinks hardly at all and he's got a job. Directing a big new amateur orchestra somewhere in the suburbs."

"I rather like the sound of Frank Merlin," I said. "He seems a bit of a Micawber. I don't know why I should say so, but—"

"As a matter of fact you're dead right," Wyster told me. "He's a really likeable man, mind you. Always optimistic when he was down, and sort of grandiose when he happened to be momentarily up. I'm told he's often seen nowadays where we stage people congregate, throwing his weight about. According to him he's still going to end up as musical director at Covent Garden. But everybody loves him."

"His wife makes him an allowance?"

"I think she does," Wyster said. "Mind you, I don't see a lot of them now. But I do know that this orchestral job is fairly well paying. Frank now has some money of his own. But I'm pretty sure he'll never go back to anything connected with the stage. That's the one thing Clara would never forgive him for. She's proud of Audrey, mind you, and she tolerates me, but after what she went through with Frank, well . . ." And a shrug of the shoulders left it at that.

"Very, very interesting indeed," broke in Wharton. "But to get back to hard facts, if you don't mind me saying so. Your wife's car. It was her own car?"

"Oh, yes." The smile was dry but not at all bitter. "She'd become rather a wealthy person. Hers was an Apollo twelve. Almost new. An expensive car but not showy. Mine's a pre-war Martlet."

"What about jewellery? Had she much?"

"There again I can't help you," Wyster said. "I've seen her wearing some really valuable stuff but I rather think it was kept at her bank. Barclay's in Hayes Street, just off Finsbury Park."

"Then it's no use asking you what she had with her here," Wharton said. "I ought to tell you that we found nothing at all. If she was wearing rings, they were taken off her fingers. There wasn't a watch, a bracelet—there wasn't a thing. The whole place as you may have glimpsed, was ransacked."

"Her mother might help you perhaps," Wyster said. "There was one ring she always wore—a diamond cluster set in platinum. And a quiet-looking but valuable wrist-watch. The bank ought to have a list of the more elaborate stuff. In all probability they have the actual jewellery there."

"What we want is to get out a list of what we're certain was stolen from here," Wharton told him. "I don't give any hopes, mind you, but there's just a chance that they might try pawning it. The sooner a list's out, the better. And what about a will? Do you know if she made one?"

Wyster merely shrugged his shoulders. Then all at once his eyebrows lifted.

"I don't see what a will has really got to do with it."

"With what?"

"Well—you'll pardon me if I'm wrong—it doesn't seem any help towards discovering who murdered my wife." His face was flushing slightly. "Those bastards who shot her—they didn't worry about a will."

"Agreed," Wharton said, and then he was giving a little chuckle. "You're not being questioned or grilled, Mr. Wyster. We're merely listening to some very interesting, and maybe vital information which you've been good enough to give us, and for which we're very grateful—very grateful indeed. All I want to know about a will for, is this: that in it she might have made bequests of certain jewellery. That might have been an additional check on any list we're able to make."

"I'm sorry," he said, and shook his head with a kind of self-reproving. "Perhaps I'm feeling a bit too sensitive. What I hated was that you should think, after what I've told you, that I was likely to profit from her death."

"Not a bit of it," Wharton said. "But there is also the matter of red-tape. Even if we catch these men tomorrow, the Case doesn't end just there. Incredible as it may seem to you, every detail that's had the slightest bearing will have to be noted in the final record."

"In confidence, of course, but everything about your wife and her family will be there," George went on. "When everything's down it'll all be tied up in red-tape and locked away, and that'll be that. I don't know, mind you, but I may even have to ask everyone remotely connected with the Case where they were at from—say—ten o'clock till midnight last Thursday, which was the probable time of the robbery. In your case, of course—"

"I've no objection whatever," Wyster told him, and readily enough. And then he was suddenly frowning. "Part of it's confidential, but I went straight from the theatre to my flat. The show ends just before ten o'clock. Later I went out in my car and spent the night with friends."

"My dear sir, why worry?" Wharton told him and almost amusedly. "At the moment it doesn't matter in the least. What I must say, though, is that Mr. Travers and I would have an easier job if every witness was as helpful as you've been. But just one other little matter that might have to be cleared up. Your wife was taking a holiday to work at a part. Do you happen to know what film or play she was working at?"

"I don't," Wyster said, and for almost the first time I seemed to detect a bitterness. "Any news I had of her work was when we ran across each other and she made a casual remark, or else I had it at second-hand. But Holberg could possibly tell you. He's her agent."

"Tom Holberg?" I said.

"You know him?"

"He used to be my wife's agent," I said. "She was Bernice Haire, the classical dancer."

His face wrinkled with pleasure.

"I remember her well," he said. "My God! What a small world it is."

"Then we might apply to the agent," Wharton said.

"It would certainly be a film story," Wyster told him. "It's some years now since she did anything else."

Wharton got to his feet. I was saying to Wyster that I didn't remember ever seeing him on the screen.

"For an excellent reason," he told me dryly. "I don't go so far as to say that I hate the films but—well, I know where I feel at home."

"The money doesn't interest you?"

"Why should it?" he said. "I make more than I need. I've no family and very few commitments."

That was all except the handshakes and thanks. As they went out I heard Wharton saying he'd give the earliest possible news about developments, and about the available date for the funeral. And there was no lingering at the gate for he was back in a couple of minutes. And he was wanting to know what I had thought of Wyster.

"A nice chap," I said, "and a very good witness. Obviously still fond of his wife in spite of that queer life they led."

"Actors!" George said; and snorted. "Putting on an act is their bread and butter. Give 'em half a second's notice and they'll squeeze out any god's amount of tears. And real tears at that."

"Damnation, George!" I had to say. "Isn't anything sacred to you?"

"Yes," he said. "My job."

"And what's it matter," I said, "if Wyster did shed crocodile tears—not that I think he did. He didn't kill her."

"Who said he did?" he told me, and glared. Then he waved a hand and his tone had changed to a kind of jovial-apologetic.

"You mustn't take things too seriously. All we're doing at the moment is feeling our way. Mind you, though, there were a couple of things that struck me as peculiar."

He waited as usual for me to ask him what they were. "Well, there was that bit about his wife having no other man. But he didn't say he had no other woman. What he said was that he'd no *particular* woman. And that fits in with the second thing— that he wouldn't say exactly where he spent Thursday night."

"You've got a nasty mind," I told him, if not too seriously. "He might have been at a bottle party or gaming house. But why all this worry about Wyster?"

"For a very good reason," George told me. "Because either my name's Robinson or else there's a damn sight more in this case than meets the eye."

CHAPTER IV
MABEL GANTON

I WAS GLAD when George made a remark about the labourer being worthy of his hire. In the refrigerator was a small piece of cheese which we divided, and there's many a worse snack than bread and butter and cheese washed down with a cup of tea, especially when the last meal was overnight.

Sergeant Tritt, in charge of prints, came to report progress while we were eating. New prints were what his people were looking for, and he hadn't found a single one except of the dead woman. The garage was still being worked on, but the most interesting thing so far was that every door handle in the house was clear of prints. The robbery had certainly been committed by what Tritt called 'some of the old hands'. As for the hurriedness of the search, that could be accounted for by the shooting and the need to get away quickly. That, at least, was Tritt's opinion.

"I wish to heaven we had some idea of the time she was in the habit of going to bed," Wharton said to me. "What the devil was there for her to sit up for? The wireless closes down now at eleven."

I said it was only surmise at present that she'd been killed as late as midnight. I also told him about the book I'd found under her pillow, though that didn't seem to interest him. It didn't, as he said, affect the problem of *when* she went to bed. All it told was what she *did* when she went to bed. And that little victory in argument made him open out a bit more.

"It's that shooting that's got me beat," he said. "Something's wrong with it. Think back yourself. Have you ever known it happen before?"

I said that in circumstances that were in any way parallel I certainly hadn't.

"An old hand would never shoot unless it was his way out when he was cornered, and that's rare enough," he said. "And it was so unnecessary. Even suppose she had a gun of her own for protection and came out of the lounge with it in her hand, there still wasn't any necessity to shoot. A gun in the hands of that little woman wouldn't have intimidated toughs like that." He gave a sideways, dubious nod. "There's far more in this than meets the eye."

"But there *was* a robbery."

"Undoubtedly. The car's gone for one thing."

"And you agree that the robbery was done by the three toughs that were in Porelli's?"

"I can't do anything else."

"Very well, then," I said. "All we've got to do is find some testable explanations for the shooting."

If he hadn't been called to the telephone, I knew what he was going to say—that he could put up with anything except my theorising. That's something I've mentioned before about George: one of the bland little manoeuvrings that make his personality the fruity thing it is. I like theorising, as I've said. A problem presents itself and the only method of attack, or so it seems to me, is the Socratic one—to put up questions and suggest answers. Besides, I've always found the method pay. Theorising may be easy to my type of mind, but at least it costs little. I suppose I'm right once in three times, and that's not a bad average. But when I put forward a theory, George has a habit of pooh-poohing it, or rather me. If it turns out to be wide of the mark, there's one more failure of which to remind me. If it turns out well, it suddenly becomes *our* theory. If it turn out an absolute winner, it's as likely as not to be *his*.

It was the Yard calling to say that the car had been found abandoned at Highbury and was being taken along for examination. It hadn't been noticed before—on the Friday morning for instance—because it had been left on a bombed site used unofficially for parking.

"Probably too hot to be handled," George said. "A car like that's too uncommon a make."

Then as he drained the last drops from the pot into his cup, Glass turned up. He had the gardener's prints, though the gardener had never been in the house beyond the kitchen. He was a jobbing gardener and Miss Harboard hadn't kept him on after the end of August when she left England.

"What about the golf?" Wharton wanted to know.

Glass said Miss Grange, or Mrs. Wyster, had had a round by herself on the Thursday morning, starting at about eleven o'clock and had had lunch at the Club. She paid a green fee and she'd only played once before during her stay at The Croft, though some years back she had played often.

"Any good, was she?"

"The pro. says she was pretty fair," Glass said. "Miss Harboard was very good. She used to have parties down up to quite recently and they'd all have lunch and tea there."

"How did she sign the book when she paid her green fee?"

"Simply 'A. Wyster'," Glass said. "I rather gathered she wasn't one for publicity. Also the secretary knew who she was and he agreed that publicity wouldn't do the Club good. People after autographs and pestering and so on."

"Then she was a damn funny film actress," Wharton said.

"Maybe she was," I said. "Remember what her husband said: 'The only thing in life she gave a damn for was the job itself.'"

And then I remembered something I wanted to ask Glass. Why was it that the constable hadn't discovered anything wrong during the Thursday night. What was the difference between that and the Friday tour of duty.

The only difference, Glass said, was that nothing appeared to be wrong when the constable came by in the early hours of the Friday morning. He was cycling, and all he had to do was keep an eye open for anything suspicious. A light on in the early hours might warrant an investigation, for instance. An open garage door would not, even if he saw it, and as it was a dark night, that was extremely unlikely.

"Early this morning was different," he said. "There was a bit of wind and the noise he heard was a garage door. That's what he saw when he got off his bike to investigate the noise. When he came back he tried the front door and it opened. Then he flashed his torch."

"The gates to the garage way were shut?"

"Shut, but not bolted down," Glass said.

Wharton told him about the car's being found at Highbury. "How many ways are there of getting to town from here?" he wanted to know.

"Literally scores, sir," Glass told him. "Go on down the hill to the station and you can turn back either way. The same with the way you came. After that you can branch out all over the place."

"Highbury convey anything to you?"

Glass said it didn't, except that if he were at Finsbury Park and wanted to avoid any traffic, he'd take the back way through Highbury and along Ball's Pond Road to Islington. Then he was asking if he might suggest something.

"About taking the car," he said. "The easiest thing in the world once the garage was open, and they'd do that with her keys. If there were two of them, one would keep an eye on the road and the other'd be at the wheel. Just a touch and the car'd run downhill through the gates. The other'd nip the gates to—so as to make it less suspicious—and then hop in, and the car'd run right down to the station without the engine being turned on at all. No one would hear a thing."

"They certainly did use her keys for the garage," Wharton said. "There's no sign of a forcible entry."

"And one other thing I think I ought to report, sir," Glass said, and I wondered why he should smile. "I don't think there's anything in it myself, but that Mrs. Ganton down the road—the Nosey Parker woman—swears blind she heard the sound of a baby crying up here on the Thursday night. She says it kept her awake and she came up the hill to find out." My eyes had bulged and so had Wharton's. Then I smiled, and for the life of me I don't know why.

"Is she serious?" Wharton asked.

"Serious, sir?" He gave a little snort. "She swears by everything that's sacred that it was a baby. By the way, sir, I don't think she liked Mrs. Wyster. I wouldn't be surprised if she'd come poking her nose in here and had got ticked off."

"A baby," Wharton said. "It couldn't be. How could a woman have a baby at night and be fit for a round of golf the same morning?"

"Well, sir, if you'll pardon me saying so, it's not impossible. I've known women have babies and be doing their housework right up to the very hour."

Wharton's lips pursed out and he was frowning away.

"It might be the reason—only *might*, mind you—for why she was here. Her mother ought to know. And the doctor certainly will."

He made a note in his book.

"By the way, I asked Wyster to break the news to the parents. No use our seeing people till they've got over the initial shock."

He put the book away and did some more frowning. Then he made up his mind.

"You've been doing some good work, Glass."

The Inspector's tail wagged.

"But this looks like being a much more complicated business than we thought. No use panicking. No use hurrying. We've hardly been here five minutes yet and all we're doing at the moment, as I told Mr. Travers, is feeling our way. And I think the best thing is for Mr. Travers to go and see this Mrs. Ganton. I've got some telephoning to do and there may be a job or two for you. After that we'll see. Probably Mr. Travers and I'll be slipping back to town."

It was still raining and that was probably why Mrs. Ganton wasn't peering from her windows. But she must have had a quick ear for she was at the door of Uani before I could ring the bell. Hers was a snug little bungalow and well enough built, but with neither the size nor the class of The Croft.

"If you're selling anything, there's nothing I want," she said, and that before I could even lift my hat.

"I'm selling nothing," I told her, and quite politely. "I'm from the police. I'd like to ask you a few questions."

Most people take a perfunctory look at a Warrant Card. She gave it a thorough inspection and while she was doing it I had a good look at her, for she was fascinating me already. If ever someone came straight out of Dickens—Betsy Trotwood, for example—it was she, for she was wearing a kind of bodice thing that came high up the thin neck and her hair was done up on a tight bun on the very top of her head. She was tall, too, and angular, and with a long, horsey kind of face. Her voice had a snappy sort of tartness, and I put her age at about sixty.

"Perhaps you'd better come in," she said, and thrust the card back at me, and I followed her through a door on the left into a stuffy kind of living-room that was a Victorian survival. But there was never a sign of dust. Mabel Ganton, I gathered, suffered from house-pride.

"What a nice place you have here," I said. "Have you lived in New Zealand?"

She stared.

"The name of the bungalow," I explained, and I pronounced it *wahnee*. "It had a kind of Maori look."

"The name is You-and-I," she told me severely. "My late dear husband and I had it specially built. And now what is it you want to ask me?"

But she didn't give me time to say. She supposed it was something to do with that robbery up the road, if it was a robbery. Not that it was any business of hers, except that she wondered why there hadn't been robberies before. Often they didn't see a policeman for weeks.

"It's more than a robbery," I told her. "Mrs. Wyster—I don't know if you've met her—has been killed. Murdered if you like."

Her mouth gaped wide. The upper plate fell and she snapped her lips quickly to. That gave me time to say why I'd come. Had she heard anything suspicious on the Thursday night. Say, round about midnight.

"Sit down, young man," she told me, and took a seat herself on the plush-covered couch. "The Thursday night, you say."

She screwed up her thin lips as if trying to squeeze some recollection out.

"It depends what you mean by suspicious. I always go to bed at ten o'clock. We always did when my dear husband was alive, and so I do now. Nothing to stay up for, and only wasting electric light, and what with the Government asking us to be careful . . ."

The spate at last oozed to nothing and I got another word in.

"Inspector Glass was here, I believe, and he tells me you did hear something suspicious—something about a baby."

"Ah, that!" she said, and fairly pounced. "Yes, it was on the Thursday night. About nine o'clock. Yes, about nine o'clock. The wireless said there might be thunder so I just had a look out, and then I heard it." She leaned forward. "It was a baby!"

My eyebrows duly lifted.

"I thought to myself, 'What on earth is a baby crying for? No one near here's got a baby.' Then I thought it might be someone coming with a baby in a pram, so I stood there and waited and it still kept on, so I said to myself I'd go and see what it was; so I went up the hill—that's where it was coming from—and sure enough it was coming from The Croft. You could absolutely have knocked me down with a feather. 'There!' I said to myself. 'So that's why she's been living there all alone.' You see, I always knew there was something fishy, as they say, about that woman. A stuck-up hussy, that's what she was. Nearly snapped my head off when I went round in a purely neighbourly way . . ."

"About this baby," I at last managed to say. "Was the crying continuous or intermittent?"

"Well, it was off and on, so to speak. Not real crying. You know how babies keep it up once they start. I ought to know; I had two of my own. But this was sort of sudden-like. Just as if it had a sudden pain and it'd give a sort of cry. Just as if it was hungry and wanted feeding. Sort of fretful. Then it would stop and then it'd begin all over again. It fairly gave me the creeps."

I gave a Whartonian grunt.

"And you'd be prepared to swear it was a baby?"

The lips clamped together.

"Young man, are you doubting my word? You're not suggesting that at my time of life and after having had two of my own I don't know. . . ."

"It was a baby," I said, and let out a breath. "We're agreed it was a baby. A newly born baby probably. But what about the house? Could you see any light?"

"Never a light," she said. "I thought afterwards that was all the more suspicious."

"Mind you, Mrs. Ganton," I said, "we mustn't rule out the likelihood that Mrs. Wyster had a caller and it was this caller's baby you heard."

"Then why didn't its mother quieten it?"

I shrugged my shoulders. Babies, I said, weren't in my line. I could only wish they had been. And then she actually asked if the fault—fault mind you—was mine or my wife's and had we seen a doctor. A friend of hers had . . .

My turn came again. I said she was a woman of discretion and whatever she told me would be regarded as implicitly confidential. So what were her considered opinions about the baby.

"Well," she began, and shot a look at me as if to say that gossip was one thing and statement another. "Naturally this is my own idea, but I thought afterwards she'd had this baby and was too faint to feed it."

"But why wasn't there a nurse or a doctor there?"

"Because she didn't want anything known. That's why she was living there. That's why you never saw a sign of her in the daytime when you used to walk by."

"I see," I said, and gave a nod that might have meant anything. "And what do you suppose has happened to the baby? It isn't there now."

"Ah!" she said, and nodded meaningly. "What *do* people do with babies that aren't wanted."

"Yes," I said, and with what I imagined was a world of meaning too. And I thought I'd better leave it at that, so I got to my feet. But it was another good ten minutes before I could get clear, and that made it one o'clock by the time I was back at The Croft. Wharton was almost ready to move off.

"She's dead certain it was a baby she heard," I told him, and gave him her very words. "A very young baby having spasmodic bouts of crying or whimpering, probably because it was hungry."

"I can't make it out," he said, and I was wishing he'd suggest a visit of his own to Uani. Wharton handling Mabel Ganton would be first-class entertainment, even if he did always say with false modesty that somehow he had a way with women witnesses. "Mind you, she might have deceived everybody and come here for the purpose of having her baby. But why worry," and he waved a dismissive hand. "I'll ring Ousten and he'll soon be letting us know."

Glass, it appeared, had the job of trying to find out how the men had made their way to The Croft. Since they'd come with the intention of stealing a car it was highly improbable that they'd come to Carr's Hill in a car of their own. And whereas the stolen car could run noiselessly downhill, an arriving car would have to come under its own power. And Glass, it seemed to me, had a pretty tough job. Main and suburban lines run from the central hub of town like the densely packed spokes of a wheel, and to get to Carr's Hill there were several choices of route. On the direct line one could get off at Carr's Hill Station, or at Redwood Park which preceded it. Half a mile to the east was another line with a choice of stations, and a mile to the west was the latest extension of the Piccadilly Tube. Two bus routes ran near Carr's Hill Station and two were by Redwood Park.

It was half-past one when we left and the rain had stopped for a time, though the clouds were still low. George said we were bound for the Seven Bells and, without hurrying, we should be there just on closing time. While I was interviewing the Ganton woman, he'd rung Bill's office again and Maudie Brown had still not returned. I thought it was time to put a pertinent question.

"George," I said, "why aren't you so enthusiastic about the Seven Bells end as you are about this end?"

"Who says I'm not?"

"Well, that's how it seemed to me," I said. "That business of the shooting seemed to damp you down."

He was so patient in explaining that I knew he had something up his sleeve.

"Look," he said. "We're enquiring into a murder—a cold-blooded, unnecessary murder. We've begun at the right place and seen enough to get on with, and now we're going to work back. The trouble with you is, you're biased. By sheer coincidence you were in on this murder before it took place. That's why you think the Seven Bells is where we ought to have gone first. Started the hue and cry for Maudie Brown and the three men."

"I think nothing of the sort," I told him. "I admit I am a bit prejudiced. I couldn't see why you worried Wyster so much about his wife's affairs and her family's affairs. Even he had to kick when you asked about a will. Anyone would have thought, as he did, that he was under suspicion of murdering his wife."

"He was too sensitive," George said, and I knew he was begging the question. "But don't run away with the idea that nothing's been done about the Seven Bells end. They're on the hunt now for those three men. And if your friend Maudie Brown hasn't turned up on Monday at the latest, a Police Message will go out. What are you shaking your head for? You don't think she's dead?"

"She was threatened," I said, "and she was followed, and for a very good reason, as we know now. Until the murder was done she didn't matter so much. Now I'm wondering if they dared leave her alive. I don't imply that they meant to commit murder. That'd be sheer nonsense. But I still think one of the three lost his head and shot. Then they had to do something about Maudie Brown."

"Who's denying it?" George asked aggrievedly. "But what about all the discrepancies? As soon as you told me about that barmaid, everything was fishy. Whichever way I poked my nose I smelt fish—and it wasn't good fish."

"Very well," I said. "What were the discrepancies?"

He hauled out his big notebook and began a regular bombardment.

"First there's the shooting. That we've gone into. It was cold-blooded and unnecessary, though that doesn't matter as much as the fact that it's unique in our experience. Now there's the supposition that this murder has been followed by another cold-blooded killing—that's number two. Number three is the car. They knew all about the car and yet they abandoned it when they were as good as back in town. There's the things they *didn't* take from the house. There's the contradiction of Maudie Brown's insistence they were spivs. There were at least two or three lies she told—according to your own statement." He snapped the notebook shut and pushed it back into his breast pocket. "Now do you see why I kept insisting we were only feeling our way? Didn't I say there's more in this Case than meets the eye?"

"Undoubtedly there is, George."

"Undoubtedly!" he told me, and gave a snort. Then he took a look out of the window. "Another ten minutes and we'll be there. Suppose you start telling me what you thought of that Quarren and his wife."

Chapter V
PUBLICANS AND SINNERS

THE CAR WAS LEFT short of the pub and George and I went along on foot. A peep into the public bar showed Quarren there, and we promptly went in. I should say that we forced our way through, for it was ten minutes short of closing time and the place was jammed with thirsty souls who needed a final spot of moisture. There were quite a few women, though not so high a proportion as in the saloon bar.

Then all at once, and when he was almost at the bar, George was shying away. Somehow I knew he wasn't up to his old trick of leaving me to pay.

"You get the drinks," he told me. "Got to do some telephoning."

He made his way out again. I got near enough to the bar to order two bitters, and my long arm could reach over. The drinks had just room for parking on the sopping mantelpiece. I took a swig at mine and kept an eye on George's. There was never a hope of a seat.

Five minutes went by and he hadn't appeared, and I was wondering what it was that had suddenly struck him. I was also thinking about that list of discrepancies that he'd hurled at me and telling myself that if he'd been in the mood to listen and had given me time, I could have found explanations ample enough. I still thought, for example, that one of the crooks had lost his nerve and had shot without thinking of the alarming consequences; not the one who had threatened Maudie—he seemed to have nerve enough for anything—but the younger one she had seen with him in Porelli's. As for the car, that had been abandoned—in Wharton's own words—because it had become too hot to hold. As for a likely killing of Maudie, what's a second murder if it's going to save one's neck from both it and a first? As for the discrepancies in her story—the ones I'd pointed out to Bill Ellice—if I couldn't find any exquisite reasons for them at least I could find reasons good enough.

Then Wharton came in, and just in time to swallow his bitter. The order to leave had gone forth and slowly the bar began to empty. But it took five minutes before Wharton and I were the last ones left.

"Time, gents, please!" snapped Quarren angrily, and was muttering something about some people thinking it was a hotel. Wharton picked up our two glasses and slowly made his way to the bar, and he had donned his antiquated spectacles.

Quarren gave him a glare, and then the glare as suddenly went. There seemed almost a recognition.

"That's right," Wharton told him, and handed him the Warrant Card. "Once seen, never forgotten."

"Well, how are you, Superintendent?" Quarren was asking him with a heartiness about as genuine as the ruby in his tie-ring. Then he was telling the younger barman to close the doors and get out.

"You'll have one on the house, Superintendent?"

"Just had one," Wharton told him. "Mustn't overdo it, you know. My wits fuddle a bit too quickly these days. Not like the old days."

It was a scene after his own heart. I've told you George was very much of a showman. That scorn he always showed of actors was merely jealousy, for he would have made an actor—if a highly original one—himself. And he knew it.

"Yes," he said heavily. "Not like the old days."

And then he was giving Quarren a peering look from over the tops of those fake spectacles.

"Let me see, now. Where did I see you last." He screwed up his crafty old forehead and then the wrinkles went. "Of course it was in that Yaxley Case. You were giving evidence."

Quarren couldn't get out a word. But his conscience seemed to be troubling him, and then he was giving a quick look at me.

"Mr. Travers—my colleague," Wharton said. "That Yaxley Case was before his time."

That somehow eased the tension. Quarren asked if he hadn't seen me before. I told him he had, and where.

"Then you'll have come about Maudie," he said, and it seemed with enormous relief.

"That's right," Wharton said. "We've come about Maudie. Suppose you come round here and we'll have a seat and talk things over nice and cosy."

There was nothing very cosy about Quarren. The room was stuffy it was true, but there was quite a lot of perspiration on his forehead and the quiff was decidedly damp.

"How's trade?" Wharton began. "Pretty good?" Quarren said he couldn't grumble. And he was claiming the house was well run. Wharton himself ought to know that.

"Not in my line," Wharton said, and gave another of those quizzical looks from over the tops of the spectacles. "And yet I don't know. Some little bird was telling me about a spot of black-marketing. What did they do to you? Five quid, wasn't it, and costs?"

Quarren spread ingratiating palms.

"You don't hold that against me, Super. What would you do? I mean, what would anyone do? You know what rationing is. I was offered the stuff and I took it. If it'd been anything serious they'd have slipped more than five pounds into me. You bet your life on that."

"Why should I hold anything against you?" Wharton asked him and beamed. "I come in here for a little information and spot an old friend like yourself, and I'm accused of harbouring a grudge. Suppose you tell us about Maudie. How'd you get her. What d'you know about her. Everything you know—and don't leave anything out."

Quarren's account, and it rang true enough, was this. He had had trouble with barmaids. Up till a year ago he'd had two, and then he'd been glad to replace one by the demobilised man we'd just seen in the bar, especially as the man was married and his wife was willing to work as a kind of general. Then he'd had to get rid of the last barmaid and as he considered it essential for trade to have one in the saloon bar, he'd put an advertisement in the *Telegraph*. The very morning it appeared he'd been rung up by Maudie Brown. An interview for that same afternoon was fixed up. Her references were in order and a day later she was on the job.

"What about the references?" Wharton wanted to know.

Quarren had to do some thinking. Maudie, he said, had been at the Bear in Kennington during the early part of the war, and as he knew the house and, if only slightly, the landlord, he knew she couldn't have been there three years if she wasn't all right.

"You didn't ring up?"

The Bear was blitzed, and Charlie Morton was dead. Half the area was wiped out in one raid, and Charlie and the pub with it. Maudie escaped because she slept out.

"And what did she do next?"

"Married, so she said. Then her husband left her and she had to do something, so she turned to the bar again. She showed me her marriage lines. Everything seemed O.K. to me. Besides, I wanted a barmaid, if you know what I mean, and she looked the very one for the job. Smart and willing and likely to know how to handle customers. I kept an eye on her, mind you, and then after the first day or two I didn't have to, Maudie was absolutely O.K."

Wharton wanted to know about dates. They were easy, Quarren said. She had come on the 1st of September.

"What address did she give?"

Quarren produced the Welman Street address, and he didn't seem flabbergasted when told it was an accommodation one. As he said, that was no affair of his. He wanted a barmaid and the right barmaid—honest, and competent. He had her, so what did it matter to him where she really lived? Maybe, he suggested, she had a kid or two she didn't want anything known about. Then he added the usual end-piece about Maudie being O.K. As to why she was absent, and with never a note or word of explanation, he had no ideas. Perhaps she'd had an accident and was in some hospital. But there was some good reason—he'd bet a lot on that.

"And now I'll tell you a few things," Wharton said. "Or perhaps Mr. Travers here, will do it. He knows more about it than I do."

I talked and Wharton listened and watched. But I could tell easily enough when Quarren was bewildered, and when he was uneasy as well. He knew about her slipping into Porelli's—that was no secret—but he was definitely uneasy at the first mention of the two toughs. He was even more uneasy when I told him how I'd heard Maudie's story, and that it had been in Bill Ellice's office that she had talked. Then he burst out.

"Well, the damned little liar!" he said. "Whoever'd have thought it of her, saying she didn't like to come to me! Any bother like that and I'd have seen she was all right."

"You mean you could have spoken to one of the heads?" Wharton asked.

"Now, now, Super; you know me better than that," Quarren told him. "The police, that's who I'd have spoken to."

"You'd have believed her story all right, if she'd come to you?" I asked him.

"Why not, sir? Plenty of the razor-slashing sort round this way. The Super here knows that."

It didn't exactly answer my question but I left it at that. And then there was an interruption. A woman's voice was calling that the dinner was getting cold.

"I'll be along in a minute," Quarren called back. But then his wife appeared—and no more. Her mouth was open to speak as soon as she came round the end of the bar but at the sight of us she disappeared again.

"Shan't keep you much longer," Wharton told him. "But what about routine? Tell us just what Maudie did."

Quarren said she arrived at ten and did her own personal tidying up behind the bar.

"Didn't she change her clothes?"

Quarren said she had the run of the upstair bathroom.

If she did any changing or dolling up, it was in his daughter's bedroom. The room was only used when his daughter—in the A.T.S.—was home on leave.

"What about when you closed down now?"

"She had a meal with us," Quarren said. "Then she could lie down on the bed if she wanted to, or go out. At half-past five we have a high tea."

"And when you finally closed down, what did she do?"

"Never used to stay a minute. As soon as I checked the cash off she used to go. Used to nip upstairs and then be away."

"No friends or followers?"

"Not that I knew of," Quarren said. "Used to keep herself to herself, Maudie did. Wouldn't stand for no familiarities. Just let 'em get so far and then pull 'em up with a jerk. Quite ladylike with it, though."

"Ever talk about her private affairs?"

Quarren did some thinking.

"Can't say she did, now I come to think of it. She was the quiet sort, was Maudie."

When I asked if it was true that she took a day or two to get back to the job, Quarren said that was only natural. Different houses have different ways, and, besides, she'd not been behind the bar for a year or two.

"Fond of make-up, was she?"

"About the same as most of 'em," he told me, whatever that might mean, and then Wharton was getting to his feet.

"Well, that's the lot—for the present. Now if we might have a word with your good lady."

Quarren didn't like it, and I wondered why. Then I thought I knew.

"I don't think she'll be any use to you, Super. She can't tell you any more than I've done. Not so much perhaps."

"I'll be the judge of that," George told him. "You just ask her to be so good as to pop in here for a minute."

It was two or three minutes before Alice Quarren came in. She had put on a different jumper and tidied her hair, and the powder was thick on her face. But she wasn't looking too comfortable.

"My husband tells me you want to see me?" she said, and her eyes went from Wharton to me. I had no doubts about being recognised.

Wharton explained. It was a question of fingerprints and where we might find one or two. Perhaps Mrs. Quarren would be good enough to show us the rooms Maudie had used upstairs. But Mrs. Quarren doubted if we'd find anything. Everyone used the bathroom, and Miss Brown had had her own small hairbrush and comb and make-up things in her bag.

"All the same I think we'll have a look," Wharton told her. "I know it's a nuisance but we shan't keep you more than a couple of jiffs."

We went round behind the bar and the stairs led up at once from the passage. Everywhere was clean and smelt of soap and there was still moisture on the scrubbed linoleum. But Alice Quarren seemed to have been right. The rooms held nothing peculiar to Maudie Brown to give us a print.

"What about aprons?" Wharton asked.

But aprons weren't used. Maudie used to put on an overall for washing or cleaning in the bar, and the overall last used had gone that morning to the wash. There were no books that she might have read in the bedroom, in fact there was nothing. Everything in the saloon bar had been washed and dusted.

"Well, that seems about all then," Wharton reluctantly said, and then, as arranged, I put my question.

"You remember my asking you in the bar about Maudie, Mrs. Quarren?"

She had remembered me all along but now she pretended a sudden recognition.

"Do you know, I wondered where I'd seen you before," she said. "So that's why you asked me about Maudie."

She had changed her tune. Previously it had been Miss Brown and a bit of a sniff, but now it was Maudie.

"Tell me," I said, "why did you say that you wouldn't be sorry if she never turned up here again?"

"Did I say that?"

"You certainly did."

"I must have been a bit short-tempered," she said. "I don't like the bar nowadays. Too much housework, and other things."

"According to that you ought to be only too glad to see her here again," Wharton said, "and not the other way round. Come on, now, Mrs. Quarren. Just what did you have against her? It's in absolute confidence."

"I don't know that I had anything."

Wharton spread his palms.

"You're a busy woman, Mrs. Quarren. You don't want to spend this afternoon at the Yard, making an official statement. All you've got to do is make a confidential statement here and now and you won't be bothered again."

She hesitated.

"Come in here," she said, and led the way back to the bedroom. The door was closed and she stood with her hand on the knob.

"She was a hussy; that's what she was," she said. "She was leading my husband on."

"Really?" said Wharton, and looked incredibly shocked.

"Yes," she said, and nodded grimly. "I caught madam up here with him in this very room."

"And she blamed him?" I said.

"Who told you?"

"Nobody," I said, "but it's a likely thing. But what did you think when she put the blame on him?"

"I gave him a piece of my tongue as well. 'Anything like this again, my girl,' I said, 'and out you go neck and crop.'"

"And when was this?" Wharton wanted to know.

"Last Wednesday," she said. "The last day she was here." That was all, but Wharton was looking like a man who's had good news. When we got to the foot of the stairs Quarren was waiting for us.

"Got everything you want, Super?"

"More or less," Wharton told him. "Just one last word with you, though, before we go."

He shook hands most gallantly with Alice Quarren and was all apologies for the nuisance we'd been. Then we went out by way of the bar.

"Sure you won't have anything before you go?" Quarren was most ingratiating. "What about a glass of real good port? The genuine stuff."

"Some other time," Wharton told him. "What I wanted to ask you again was this. You're still dead sure you've seen no party of three like those Maudie described?"

"Never, Super. I'd swear to it anywhere."

"What about the eldest one? The one with the streak of a moustache?"

Quarren's gesture was almost a cringe.

"I told you before, Super. I could tell you a score but they wouldn't fit. That's a sort of craze now, wearing a moustache like that. I reckon they got it from the movies." He ventured on a smile and looked at me for confirmation. "Look at the photographs of band-leaders and crooners and so on that you see in the *Radio Times*."

"Good enough," Wharton told him, and heaved a sigh. "Well, we'll be pushing along. Much obliged to you, Quarren. Next time you get hauled in, apply to me and I'll see you get bail."

Quarren pretended to see the joke.

"Where now?" I said as we made for the car.

"A square meal, if we can get one," George said. "I'm feeling a bit peckish."

We found a little place in Moorgate where George knew the proprietor and had a kind of high tea and warmed-up lunch. I wanted to know why George had looked so relieved when Mrs. Quarren had said it was on the Wednesday when she had caught her husband making a pass at Maudie, for that seemed to me to be the real truth of it.

"What makes you think so?"

"Maudie didn't look at all provocative to me," I said. "She didn't seem to me to have a roving eye."

"I thought you said she was made up to kill."

"Not a bit of it," I said. "She was made up for the benefit of this pal she was going to see at Chingford. What she looked like normally in the pub I don't know, but in the evenings probably just about the same. And don't forget that she may have used the heavy make-up to conceal some skin affliction."

"Well, you asked me a question," George said, "and I'm going to give you the answer. Why was I interested to hear that the shindy had taken place on the day before Maudie disappeared? For this reason—and I'm laying myself wide open. *If*—if mind you—if it weren't for one thing I could explain Maudie Brown. I'd say she had a neurotically romantic mind. After that shindy she knew the Seven Bells wouldn't be much of a place to be in, what with Alice Quarren having her knife into her and Quarren afraid to look or speak. Very well then. She made up an excuse to leave. All that yarn about Porelli's and the three spivs was sheer imagination. She tried to get even with Quarren—for getting her in bad with his wife—by telling you and Bill Ellice that he was in with the gangs himself." He waved an impatient hand to stop my question. "I know what you're going to say, and you're right. Quarren probably keeps some pretty bad company, but that doesn't affect the argument. Now what have you got to say?"

"The flaw sticks out a mile," I told him. "Whatever Maudie made up, she couldn't have fabricated on the Thursday morning what didn't happen till the Thursday night. I mean the Grange business."

"I know," he said, and gave a puzzled shake of the head. "But for that my argument's perfect. There must be some truth in that yarn she told. And yet the whole thing stinks. Spivs who couldn't have been spivs. A spiv who picked her up outside Ellice's office and didn't see her on the way to it. There's something wrong—damn wrong. And something tells me my explanation is right—but for that flaw. A romantic neurotic—that's what she was. Got her ideas from cheap novelettes and pictures."

"Let's wash out the Porelli side as invention," I said. "But why shouldn't the rest of it—overhearing about the job at The Croft—have been to do with Quarren? Why couldn't it have been him and some crooks she overheard? Or again, why couldn't it have been that husband of hers?"

"Leave it," George said, and waved an impatient hand. "No use trying to worry the guts out of something when you're too close to it. Give it a rest and something else may crop up."

"That suits me," I said, "except that I'd like to add just one thing. Quarren was a badly scared man. He may be wise to that business at The Croft. Also he may have known infinitely more about Maudie than he let out to us. He may even be responsible for her disappearance. I'm not hinting at anything like murder but that doesn't mean he mayn't have parked her somewhere. He may be paying her to keep her mouth shut."

"Theorising's no good," George told me with the usual contempt. "We've got to get hold of something solid. Let's get along to the Yard. Maybe they've got something there."

At the Yard nothing had come in about the search for the three toughs, and there were no developments from The Croft. At six o'clock George had an appointment with the bank manager, and he rang the Greenford Street number to fix an appointment for me with the Merlins. But the stepfather was out and wouldn't be in till late that night—business with the new orchestra, George gathered—and as the mother still seemed very upset, my call was fixed for ten the next morning. After it I was to get in touch with George through the Yard, and, if he wanted me, he could get me through the flat.

Before the evening meal I wrote up my notes and then the evening papers arrived. The story had been released and both papers carried banner headlines and pictures of Audrey Grange. But George had let out so much and no more, and most of the letter-press was sheer padding. Robbery with murder was the general impression.

After my meal I thought I'd try to get Tom Holberg, for I was feeling the urge to do something tangible instead of twiddling my thumbs or racking my wits and getting nowhere. Just what I hoped to find out I didn't know, but maybe Holberg might miraculously provide something that would give us a lead. He certainly ought to know what part she'd been studying, though that was of little importance to us. What mattered was not *why* she was at The Croft, but that she *was* there. Did the men who murdered her know her as Mrs. Wyster or as Audrey Grange? If as the latter, had there been some snippet of information in the papers about her going to The Croft?

I rang his private number and by sheer luck he was in, and it was his quiet, rather mumbling voice with its faint suggestion of a lisp that answered my call.

"Travers?" he said.

"Ludovic Travers. Surely you remember?"

"Good lord, yes," he said. "And how are you, Travers? And how's your wife?"

We had a sort of domestic chat and then I asked if he knew about Audrey Grange. He said he'd heard the news about an hour before. I told him I was with the Yard in the matter of the enquiry and I said the story in the papers about robbery was very likely true.

"It's hellish," he said. "I still can't believe it. The only real woman genius the English screen has produced. I hope to God you get the swine who did it."

"We shall try," I said, "and we'll probably be round to see you in a day or so. Meanwhile can you tell us just why she was at Carr's Hill? We understood she was studying some new part. Do you know what part? Just for the records."

"I might have vague ideas," he said, "but that wouldn't help. Tell you the truth I hadn't the faintest idea she was at June Harboard's place. All she told me—I can show you the letter—was that she was taking a rest and I wasn't to worry her about business."

"Then it's no use my asking if there was any snippet in the papers about her being there," I said.

"Nothing in the papers that I know of," he said. "She didn't need that sort of publicity. My guess is the crooks simply saw it as a likely kind of place to burgle. They're supposed to have scouts out, aren't they?"

"Maybe you're right," I said. "But why was she taking a holiday at that particular time?"

"Well, she'd just completed a three-picture contract with Empire Associated. They wanted a new contract but she preferred to wait and see."

"See what?"

"Just wait and see. I think she had some scheme on. Don't ask me what because I don't know. She could be very secretive when she liked, but I judged as much from her manner."

That seemed to be all, so I thanked him and said we'd be seeing each other soon. And that left me to puzzle my wits again, at least till half-past nine when the telephone went. It was George. I said nothing had been happening as far as I was concerned.

"Just had a preliminary report from Ousten," he told me. "There's not an atom of truth in that baby yarn."

"Then it was a caller with a baby?"

"How the devil should I know?" he told me testily, and I was telling myself that he hadn't had the job of being convinced by the Ganton woman.

"The bullet that killed her was probably from a little French automatic," he was going on. "They're working on it now. Funny thing for crooks to be armed with, wasn't it?"

His tone had been a kind of, "Now work that one out," and before I could say a word he was repeating the routine for the morning and then he rang off. No wonder that that night I took the devil of a time to get to sleep, and trying to recall the details of *Three Angels* wasn't any help.

CHAPTER VI
GREENWOOD STREET

GREENWOOD STREET had once been a fine residential quarter but now it had an air of the shabby genteel. Some of that was due to bomb damage and to an inability to repair and redecorate, and there Number 2 was an exception. Apparently one of the first uses made of Mrs. Merlin's legacy had been to give the outside of the house a thorough painting, though how the permit had been obtained was no business of mine, and the result was that in the long, early-Victorian street that one house stood out like something almost continental.

That was a minor surprise and the second was when a woman opened the door and announced herself as Mrs. Merlin. I'd been expecting someone tall, thin and rigid, and with an air of the Puritanic—another Mabel Ganton, in fact—but here was a short and rather dumpy woman with a quiet, pleasant manner and quite a charming face in which it was easy to discern the mother of the daughter. It was almost a pity, as I quickly thought, that I couldn't reverse the hackneyed compliment and say, "Mrs. Merlin, your daughter will never be dead while you are alive."

Then there was the sitting-room into which we went. The hall had been commonplace with the usual row of pegs for hats and a perfectly frightful umbrella stand, but the room was airy and modern, with a keynote of comfort and innumerable signs of taste.

"My daughter loved this room," Mrs. Merlin told me, and it was as if she had to mention her daughter at the very first opportunity and ease at once a likely strain.

I said it was a charming room and she said I must excuse her husband for a few minutes. He had been rather later than usual the previous night and she had wanted him to have a good sleep. Then I managed to offer condolences.

"Your daughter must have made you a very proud woman," was one of the things I said.

"Yes," she said thoughtfully. "Yes, Mr. Travers, she did. But it was as a daughter that I was proud of her, not as a film actress. I oughtn't to say it of my own daughter but she was a good girl. A fine girl. Never a bit of silly pride. This was her home and we were her parents, and we always came first. There was nothing too much for us that she could do."

I said that was wonderful hearing and better than all the encomiums there'd be in the newspapers. But I wouldn't intrude on her grief. Perhaps she could give me a list of any jewellery that her daughter might have taken with her on her holiday.

"To tell you the truth," she said, "I don't know what she took. She came to see me on the Friday—that'd be the day before she left—but my husband saw her last. That was on the Saturday when they had lunch out together."

I think she must have noticed the quick, enquiring look.

"I haven't gone out with Audrey for quite a long time," she explained. "People had got to recognising her and it would be very uncomfortable for us both. I didn't like it a bit."

"I can quite imagine," I said. "But your husband didn't mind it."

"No," she said, and a slight frown went across her face. "Frank has been more used to that kind of publicity than I have. He was once quite a famous man, you know."

"I know his name well enough," I said.

"But like a lot of other people we had our bad times," she went quietly on. "But Frank was always the best of fathers, and the best of husbands. He simply adored Audrey, and she him." She gave a quiet smile. "They never really grew up—either of them. Just like two children sometimes."

And there, had I known it, was the germ in which lay the identity of the murderer of Audrey Grange. But how could I tell? I remember that all I could say was that it must have made for a very happy house.

"Yes," she said. "This was always her real home in spite of her marriage. I think you've met her husband?"

I said he had struck me as quite a charming man.

"He is," she said, and sighed. "But I'm an old-fashioned woman, Mr. Travers. Homes like my daughter's aren't my idea of a home. There was he working at this and she somewhere else working at that, and often they'd never see each other for weeks on end."

"And no one really to blame."

"Oh yes. It's a hard thing to say of my daughter now, but she was most to blame. Her own home came last—not first. I'm old-fashioned enough, Mr. Travers, to think that people get married for love, and company and children. But no. Everything in Audrey's life—except perhaps us—had to be subordinated to her career. Nobody can tell me that was right."

"A difficult problem," I said, and I knew how right Wyster had been when he had said that his mother-in-law had hated both stage and screen. But I had imagined a different kind of hatred. This of hers was far deeper in that it had so firm a restraint.

She began telling me about the jewellery, and it was merely a confirmation of what Wyster had said, except that she divulged that the diamond ring had been her engagement ring. There was also, of course, the platinum wedding ring. Audrey had lost weight since her marriage and had difficulty in keeping her rings on. As for the wrist-watch, that had been a present—a far too valuable one in her estimation—from a Mr. Kraaf, an American film magnate on a visit to England the previous year when Audrey apparently had helped him in certain little ways. It carried the name of Tiffany of New York, and I said that would be a tremendous help.

"Before you see my husband there's something I'd like to show you," she said. "It's a letter I had from Audrey only as late as Wednesday. I think it bears out what I've been telling you about her."

I said I should regard it as a favour and at once she was taking it out of her handbag. The first thing I noticed about it was that it bore no address.

Dear Mummy,

I'm still having a very peaceful and restful time, and I'm sure you are now Daddy's settled down to his new job. I'm still sure it's going to be a stepping-stone to something even bigger. Heaps of people have had to drop out of things, like Daddy, and then have managed a come-back. He's going to surprise us all yet, so mind you get ready. I only hope it won't be too much of a shock!

I've had a lovely time, as I said, and I know by now you'll have forgiven me for not letting you know where I was, but you know yourself how it would have been. You'd have come to see me, and Daddy would, and before I knew where I was I wouldn't have been doing any work at all. And Harlan would have got to know as well. It's awfully hard for Daddy sometimes, as you know, to keep quiet about things.

I haven't even been worried any more by that dreadful old woman I told you about who came poking her nose into everything. I don't think I left her in any doubt that I hadn't any use for her at all. At any rate I haven't seen her again, openly that is. I've seen her going by once or twice and giving little sneaking looks out of the corner of her eye.

Another day or two and the holiday will be at an end and I shall be seeing you. I have to spend today in town so I'm posting this there. Give Daddy my love and tell him I have a little bird who is keeping an eye on him.

Much love to yourself,

Your ever loving,

Audrey.

"It's a lovely letter," I said as I gave it back. "Something you'll treasure as long as you live."

It was then that her lip began to quiver, and it was then too that steps were heard descending the stairs. That momentarily checked the tears.

"My husband's just coming," she said. "Do stay here."

She almost ran to the hall, and through the closed door I could hear faint voices. Then the door opened and Frank Merlin came in, alone.

He was of medium height and thin, with dark hair, worn long, and the grey by the temples and the beak of a nose gave him the look of a rather emaciated Irving. But the face was veined and purple like the face of a heavy drinker, and that rather detracted from a possible nobility. But he carried himself well, if with just a touch of the flamboyant, and his voice was slightly fruity and his choice of language what I might call inclining to the grandiloquent.

"Mr. Travers?" He came forward with outstretched hand. "Pray sit down, my dear sir. You are, I believe, from Scotland Yard."

He waved my Warrant Card gracefully away.

"At my time of life, sir, I can tell a man—a gentleman, I should say—when I see him." His head went sideways. "The matter, I believe, concerns my daughter's jewellery."

What he told me was little more than a repetition of what I had heard from his wife and son-in-law. Then there seemed little more to do than offer condolences again, and in a flash of a second he was a different man. The pomposity had gone and he was a stricken man. And yet somehow I didn't feel uncomfortable at the sight of his tears. What I was feeling was an enormous sympathy and almost an affection.

"Forgive me," he said. "It takes a lot of getting over. I'm a man with a broken heart, Mr. Travers, and I shall be for the rest of my days. But there. . . ."

He dabbed again at his eyes and then almost as quickly he was himself again.

"Don't go," he told me quickly. "It's so rarely we have company." He even ventured on a smile. "You don't mind being called company?"

"I like it," I said. "I've already met your wife, by the way, and I thought she was charming."

"They don't make women like her nowadays," he told me, and drew himself up with a kind of resolution. "The mould's been broken, sir. The best woman in the world, sir. The best wife. The best mother." Then he was thrusting out a hand. "Sooner than hurt her feelings, I'd cut off the fingers of this hand." Then as quickly he was shaking his head. "Pardon me, sir. Perhaps I spoke too warmly."

"It was good to hear you," I said. "And I can quite believe all you say. Your son-in-law was telling me much the same thing."

For some reason or other he was suddenly deflated again, and then I knew why, if only from his quick, enquiring look. Maybe he was wondering if I knew about that besetting sin of his, and what it had cost him, and, above all, the woman he had just so lavishly praised.

"Harlan's a good fellow," he told me. "He has his faults like all of us, of course"—another quick look which I appeared not to notice—"but a good fellow at heart. And much esteemed in his profession. The sort of man, sir, who one day might end up with a knighthood."

I didn't contradict, even if in my judgment Wyster's acting lacked that vital distinction.

"By the way," I said, "am I right in thinking you were the only one who knew your daughter was at Carr's Hill?"

I could see him debating his answer. The whole man of him was for a moment as if in a state of suspension. Then the truth came, and not the prevarication.

"Yes," he said. "I was the only one. All our lives my daughter and I have had our secrets. You'll understand why I call her my daughter. In every real sense of the word she *was* my daughter and I was the only father she knew." His face lighted up. "When she was no higher than this we used to have our little secrets. Not even her mother would know. Not that Clara was ever jealous."

"I think your daughter must have owed you a lot, too," I said. "It must have been through you that she got her chance."

"Well, perhaps—yes," he said judicially. "I had had misfortunes, sir, and things hadn't gone well with me, but I wasn't without influence. A word here and a word there and she had her chance, as you say. But the spark was there, sir."

"Yes," I said, and felt the triteness, "but it was you who gave it the chance to burn. And what a spark it must have been! *Three Angels* was the last film I saw of hers, and it was a real emotional experience. Something I'll never forget."

"A fine film," he said, and then raised his hands in horror. "But the music, my dear sir! Why in God's name did they have to have Sibelius? Sibelius—I ask you. Vikings and forests and icebergs in a film like that!"

"To tell you the truth," I said, "I was so engrossed in that picture that the music was hardly a background."

"Cesar Franck," he said. "You know the Cesar Franck symphony? That's what they, should have had. Three perfect themes for the three main characters. And they shouldn't have allowed that gross overacting of Merril Holme. In my judgment that was a definite blot on the picture."

"She was the elder daughter, wasn't she?"

"Yes," he said. "A thrustful, aggressive woman, and that was how she played it. An error of direction. A palpable error." He let out a breath. "But there we are. It's too late now."

"Isn't she playing with Wyster at the moment?" I asked.

"Yes," he said, and his lip curled. "If you haven't seen the play, my dear sir, go and see it. You'll find my judgment still holds good."

I asked him what he was doing himself, and at once he was telling me about the new orchestra. It was a rather confidential matter at the moment because of publicity timing. Conducting—if he might say it—had always been his forte.

"It's not unlikely," he said, and his thin chest had gone out and his head was high, "that I may take up the whole thing seriously again. A little composing, perhaps in my spare time, but musical direction mainly."

I said I was sure he'd be the very man for that kind of job.

"We shall see," he told me, and his tone had more than an optimism. "When a man has bad luck, my dear sir, he has few friends. Most of those who made a pretence of friendship proved mere broken reeds. I think I may safely say that I'm already in a position to prove to some of them that I'm not the man they mistook me for."

"An excellent thing to be able to do," I told him. "But before I go, there's just one little thing you might tell me. Your daughter was supposed to be studying a new part, or whatever you call it, at that bungalow of Miss Harboard's. Do you know what that part was?"

There was again that sort of dramatic pause. Again there seemed the quick question of the truth or the lie. And this time— an old hand like myself rarely makes that kind of mistake—I was sure he was telling me the lie.

"No," he said. "I know she was studying some part or other." His eyes went questioningly up. "Or wasn't she? Am I thinking of something else? I really can't say."

I got to my feet and we went together to the door. His hand went out to grasp not my hand but my arm, and suddenly he was an old heart-broken man again.

"You'll catch those who did it?"

"I hope so," I told him gently, and as his hand withdrew I as gently patted his shoulder.

"I want to live to see them hang," he said. "Just to see them hang."

A voice called then. I couldn't distinguish the words but he could hear them well enough. Once more his face was lighting up.

"My wife, sir. She asks me to make her apologies for not coming personally to thank you and say goodbye."

"It's I who owe the thanks," I said, "and to yourself as well. It's been a great pleasure to meet you both, Mr. Merlin."

"And to meet you, sir." He cleared his throat. "Perhaps in what I might call happier circumstances you'll pay us a visit again."

There was no denying that in some ways it had been a delightful visit, even if I'd learned nothing that looked like helping to solve the Case. In fact I hadn't learned much more than Wyster had already told us, though it was somehow reassuring to have everything so delightfully confirmed. Merlin was certainly a remarkably likeable man, and though his lineaments were as unlike as could be from those of the imaginary Micawber, yet in many ways he was Wilkins Micawber to the life. A gentleman by ancestry and doubtless first-class at his job, and yet an incurable optimist, and one with a convenient memory. I could imagine him, as Wyster had more formally said, where actors and people theatrical most do congregate, showing the world that a come-back had been accomplished and hinting at still greater things to come. But what I liked most about him was that genuine devotion to his wife, and what I could feel was the incredible, stunning tragedy of that loss of a daughter. A many-sided man, Frank Merlin, and it was his ready emotion that was not the least of the characteristics that had made me respect and like him.

My thoughts had taken me out of my way but I happened to see a call-box as I came to the end of the road and I rang up the Yard. I was put through to Wharton, and he wanted me at once. Bill Ellice was there and we were to compile a description of Maudie Brown for that Police Message.

It took the two of us best part of an hour and when we'd compiled it, we were far from satisfied, for the general effect was so vague. Bill said it was because women of that type looked very much alike. Everything about her had been what he called sort of medium. But for what it was worth, this was the description.

> Five-feet six in her shoes. Full-busted but with rather peakish face. Upper lip prominent but teeth small and regular. Face oval and nose somewhat pointed. Eyes (we disagreed about that and settled on a compromise) brown or dark grey. Hair black or dark brown. Heavily made up and probably to conceal a blotchy skin. Voice thin and rather high-pitched, and with a definite London accent. Age about thirty-five. Married but may not be wearing wedding-ring. When last seen was wearing a ready-made costume of brownish tweed, with a yellow

jumper beneath. Hat black with yellow and red flowers. Carrying worn black handbag with single clasp.

George said it would be edited and maybe pruned, and bits inserted about her being a barmaid and being last heard of at Liverpool Street Station when on the way to visit a friend at Chingford. Would that friend at Chingford or any other person who had any information whatever about the missing woman get in touch, etc., etc.

"No news about her at Liverpool Street?" Bill asked.

"Not a thing," Wharton said, and he didn't seem despondent nevertheless. "She rang your office and disappeared into thin air, as they say. Still," and his knuckles rapped that description of ours, "this may produce something. Let's hope it will."

To my ear he sounded as if he might have added, "But I'm damn sure it won't!" But Bill left and then he was asking me about my call on the Merlins. I told him the very little I'd learned and we settled down to the list of jewellery. The main items had been at the bank, so not a great deal was missing.

George went out to deal with the official description and I had a look at one or two of the Sunday papers lying on his side table. Then something caught my eye—the name BOBINOT.

In a flash I was seeing that bedroom again and the newspaper photograph wedged in the mirror corner. The paper rested on my knees and I was thinking back. Once more I thought that it could have been only the comical face of that clown that had appealed to anyone so vastly different as Audrey Grange. If she had known the man or been friendly with him in any way there would have been a studio photograph with a signature. And then I was thinking that there was a side of Audrey Grange about which we'd heard never a word—that she had a sense of humour. Wyster and Tom Holberg had both described her as living for nothing but work: not a ruthless kind of living but an absorption in only the things that mattered for some final consummation of ambition.

And then again I knew I was already forgetting something. Only an hour before I'd heard something about that sense of humour. It had been implicit in those remarks in her letter when referring to Mabel Ganton. Her mother had said that she and her father had never quite grown up. Merlin had talked about little humorous secrets that even the mother did not know. And so there it was. Audrey Grange had seen that photograph and had cut it out. Every time she went to her mirror it must have been a kind of tonic.

George came back then and I laid the paper aside. There was nothing I could do, he said. There was nothing either of us could do that our subordinates couldn't do as well and better. But if nothing turned up before the morning, I was then to give him a ring. Maybe we'd go to Carr's Hill, if only for the lack of something better.

"Never a print, never a word about the crooks, nothing about that barmaid," and he shrugged his shoulders. "The best thing we can do is have a good dinner, like a couple of ruddy camels. Let's hope tomorrow we get so damn busy we haven't time to eat."

I had a service lunch at the flat and didn't have to loosen a button. After it I had a look at all the papers I'd been able to buy of the What-the-butler-saw type in the hope of picking up anything that might even begin to look like helping, but there was nothing at all. Never a bit of scandal had apparently attached itself to the name of Audrey Grange. But when I came to the other kind of paper I did see something that interested me, if only slightly, and that wasn't the actual name of Audrey Grange but that of Merril Holme, the lady for whom Frank Merlin had had such little use and whom he had virtually accused of trying to hog the limelight of *Three Angels*. The paragraph was this:

It is now thought in film circles that the part of Jinny Patman in the eagerly awaited film version of Matthew Riche's famous best-seller *Number Thirty* will be played by Merril Holme, now appearing by a somewhat macabre coincidence with Harlan Wyster in *Round Square* at the Orpheum. Israel Kraaf of Kraaf Pictures Inc., who purchased the film rights, is due in England at any moment for casting.

In that paragraph were quite a number of flashbacks. It told the probable reason why Audrey Grange had gone to Carr's Hill—to study that part herself—and it explained the book beneath her pillow. Or maybe she hadn't been interested in the part but in the book for its mere self. I didn't know and, after all, it didn't really matter. Then there had been that mention of the Kraaf who had presented Audrey Grange with that valuable wrist-watch.

But, as I said, all that was interesting and no more. *Why* Audrey Grange had been at The Croft had no bearing whatever on her death. Nor had Wharton and myself any too much that did have a bearing, and that was why mere snippets from the Press had at least an interest. And it so happened that as I turned over the page of the paper I was then reading I saw once more the name BOBINOT, and maybe because of its large type. It was in connection with a gala charity concert that same afternoon at the Palliceum. A formidable list of stars was billed as positively appearing and among them was Bobinot. I looked at my watch and I had twenty minutes in which to make it. I did it with five minutes to spare, and there wasn't a seat left in the house.

I suppose I have an almost scandalously long list of social acquaintances, and if there is a reason for it, it may be that in my job I have to question or solicit favours from or ask the co-operation of all sorts and sizes. In fairness to myself I ought to add that I haven't an atom of snobbery in me, and I'm passionately interested in my fellow men, if only as types for private dissection. At the Palliceum, for instance, I wasn't in a dither when there wasn't a seat. I flashed my card and asked to see Newton Crole, the manager. But even he couldn't find me a seat, though he did find me a first-class observation post on the stairs that led down between two of the more ornate of the boxes. He even wanted me to have a cigar.

Most of the show didn't matter, though I will say it was uncommonly good. But it didn't start too well with—need I say it?—a famous croonerette: start well for me, I should have said, for the audience wallowed. She was followed by a light comedian and he by the first of the spectacular pieces from the current Palliceum show *Skip and Jump*. Then came quite a clever troupe of acrobats, followed by a singer of bass ballads. When the curtain fell on him there was a kind of anticipatory rustle among the huge audience. A minute or two of waiting and there was just a short fanfare. The curtain rose on Bobinot.

I should warn you that this isn't going to sound at all funny as I describe it. Bobinot's act was one of the kind that even a skilled radio commentator can—and so often does—make merely irritating. It was something essentially to be seen and only in minor moments to be described.

But the curtain went up, as I said, and all one saw was an empty stage and a huge backcloth. Now that backcloth consisted of a whole series of Bobinots sitting at pianos, and they were graded from a midget painted on the left to a gigantic Bobinot on the right. Each was depicted as the real Bobinot would be: flaming red hair, plump face, with bulbous nose, and wearing the usual clown's costume of bulky black pantaloons and jacket, set off by an enormous red bow. So much for the backcloth.

But nothing happened. Seconds went by. A minute went by. Almost two minutes went by, and then through the audience went a faint ripple. It grew to a monstrous chuckle and then to a deafening roar. For one of those painted clowns had been the real thing. While the impatient crowd—but for those in the know—was shifting restlessly in its seat and one could almost hear the incipient cat-calls, something stirred on that backcloth. It was a hand. It moved. It seemed nervous and went back to its immobility. It moved again and again went back. Then as if the matter had gone beyond all urgency, the hand shot round and the fingers began a frantic scratching of the posterior. So frantic was the scratching that the scratcher tumbled head-first on the stage.

"What an entry!"

Crole had slipped in beside me and we were both watching, and, as he said, he saw that act of Bobinot's eight times a week and yet it never failed to fascinate. But to get back to the clown. The space from which he'd fallen was now filled by some mechanical device and when he went back to his painted piano it wasn't there. His look of bewilderment was the very one on the face of his photograph as I'd seen it in that mirror at The Croft, and it was even more funny in that it had such utter despair. Then he clasped his hands, shut his eyes and the lips began a prayer, and gabbled with such grimaces of intensity that my belly rumbled with laughter that hurt. Then he opened his eyes but nothing had happened. Another tragic look and another clasping of the hands. But a step back accompanied it, and suddenly he was tumbling over a piano stool that had shot up from nowhere.

And his joy! That stool seemed to have a clever universal joint and when he tried to mount, it acted like a bucking horse. But he was determined to master it. On he would leap and off he would go. Then it did seem as if he'd got the hang of it, but just when he'd given us all—and himself—a huge grin of complacent congratulation, off he suddenly shot again. Then he lost his temper. He took a kind of running jump at that stool and gave it a tremendous kick, only to stub his own toe and stagger round the stage holding the foot in agony. And all the time he seemed unaware that a grand piano had suddenly shot up from nowhere to join the stool.

Then he saw it. He looked at it and he looked at us—eyes bulging like marbles. He began a crafty approach.

He got on his belly and stalked that piano. He got within range. He leapt, and the piano stool didn't buck. Like a child let loose for the first time at a real piano, he touched a key. It sounded and he chortled. He touched another key. All his fingers went to the keys and the cacophony was awful. Even he couldn't stand it. He went to give that piano a hearty kick—and remembered just in time.

The hands were clasped again and the eyes closed. Paper fluttered down and there was a sheet of music, a huge sheet with single notes as big as one's fist. And the joy of that again! The paper of course wouldn't stand on the rest so he folded it till one line only could be seen. Then he went through various Pachmann-like preliminaries and finally settled to play what? *God Save the King*, and with one finger and with the most intense laborious care, and even then he got the last note of the first line wrong. And the agony! He tried it again and again, and all the time with nervous glances at the piano stool that had bucked, and then at last he knew and we knew why he couldn't get it right. That strip of music was upside down!

We shared the joy of that discovery. We shared the almost agonising anticipation of a perfect one-finger rendering. And so to the curtain, as superb as the entry. The first line was played, and it was perfect. Another finger joined in. Both hands joined in. A minute and we were hearing a—to me at least—magnificent improvisation on the theme of that original line. It merged subtly into something else, and we were hearing the finale of Greig's pianoforte concerto. The orchestra had as subtly joined in, and so to the last crashing, overwhelming chords.

Bobinot took a bow. If the audience had had their way he'd have had twenty bows after as many encores.

"What an act!" I said to Crole. "When I've laughed so much I don't know."

"Clever," he said. "Very clever. That chap'll have a European reputation before long."

"He's ruined this show," I said. "You ought to have kept him till almost the last. Everything's going to be anti-climax."

Crole slipped away and I sat on. Anti-climax it was, at least for me, though the audience seemed to find the rest of the show sufficiently enthralling. I went out early to avoid the rush, and as I waited for a bus in the drizzling rain I didn't need to hunt for reasons why Audrey Grange had made a pin-up boy of Bobinot. "Once seen, never forgotten," as George Wharton would say. "Once seen, always remembered," was how I'd prefer to put it, and that afternoon had been such a tonic that I wouldn't have minded a pin-up photograph of Bobinot myself.

Chapter VII

HOLME THE UNEASY

THE HALL PORTER gave me a message that Wharton would like to see me at the Yard. I felt like a cup of tea and obstinately had it. The Yard is only a five-minute walk for me, and I didn't apologise for being late.

"Glass sent something through this afternoon," George told me. "Something he unearthed at the golf course. I don't think there's anything to it but you might like to follow it up. In our job you never know."

Had I been a prophet I should have said, "How right you are!"

"It's about Audrey Grange and that golf she played last Thursday morning," George was going on. "She let two men players through and one of them stayed talking to her while his partner went on. Talking quite a time they were, like old friends. The name convey anything to you? It's Holme. James Holme."

"It does," I said. "That is if he's any relation of Merril Holme, the actress."

"We haven't got that far," he told me, and passed me a booklet with a list of the members of the Carr's Hill Golf Club.

"Holme J.," I said. "Address—Thorngate, Russley Road, Finchley. Telephone: Finchley 7171. Anything else about him?"

"Not a lot," George said. "He's pretty well off. Managing Director or Chairman or something or other of some business near town. Drives a damn great American car. The sort of chap who can play a round whenever he feels like it. You know the type. He should have been playing this morning with three friends, by the way. They'd booked their time and then early this morning Holme rang and cancelled for himself. The others played a threesome starting off at the tenth."

"Well, what's his importance?" I said. "How's he going to help? After all, he wasn't even the last one to see her alive."

"You never know," George said. "It might look pretty on the records, that's all." He gave one of his ersatz sighs. "I'd go myself if I hadn't a conference."

He pressed the buzzer and asked for the number. He got it, and a woman—the housekeeper—said Mr. Holme was out. But he'd be in at seven o'clock for certain. And who was it speaking, please?

George didn't tell her.

"There you are," he said. "In at seven. Just gives you nice time to make it." And he was adding largely that I might as well take a police car.

It was just short of seven when we drew up outside the house. It was in a good residential neighbourhood and the house itself was a detached one of medium size with plenty of garden. The garage doors were open and I had a rear view of that American car, still a-drip from the drizzle. The housekeeper answered the bell.

"Mr. Holme in?"

She gave me a good looking over.

"Well, he is, but he'll be having his dinner at any time now. What is the name, please?"

I gave her a private card and wrote 'Most Urgent' on the back. She asked me to wait in the hall and it was two or three minutes before she came back. Then she showed me into a room on the right and said Mr. Holme would be along in a moment. He was quite a time before he turned up.

And he again was not as expected. He wasn't beefy and prosperous, so to speak, but a good-looking, quiet sort of chap almost as tall as myself, and I put his age as under forty.

"Mr. Travers?" he said, the card in his hand, and his eyes were giving me what I could only call an uneasy inspection.

I gave him the Warrant Card. He looked at it and he looked at me. He looked at it again and he nervously moistened his lips. When he handed it back he had a little laugh all ready.

"Scotland Yard? Now what have I been doing now?"

I said I was not too official—at the moment. That always puts a guilty conscience in a dither. He wasn't in a dither but he was still uneasy, though that might have been the old, old story of the black market, except that he looked too decent a sort.

He waved me to a chair and I took one of his cigarettes, and then I told him just why I was there. I couldn't help seeing his enormous relief, so I gave him another damper at once.

"You must have read the Grange story," I said. "Don't you think you should have got in touch with us and told us what you knew?"

He was indignant, and with good reason. What was the point in reporting a conversation with a friend, even if that friend was subsequently killed by burglars? He seemed to stress that last point.

"You never can tell what's of consequence and what isn't," I told him, but not too severely. "The tiniest little hint might lead to something vitally important. Still, let's wash that out. You were a friend of Miss Grange?"

"I've known her for quite a time," he said.

"Tell me. Are you by any chance a relation of Merril Holme, the actress?"

"Her brother," he said tersely, and there had been a faint frown. It almost looked as if the two had been on not the best of terms.

I suppose I've made fun enough in my time of the old-school tie, and that is the basest ingratitude, for it can be useful enough. It was so now, when I wanted this chap to talk.

"Pardon me," I said, "but were you at Radley?"

"I was," he said, and waited.

"Then you look as if you were a contemporary of a cousin of mine—Peter Vannley. Chubby was his nickname."

"Good Lord, yes," he said. "I knew Chubby Vannley. Quite a good chap. A cousin of yours, was he?"

I said he was, and he seemed sorry to hear he'd been killed in the last year of the war. But the ice was really broken and we settled down to quite a good chat. He even called through to the housekeeper to keep things hot, and after I'd pleaded further business as an excuse not to take pot-luck. He was suddenly being most friendly—almost too much so. He told me quite a lot about himself, how he was a bachelor and up to three years before had lived at Thorngate with his widowed aunt. Now he lived there alone with a housekeeper and an elderly maid. It was handy for his works—Holme and Son, Electrical Engineers, Edgware Road. Refrigerators and electrical gadgets, as he explained.

I drew him gently back to the Thursday morning, but all I could get out of him about the talk he had had with Audrey Grange was that it was personal and trivial. Just the usual things people talk about when they meet after an interval.

"What interval?" I persisted, and he shot a look at me before he said about a month or so.

"We're interested in what *she* said," I told him, and again it seemed that nothing had been said but the trivial. Then all at once he got up to knock the ash from his cigarette, and then he stayed at the mantelpiece, lounging against it, the ashtray ready to hand. And that was unnecessary because there had been an ash-tray on the low table between our chairs. So I got up to flick off my ash there too. His elbow moved back, deliberately as I thought, and a framed photograph fell to the rug.

"Sorry," I said, and stooped.

But he was too quick for me, and picking up the photograph and keeping it face downward till it was laid on the piano top. I didn't even lift an eyebrow as I went back to my chair.

"Personally I hate photographs cluttering up a room," I said off-handedly. "By the way, that was a photograph of Audrey Grange, wasn't it?"

He didn't like that a bit. He looked down at his cigarette and I almost expected him to ask what the hell that was to do with me. Then he was going through the formality of having a look at it. It was so silly of him that I felt a bit ridiculous too.

"As a matter of fact it is," he said. "I don't know how you knew. It isn't at all good of her."

Then he was taking the trouble to explain that he was rarely in that room, and how Audrey was an old friend and he'd forgotten all about that photograph.

"I saw her in *Three Angels*," I said. "Your sister was in it too, if I remember rightly."

"I think she was," he said, as if he didn't know. "But I don't run up against her a lot these days."

"Married, is she?"

"Well,"—he gave a wry smile—"yes, and no. Divorced, actually. Then her ex-husband was killed in the war. I should say that she divorced *him*."

That seemed about all but I did ask him how he liked Carr's Hill as a course. He merely said it was quite good, and the bite, so to speak, seemed to have gone out of our talk since that episode of the photograph. Though I got to my feet I decided to give it a last gingering up.

"And so Miss Grange didn't tell you she was staying at The Croft? Or did she?"

And there at once was the uneasiness again. First the looking away and the looking down and the hesitation.

"She didn't," he said. "She sort of gave me to understand she'd just run along for the morning."

"That settles that," I said, and gave a little laugh of my own. "And it's no use asking you then if you went to The Croft after you'd seen her."

"Afraid not," he said, but there'd been a rather longer pause.

"By the way, shouldn't you have been playing there this morning? Didn't I hear something about your having to cancel?"

He didn't like that either, though he did say it was the weather principally. And then at the very door he changed, his mind.

"Look here," he said, "I don't mind telling you the truth. I didn't feel like going. That dreadful business knocked me all of a heap. I just couldn't face Carr's Hill again—after seeing her there last Thursday."

"Very understandable," I told him, and held out my hand. "I'm afraid I've been a bit of a nuisance."

"Not at all—"

But I wasn't leaving him as cosy as all that.

"And I may have to be a nuisance again. It all depends."

"Depends?"

"Yes. Sort of on what turns up. We might need your help again. You never know."

I said he wasn't to risk the drizzle and I waved a cheery farewell from the gate. It was then just after half-past seven and when we got back to the Yard, George was still having his pow-wow with what he called the Big Bugs or the Powers-that-Be. And when he did come in he was none too pleased. All that had been decided on after an hour's talk had been the intensification of the search for the three men. I didn't see anything to grumble at in that; in fact it was the only thing to do. Take my evening, as I told George. Suppose I *was* of the opinion that Holme had been in love with Audrey Grange and that he was on none too good terms with his sister, just what use was the information? Where did it get us?

"You keep harping on him being uneasy," George said. "Why was he uneasy?"

"Because he was in love with another man's wife. That's why he didn't want me to see that photograph."

"Look," said George, and very patiently, "he needn't have minded you seeing that photograph. He'd just told you he'd been friends with the lady for years. That explains the photograph."

"Who's theorising now?" I said.

"Theory be damned," he told me. "It's simple deduction. He didn't want you to connect him too closely with her, even as friends. Therefore there was more in it than friendship. He probably knew she was at The Croft, for instance. You thought he was telling you a lie when you asked him if he knew."

"Admit all that," I said, "and where does it get us? He didn't kill her?"

George let out a breath and shook a sad but still patient head. Now he was the schoolmaster and I the prize dunce.

"Take that theory of ours"—that word *ours* was a bit ominous—"that the whole yarn of that barmaid might have been a fake." Up went the same old hand. "I know the flaw. You needn't remind me. It's that word *Grange*, and she couldn't have made that up. But wash the flaw out—"

"A pretty high-handed kind of argument?"

"Let me finish," he said, and his patience was getting thin. "But for that word *Grange*, the whole yarn might have been a fake. The robbery may have been a fake and the car theft a fake. *And* the murder a fake."

"I get you," I said, and I own frankly that I was only trying to humour him. "And that's why you're on the look out for likely suspects—"

Then the buzzer went. Inspector Glass was on the line.

"Hallo, Glass," Wharton said, and genially enough. "What's worrying you?"

Then his eyebrows were lifting and I was treated to a series of grunts. Then came an interruption.

"But dammit! She told Mr. Travers quite different."

He calmed down again and there were more grunts. The farewell was that someone called *he* would be along first thing in the morning. A final bit of back-slapping and he hung up.

"Have a look here," he said, and reached for a sheet of paper. "Remember those bungalows along Hurst Avenue? This is the way we came. First there's one called The Rosery. Then comes Uani, and there're only those two this side of the hill. The other side there's The Croft—just here. Then there's only one more—Homeland—to the end of the avenue. That's owned by the head green-keeper at the golf course. Now the point's this:

"Cars rarely come that way except during hours of daylight. They don't make a Piccadilly of it, so to speak. It's what you might call golf-club traffic. Well, Glass has been scouting round and he's found a couple of things. At about half-past eleven—that's as near as he can pin the man down—a car went past Homeland up the hill and in about twenty minutes a car came back. No one can guarantee it was the same car. Got that?"

I said I had.

"Now the other side of the hill. We start with Uani. Your friend there now says she heard a car going up the hill at about the same time. Glass again can't get any nearer. She'd told him what she told you, that she hadn't heard anything unusual on the Thursday night, but now she says she didn't regard a car as unusual. A car in itself, she means. And one other thing. Both she and the green-keeper confirm something remarkably strange and that's why Glass wanted to report it at once. It's this:

"What strikes people in those bungalows when a car does happen to come by at night is not so much any noise as the fact that the headlights light up the front rooms. That green-keeper sleeps in a front room and so does that Mrs. Ganton. The people at The Rosery sleep in a back room. You get me?"

I said I did.

"That's really what made them aware of a car—what woke them up, if you like. It was a hot night and both bungalows had curtains drawn back. Right then. Back to the Uani side of the hill. A car came up the hill, as I said, and about the same time as the one on the other side of the hill. It went back again after about the same interval, but in each case the car now hadn't its headlights on. In other words, this time they were just aware that a car had gone by. They didn't see a flashing of lights. You've got all that?"

Again I said that I had.

"Now here's the vital question," George went on. "Two cars, mind you. Did one car come from the station way and go right through and the other come from the other way and go right through to the station? Was it just ordinary traffic passing along Hurst Avenue? Or did a car come from the station to The Croft, stay there for a quarter of an hour or so and then go back the same way? And did another car come from the other way to The Croft, stay there roughly the same time and then go back the way it came, the same as the other car did?"

"It's a problem," I said, and found myself polishing my glasses. "On the face of it I'd be inclined to say two cars met at The Croft, reversed, and went back the way they'd come. And there'd been something fishy going on at The Croft because whereas they didn't care a hoot who heard or saw them going there, they used only their sidelights going back."

George beamed. The dunce had achieved a miracle.

"Exactly! And now do you wonder why I'm scouting round for suspects?"

He leaned back in his chair, then leaned forward again with a finger thrust out at me.

"Let's give Maudie Brown and her story the benefit of the doubt. Even then both those cars couldn't have belonged to the crooks. I don't think that even one did. They wouldn't have arrived with headlights full on. Dammit! They might as well have brought a brass band with 'em. I own they could have done in a quarter of an hour just what was done at The Croft, but that doesn't affect the argument. And why should they have come in a car when they were taking another away?"

"Wait a minute, George," I said. "When does Ousten now say she was killed?"

George shrugged his shoulders.

"If she had that meal of hers at about half-past seven or eight o'clock, then she was killed at about eleven o'clock. In other words, the two cars came after she was dead!"

"It beats me," I said. "And any more news about the gun?"

"What I said it was—a little French Lautrec."

"A pity the weather hadn't broken before," I said. "There was never a trace of a tyre on that hard road."

"Well, there we are," George said. "First thing in the morning you'd better nip along. On the spot's the place to get ideas—not here. I shall have a look in at the inquest."

Then he was giving an exasperated click of the tongue as he glanced up at the clock.

"Dammit! I've missed that broadcast."

But it would be repeated at eight the next morning and I said I'd like to hear it then, if only to know what sort of a massacre had been made of that description Bill and I had drawn up.

But I didn't hear that Maudie Brown message after all, and for the simple reason that I was away at half-past seven and at The Croft just after eight. Glass said there'd been hordes of sightseers on the Sunday and his men had had quite a job moving them on. But it was peaceful enough that morning. Even the weather had improved, though it was still far too chilly for September.

And now I was there, there wasn't anything to do. Glass had rough statements from the bungalows concerned and all we could spend our time at was theorising. Two cars at The Croft and almost certainly *after* Audrey Grange was dead. Neither owner had come forward and therefore neither presumably had been there for reasons that were open and above-board. So much for a start, but after that—what? We didn't know.

So we had a good look along the grass verges that Tritt's men had already searched and we did find one patch of oil that might have been made by any car. I asked about tradesmen's vans and milk, and Glass said both grocer and milkman delivered in light vans. If Miss Grange wasn't in—or if she were, for that matter—they didn't bother the house. Each knew where the key of the shed was kept and they simply opened the door, put milk or whatever it was in, and hung the key in its place again. The newspaper was delivered by a boy on a bicycle and he merely pushed it through the letterbox of the front door. One paper had been on the mat on the Saturday morning, for instance.

"She didn't want to be disturbed," Glass said. "Those actresses and film people sleep all hours of the day, so they tell me."

So much for that and we went back to the bungalow. Glass's two men had tea and milk and we made a pot of tea and did some more thinking while we drank it and smoked. Just why, we were asking, should two different cars meet at The Croft as if by appointment, and at such a late hour? Glass had a tentative idea.

"Remember what we were just saying, sir, about actors and actresses keeping late hours? That might fit the case as she was an actress. People like her work till all hours and then sleep it off till best part of midday."

I said he'd got something there. Maybe there'd been a pre-arranged party or conference. The cars had arrived and found the place in darkness and the car gone, and so they'd gone away again. That was when hopes were suddenly high, but seconds later they were down again. In less than no time that theory had gone bust, and for three simple reasons.

If it was a question of conference or party, then the callers simply must have come forward. They must have been friends of hers and only too anxious to help the police. The second reason was that friends or close acquaintances would have tried the front door and found it unlocked. And thirdly, while one departing car might for some reason or other have switched off its headlights, the idea could hardly have occurred for the same chance and legitimate reason to the other car as well.

"And there's one objection which covers everything," I told Glass. "She was supposed to be here strictly incognito. Her own husband didn't know, or her own mother. Then why should these mysterious callers know?"

That about put paid to argument. Eleven o'clock came and we decided that both of us were wasting our time. Glass said he'd have another forage round and I said I'd get back to town. I heard him giving orders to his men and then he went. I strolled more or less aimlessly through all the rooms again. Then I was in Audrey Grange's bedroom. Everything was as I had seen it last. I pushed my hand under the pillow and there was the book—*Number Thirty*.

I took it to the lounge, got my pipe going, and settled down to a good look at it. And as soon as I opened it—it was the first time I had actually scanned the letter-press—I could see that Audrey Grange had read it with extraordinary care. Passages, chiefly of conversation, were underlined. There were notes in the margins, and heavy under-scoring and lines drawn along whole paragraphs. Now and again there were marginal comments, some of them highly critical. This is a mixed sample of the kind of thing I mean.

'Not in character.' 'Rubbish—she wouldn't say that.' 'Far too melodramatic.' 'A good point.' 'Ought to be heavily cut.' 'Why no mention of her aunt?' 'Make more of this.'

You see the kind of things I mean? They interested me so much that I got out my notebook and began laboriously to make a list of them, for as far as I was concerned they answered one question—just what Audrey Grange had been studying in that so-called holiday of hers at The Croft. Then I had a look towards the end of the book, thinking perhaps that she hadn't finished reading it, and I was wrong. The book was annotated to the very last word. In fact, against the final paragraph was the note—'Rotten curtain'.

Why then, I asked myself, had the book been beneath the pillow, and the answer seemed to be that she was reading it a second time. Then I made another check and found that annotations were far more frequent up to about three-quarters of the way through the book and that seemed to be as far as she'd got on that second reading. Then I had another idea—to ring Tom Holberg. I thought it was a certainty he'd be in his office.

"Travers worrying you again, Holberg," I said, and told him in strict confidence what I'd discovered. Then I wanted to know if he was surprised.

There was quite a second or two of silence before he answered me.

"Sorry, Travers, but I can't reveal clients' business unless I'm subpoenaed, if you know what I mean. But—well, I'm not surprised."

"Thanks," I said. "That's all at the moment. If we have to make any official use of it, then we'll be seeing you. Meanwhile, thanks again."

That was that, but copying those annotations was far too long and wearisome a job, so I found a large envelope in the desk and called in one of Glass's men to witness where I'd taken the book from and to put an identification signature inside. Just when I'd done that, Wharton rang up.

"Anything at your end?" he wanted to know.

I said there was nothing of any great consequence.

"Well, there is here," he said. "I'd see to it myself but I'm in the middle of this damned inquest. It's about Maudie. We've got something."

I made appropriate noises of surprise.

"This is going to stagger you," he said, "but Wyster heard that broadcast. He's here, of course, and he told me the Merlins used to have a maid called Brown. He can almost swear her name was Maudie!"

Chapter VIII
THE MAUDIE MYSTERY

I WAS DRIVING my own car that morning—at Government expense—and that was why I pulled up so suddenly as I rounded the corner into Greenwood Street. Had it been a police car with a driver, I'd have had to give an order to stop and by then I'd have been practically at the house. As it was I pulled up about the length of a cricket pitch short of it, and on the opposite side of the road.

It might have been a kind of instinct that made me pull that car up. Through my mind there may have flashed Wharton's remark about scouting round for suspects, so that the slightest unusual thing put one on the alert. And yet, as I immediately thought, there was nothing so unusual in Frank Merlin's going away. A free country and a free citizen, so why shouldn't he go away? Then other things must have come—the bag that the taxi-man was carrying to his cab, which meant that Merlin wasn't going away just for a day. And the cremation, as I remembered, was to be on the Wednesday morning, and there was Mrs. Merlin waving from the door as if her husband was going to be absent for weeks. I suppose it was the cumulative effect of all that that made me jot down the taxi number.

The taxi moved off. Mrs. Merlin waved till it had passed my car and turned the corner. She was still there when I had another look from over the newspaper that had hid my face, and then she was gone. I looked at my watch and the time was exactly half-past twelve, so I told myself I'd stay where I was for five minutes. Then I changed my mind, and a minute later Mrs. Merlin was showing me into the room which I'd been in before. She seemed absolutely normal and quite pleased to see me.

"Did I pass your husband just now in a taxi?" I asked her with a kind of smiling bewilderment.

"Perhaps you did," she said, and was smiling too. "If you'd been here a minute or two earlier you'd have just caught him."

"What a pity," I said. "But he's not going away, is he?"

"Only for a day or two," she told me, and said it was to do with that new orchestra. The committee had decided that a professional leader should be employed. Her husband had heard of the very man in Scotland—at Edinburgh. Personal contact was so much better than correspondence, as she said, and her husband had been given full powers to arrange everything. Then her face rather fell.

"It will be an awful grief to him if he can't get back on Wednesday. You know perhaps that they're. . . ."

I hastily cut in and said that I knew. Tears were very near the surface.

"I suppose you know why I'm troubling you again, Mrs. Merlin?"

"Yes," she said, and her face was lighting again. "Harlan rang us up this morning about a police message he'd heard on the wireless. We so rarely listen to the wireless ourselves. My husband doesn't care for it. The music, you know. The terrible reproduction. He agrees with Sir Thomas Beecham."

I could have said a whole lot about that, but I didn't.

"Harlan said he'd mention it to the police and he warned us that someone would be coming to make enquiries. Of course I'd no idea it would be anyone like yourself. I thought it would be a police constable."

That was quite a little joke. Then she was saying how extraordinary it was.

"And it's all so queer," she said. "After all this time, fancy our Maud being wanted by the police! Do you think it's something to do with what happened to her? I mean, do you think they've found out after all this time what really happened?"

That conveyed nothing to me.

"How'd you come to be connected with her?" I said. "And was it the same Maud? Was her full name Maud Ethel Brown, known to her friends as Maudie?"

That was her, she said, and Harlan had said she answered to the description, except that she'd never had any great liking for making herself up. Even when she went out she was quite nicely dressed and with only just a little make-up.

"We think she'd developed some skin disease," I said. "Acne, you know, or something like that. When I saw her she was very heavily made up."

"You saw her!" She was staring as if I'd said I'd had a chat that morning with Napoleon or Queen Anne.

"Why, yes," I said. "I was as close to her as I am to you now."

She let out a breath and her whole body went limp.

"Well," she said, "so I was right after all. I always had a sort of feeling that Maud wasn't dead."

Maud—her name in the Merlin household—was a foundling brought up by a charitable institution. She began life as a maid in a private house, then changed to a pub, and then graduated to barmaid. Her last job as such had been at the Bear at Kennington and then that had been wiped out in an air raid. Maud had slept out and so escaped. Some weeks after that, Mr. Merlin had been caught in a day raid and had gone down to a shelter and Maud had been sitting next to him. They had got into conversation and had apparently taken to each other, and the upshot was that she came to the Merlins as a general help. In 1941 she had married a soldier, but he had been killed and she was a pensioned widow.

She was with the Merlins till the time of the V2 bombs, and then she had a day off to see a friend at Lewisham. It was the day of the terrible disaster there. The friend had definitely been among the victims, but no trace of Maud was ever found. The police had been informed, and indeed every necessary authority, but nothing had happened. Her savings book must have been with her in her bag but the rest of her personal possessions had been handed over. But for some reason or other, two or three personal papers had been forgotten. Merlin had said they'd had trouble enough over Maud and what did it matter, so Mrs. Merlin had kept the papers. As she had said, she had always had a curious feeling that Maud wasn't dead after all.

As for her conduct in the house, that had been exemplary, though the Merlins were glad they had not made her a companion-help. She was nice, as Mrs. Merlin said, and agreeable and cheerful and very competent, but not the sort of whom to make a companion. She spoke a different language, if Mr. Travers understood what she meant. Mr. Travers did.

"I wonder if I might see the papers?" I asked.

"Of course," she said, and got to her feet at once. Then she paused.

"Now I wonder where I had them last." She gave me an apologetic smile. "I do forget things so. But I think it was in a drawer upstairs."

It was quite a time before she came down again, and empty-handed. She couldn't find them anywhere, but when she did, she'd let me know.

"Do you remember what they were?"

"I do remember there was a marriage certificate, and—I think—two letters. Or perhaps three. I just tied them round with a piece of ribbon and left them."

And then of course she was asking me how I'd met her, and there she was, all bright-eyed and agog while I concocted a story to meet the occasion.

"But how extraordinary of her!" was all she could say. "Never coming to see us or dropping a line or wanting to know what had happened to her things."

"What you've got to remember, Mrs. Merlin, is this," I said. "Maud may have been a perfect maid, but that isn't to say she mightn't have had good reasons for disappearing and starting a new life. She may have been all sorts of things that you never suspected. She may have taken advantage of that disaster to disappear."

She was staring again, and then I could almost hear her telling herself that if I said such things, then they must be true.

"But what about her pension?"

"It may have been worth her while to lose the pension. Or there may be another solution, Mrs. Merlin. She may have lost her memory."

But I hadn't realised that I was talking to a woman of very considerable intelligence.

"But she hadn't forgotten her name? And—" something had almost startled her—"what about the marriage certificate she showed to that Mr. Quarren? How could she have it when I have it?"

"You can always get a copy from Somerset House," I said. "Perhaps she remembered so much and no more."

"It's a mystery to me," she said. "And now she's disappeared again. I can't understand it."

"Nor can we," I said. "That's why we want to get into contact with her. And there's something else I might tell you which seems to show she hadn't remembered everything. Was she strictly truthful, by the way?"

"Most truthful—and honest."

"Well, this is all I know," I said. "She told you she was married in 1941 and she was a widow drawing a pension when she came to you. That isn't what she told Mr. Quarren at the Seven Bells. She told him that she got married after the Bear was blitzed, and then her husband left her, and that's why she had to go back to the bar."

Then I had an idea, and I was asking if I might use her telephone. In a couple of minutes I was speaking to Quarren at the Seven Bells.

"Travers is the name," I said. "I was with Superintendent Wharton when he called on you a day or two ago. I'd just like to ask you a simple question."

Quarren's 'Yes, sir?' was a bit nervous.

"Maudie showed you her marriage certificate, according to your own statement to us—"

"She did."

"That's all right, I'm not questioning it. But this is what I want to know. Did you take it and examine it?"

"Well,"—he was thinking back—"now you come to mention it, I don't think I did. She showed it to me and I saw what it was, but I didn't actually take it."

"Let me suggest something. She had it in her bag and she took it out just so far, and let you see what it was, and then she put it back again."

That was it, he said, so I thanked him and rang off. When I told Mrs. Merlin what had happened, we agreed that what she'd had in her bag had been a copy, but even that didn't explain the lie. Unless—and that was something I didn't mention—it had been Quarren who had been lying.

But there seemed nothing else to say, so I thanked her and left. I did ask her to give my regards to her husband when she saw him and, as we were at the door, I ventured to hope he'd manage to get back after all in time for the funeral. Then I managed to get a hasty meal out, and after that pushed on to Wharton at the Yard.

George was triumphant. If there'd been any going I believe he'd have handed me a medal.

"There you are!" he said. "Now what about that theory of mine?" You notice it had once more become his. "Didn't I tell you there was something fishy? The Old Gent's not dead yet—not by the devil of a long way."

The title was one which George would confer on himself in hypocritical and deprecatory moments. I said it certainly looked like it.

"What'd she have to lie for?" he was asking me.

"Why ask me?" I said. "If we knew that, we'd know a lot of other things."

"But she did lie."

"Either she or Quarren. And I wouldn't trust Quarren as far as I could throw a battleship."

"I think Quarren told us the truth," George said. "Where's the significance in lying about a little detail like the date of her marriage? How could it make any possible difference to him? I say she lied. And if she lied about one thing, then she could lie about another—that yarn in Ellice's office, for example."

"You're still forgetting the flaw," I reminded him.

"Damn the flaw!" and there was a real old-time glare. "Suppose you suggest something yourself."

"I will," I said, "but it's about Merlin."

"Merlin? The stepfather?"

"Listen patiently, George," I said, "and then you can riddle it with holes when I've finished. Merlin didn't listen to the broadcast. He doesn't like the wireless and he's not unique. In fact it's a strong case for his absolute sanity, even if he has been a heavy drinker. But he heard about it over the telephone from Wyster this morning, and he was warned that the police would be making enquiries. Now then, doesn't it strike you that Merlin might have decided to go to Scotland—*might*, mind you—because he didn't want to see the police and be questioned?"

"You can prove whether or not his story was true."

"Just how?"

"By asking any member of that committee."

"What committee? If you mean the committee of the orchestra, I have to ask what orchestra? His wife doesn't know. The whole thing is to be a surprise. And you haven't met her, George. She's a nice woman; a fine woman. Not a word of blame for her husband in spite of what she's been through. She still idolises him, and she trusts him. If he says something's a secret, it *is* a secret."

"I see," George said, and as if he didn't quite believe it. "But go on with your theory."

"It's this," I said, "and for what it's worth. Merlin didn't want to be questioned about Maudie because he's known all along where she's been. He may have her installed somewhere in an apartment—"

"How could he when she's been working at the Seven Bells!"

"What's that matter," I said, "provided he knew where she lived? But in any case there'll be one sure test—or reasonably good test. I don't think Mrs. Merlin will ever find those papers."

"Why not?"

"Because her husband took them and gave them back to Maudie."

George leaned back in his swivel seat and he wasn't looking at me but across the room.

"Do you know," he said slowly, "I think we've got something there."

And then he was sitting up.

"But what about the flaw?"

"What about it?" I said. "I might have used your own retort and damned the flaw. But let's think it out instead. And when we do we get some pretty nasty implications. Or need we?"

I checked his impatience.

"Two ways of looking at it," I said. "Maudie spun her yarn because she was tired of Merlin and the Seven Bells both. She knew Audrey Grange well enough, so she used the word *Grange*. I admit that doesn't explain why that yarn of hers came true: why The Croft was burgled and Audrey Grange killed."

"What's the other way of looking at it?"

"Forget it," I said. "Now I come to work it out, I don't like it. It was that Merlin for some reason may have put Maudie up to it, and therefore he knew The Croft affair was coming off. But he's not the type to be mixed up in that sort of thing—robbing a daughter everyone says he idolised—even if the actual murder was beyond his control."

George sank back in his seat again. There was the very devil of a lot to think about, as he said.

"I know someone who'd be able to answer a few questions about Merlin and his orchestra leader," I suddenly said. "Nine days out of ten he lunches at my club. I might catch him now."

"It couldn't do any harm," George said. "Leave me that taxi number and I'll bring in the driver. We'll find out if Merlin really did go north. Not that he couldn't have given the driver the slip at the station."

I went off to the club and was there in under five minutes. My man had finished his lunch and was having a glass of port and reading *The Times* by himself in the lounge. I'm calling him Vidler, which seems a name as good as any, for he was a concert violinist who'd been an orchestra leader in his time. I told him I was on official Yard business and wanted to put up a hypothetical case.

"We begin with an amateur orchestra being formed somewhere in London—where, I don't know It's going to be a big affair that requires a professional leader, is that feasible?"

"Quite."

"The committee decides that the orchestra needs this leader and it deputes the conductor to find a suitable man. All right?"

"Quite in order—yes."

"The conductor knows of a likely man in Scotland and has just gone there to make an agreement. That sound all right to you?"

He pursed his lips and then said no. Not unless there was some personal graft. I asked him to explain.

"Well, why Scotland?" he said. "I could name scores of men in London who'd jump at such a job, if the orchestra's going to be as good as you say."

"Anything else against it?"

"Yes. The question of finance. Such a leader would want at least six or seven hundred a year. He might want a lot more. Where's the money to come from? Amateur orchestras couldn't possibly stand up to that. *Amateur* sounds good to the uninitiated, but what about hire of a hall, and the bigger the audience and the receipts, the greater the cost of hire. Then there's any amount of other expenses."

"But why couldn't this leader supplement his salary by playing in a professional orchestra himself when he wasn't needed for the other job?"

"Because no professional orchestra would possibly agree to fix its dates so as to fit in with those of any amateur orchestra. A professional orchestra's a business proposition. It's touch and go whether or not it pays."

"Couldn't he have a deputy when dates coincided?"

"I more than doubt it," he told me. "The deputy system's not tolerated to anything like the extent it used to be. As I've just said, a professional orchestra is big business. And it has tremendous competition."

I went over what he'd told me to see if I had it pat, and then he thought of something else. Was this man in Scotland married? Was there a London house for him? Had he one, and a job, in Scotland, and so wouldn't he be a fool to move? I could only say that I didn't know, but it all helped. I also said that if his opinion was acted upon, his name wouldn't be used, and then we switched to a minute or two of general chat and I thanked him and left.

I won't say George was hilarious over what I told him, but that may have been because he was waiting for news of that taxi driver. He'd been located at a stand near Mornington Crescent but was out on a job and Wharton's man was waiting for him to come back. George said we might as well have an early cup of tea for it might be some time before we saw another meal.

"I'd really intended to go to Carr's Hill this afternoon," he told me. "I want to test the sound a Lautrec makes."

He opened his small safe and showed me the gun he'd been furnished with. Compared with a Colt it was like a coral snake to a cobra. It was so small that had I been an expert in palming, my hand could have concealed it. And the bullets didn't look much bigger than those of my old .22 rifle.

"It can kill all right," George said, "and at a much bigger range than point-blank. No great penetrative power, of course."

"Sort of thing to go snugly into a woman's handbag," I said.

"Or a man's pocket," George said, and put it back in the safe. "But what I think we'll do now is try it out at the same time and as near as we can get to the same conditions. If there's time we'll do it tonight."

We finished our tea and George was just lighting his pipe when our call came through. That taxi driver had deposited Merlin and his bag at 76 Carris Street.

"That's it," George told him. "Just take a formal statement, then report back."

Then he was ringing through for a police car.

Carris Street might be said to have caught us both clean in the wind. It lies in the maze between Regent Street and Shaftesbury Avenue, and we'd expected to find that No. 76 was either a grubby hotel or an apartment house. But it was nothing of the sort. It was a somewhat dingy though perfectly respectable suite of offices, and there was the usual list just inside the door.

GROUND FLOOR
Harper and Webb, accountants.
Fenley Bros., Importers.
FIRST FLOOR
British and Empire Educational Press.
Miles and Co., surgical instruments.
SECOND FLOOR
Alberton Publications, Ltd.
Trewman, Ltd., Stamps.
THIRD FLOOR
A. Levin, accountant.
Hammerford and Pryce, brush manufacturers.

"Wonder what the devil he was doing here?" George said to me.

"Probably nothing at all," I said. "He got out of the taxi, saw it drive away, then went out again and took either a bus or another taxi."

"You stay here," George said. "I'm going to do some telephoning. Just scribble down a description of this Merlin."

He was soon back. A couple of men would be along in a jiff, he said, and they'd take that description and go to every office in the building to see if Merlin had had business there. He'd wait where he was and I might have a look round.

I went over each floor of that building and had a look at every door, and the tenants were a mixed lot. Some were obviously sub-departments of firms with other offices elsewhere. Some were the now cramped offices of firms bombed out and still unable to find their old-time accommodation. But quite a few names were not on the ground-floor list. The third floor, for instance, had two small businesses each using a single room. The second floor also had two, while British and Empire Educational Press on the first floor—W. Harper was written under it—had two small rooms at the most and the rest was occupied by Miles and Go. No doubt some of those small concerns were shoddy or shady, and the high-sounding British and Empire Educational Press—the door was locked, by the way, for it was the only one I had the nerve to try—might have dealt in anything from the mystico-religious to the slightly pornographic.

George is a believer in the dignity of work, and he and I lent his two men a hand. The job took us till five o'clock when some of the offices closed down, and all we found was a clerk in Fenley Bros, on the ground floor, who'd seen a man with a bag and wearing an overcoat going up the stairs to the first floor. But nobody on that first floor had seen him, so maybe he had dodged down again.

"Surely he can't be still on the premises," I said.

"I'm taking no chances," George told me. "This place is going under observation from now on. If Merlin pops his nose in or out of here again, he's going to tell us why."

The preliminaries were arranged and we set off back to the Yard, and even if the couple of hours had been a disappointment, we knew we were close to something that George would call fishy. For instance, why did Merlin ask to be set down at a particular street and a particular number? He must have known both street and number, and that there was really a 76 in that street. But in all that street there wasn't a shop that seemed in any way to do with music or an office connected with a music-publishing concern. Yet—and it had to be underlined—Merlin had asked to be driven to that street and that number. Then he had gone in but had he gone out? If he had, why ask to be driven to a particular place when he could have stopped the driver anywhere and just got out!

There was nothing for us at the Yard and then George changed his mind about the visit to The Croft. He thought he'd go there with just a ballistics man.

"It's a pity you don't go a bit early and have a word yourself with Mrs. Ganton," I said. "She was so insistent about that business of hearing a baby. It's been worrying me, though I haven't said anything. Either Mrs. Ganton was right or she was wrong. If it *was* a baby, then whose was it? If it wasn't, then what was the noise? But she swears it was a baby."

"Perhaps I'll see her," George said, "though having had a couple of kids of her own doesn't make her omniscient. But about you. Why shouldn't you go and see that play that Wyster's in?"

It was on the tip of my tongue to ask why, and where would it get us.

"That Merril Holme," George went on. "There's someone we haven't had a look at yet. Rig up some excuse and go and see her after the show. Wyster will fix that for you."

"And what then?" I said. "Do I tell her that I'm one of the unfortunates whose wife doesn't understand him?"

"You don't want me to tell you," George said, and that oily smile of his was more like a leer. "Just lead her along. Get her talking." The gesture became one of impatience. "It's a job right up your alley."

"Orders are orders," I said. "I'm to start a beautiful friendship. And if it slips just a little bit past that, then you'll put things right with Bernice. This is going to be one of my red-letter nights."

So off I went with George telling me I would have my little joke. But as a matter of fact he was only telling me to do what I'd thought of doing on my own. I don't mean a vamping act. In a competition of that sort I'd be well at the tail-end of the field. But I did want to see in the flesh the Merril Holme I'd seen on the screen. Merlin had advised me to see that play, and, after what had happened, it had struck me that he must have had a good reason.

CHAPTER IX
ROUND SQUARE

IF ONLY in fairness to that show at the Orpheum, let me say that I am a man of varied tastes. I like the old-style music-hall, and the cinema and the theatre, and of the three, I like the theatre least. If I do go to the theatre I like to be amused—and not necessarily to the point of hilarity. I like, say, to go after a good dinner and relax in a comfortable seat and have the chance of an occasional chuckle. Tragedies, except maybe the world's greatest, leave me cold, and a problem play is one of the few problems that has for me not the least glimmer of interest.

That, as I said, is why I apologise to both the author and the actors. At the Orpheum that night I was rather like a baseball fan who sees a cricket match—say Lancashire *v.* Yorkshire—for the first time. I, for instance, was ready to admit admiringly that I could never have done what the actors did, but at the same time the whole thing struck me as much adept ado about a very little and uncommonly slow nothing.

Perhaps you loathe synopses as much as I do, if only as exemplified in a synopsis you may find preceding a serial story in a magazine. It is bald and its bare bones are almost repelling. If so, you'll pardon my synopsis of the play I saw that night. Why it was called *Round Square* I don't know, unless it was that the husband-father—Harlan Wyster—was to find himself suddenly a round peg in a square hole. The scene was a fine house in the country but on the fringes of a manufacturing district. He was county and all that goes with it: a magistrate, a patron of this and that, blameless in reputation and just about at the head of the queue for a knighthood. He was also chairman of a local and big business company.

Merril Holme was his wife, and very much county too, though in her case one gathered that there was just a bit of veneer above the questionably genuine heart of Tudor oak. There was a daughter of about twenty with her fiancé and a son of twenty-three just demobilised. There was the girl he was hoping to get engaged to, though the family weren't too happy about her. There was also a butler—the Polonius, not the comic type—and also an old family housekeeper, and she, played by Agnes Farmer, was really funny. In my view she stole the show. There was also a family solicitor, all spectacles, grey hair and benevolence.

As for the plot, you may have guessed it already. We saw the family at its suavest and best, and then came the shock. A rascally general manager of the company had committed a series of frauds and there seemed nothing for it but bankruptcy. In Act 2 the news came, and then one saw the other side of the family, and it was with their reactions that the play mainly dealt. The father was for the honourable way—selling everything and paying what he considered just debts, though of course, with no legal obligations. There was a gorgeous family set-to, with the wife spitting like a cat and ready to wipe her hands of the man whose neglect of business and simple trust in others and fantastic ideas of what constitutes honour would cost her a title and heaven knew what else. The son was on her side and so was the daughter's fiancé. The daughter stood up for her father. The solicitor wobbled on the fence. The butler uttered aphorisms, and the housekeeper contrived to talk common sense.

And what happened in the end? Just what you're guessing. It's discovered that the company can undergo reconstruction. The fiancé—love finds a way—can put up the money, and there is heaven-sent news of a new big contract. With a flagrantly Noel Cowardish ending, the family is itself again, with the old suavity and unruffled routine. The curtain falls with the butler bringing in the usual nightcap to the master when the family at last have dispersed. Hot whisky or milk?

I couldn't say. It's a long time since I was in an old country house.

Had not long association with George Wharton made me impervious to shame, I must have blushed at the card I had sent round to Wyster at the end of Act 2, for I wrote on it, "Am enjoying show immensely. Hope to see you afterwards." Not, mind you, that there weren't things that I enjoyed. The family shindy was good, and it was a good theatre. I've said I loved the housekeeper, and the daughter wasn't bad if only because she was young enough herself to ring very nearly true. Wyster was most competent, if no more, and he owed an enormous deal to that fine voice of his. It was a part that might have been written for him, and in my judgment he could have made more of it; have made it less stereotyped, shall we say. But it was in Merril Holme that I was most interested.

On that stage she looked a remarkably handsome woman, though that may give perhaps a false impression. She was not regal and bosomy, even if her make-up did make her a woman of forty-five instead of the thirty-three that she actually was. But she was about five-foot seven and slim and her movements were what I believe are called slinky, with a slight swaying of the hips. She didn't, in fact, slip any too well into the niceness of Act 1. But when it came to Act 2 and the shindy, she was absolutely first-rate. Merlin had been right. He had called her a thrustful, aggressive woman, and it had seemed to me that in that Act 2 she had had no need to be other than her natural self, and if that doesn't make for first-class acting, what does? And at the very end, when the whole company took a bow, there was what seemed to me yet another Merril Holme. Now she was all womanliness and human. Wyster and she were hand in hand and bowing to the audience and each other, he all courtesy and charm and she all smiles, and her lips would be moving and I was thinking cattishly to myself that in the din of applause the unheard words would be something about you dear people.

But before the absolutely last curtain I was making my way, as arranged, behind the scenes. I had to wait for a bit and then was handed over to an attendant. The curtain was finally down as we went past and then at the end of a short corridor I was told that Wyster's room was the second door on the left. I said thanks very much and walked on, my feet making no sound on the strip of carpet. I was perhaps ten feet from that door when I heard voices, and something made me stop.

"Darling, you'd be mad! Don't say a thing. How could he possibly find out!"

That was Merril's voice. Wyster's was only a mumble. But I turned back, intending to make a new approach with a warning cough. Then as I turned again, there was Merril Holme in the corridor just beyond Wyster's room.

"Are you looking for someone?" she was calling, and with the most charming of smiles.

I said I was looking for Wyster and she smiled again and pointed, with a sort of moue, at his door. Then she disappeared round the corner.

I tapped at the door, Wyster called a come in, and in I went. He saw me in the mirror and was at once on his feet and coming to meet me. His manner was a nice blend of pleasure and reserve—Wyster the friend and Wyster the bereaved; Travers the caller and Travers the sleuth.

"Nice to see you here," he said. "Take this chair, it's reasonably comfortable. Cigarette? And what will you drink?" And then the real question, so smoothly added: "Or are you partly on duty?"

"Duty be damned," I said. "This is my night off."

I had a whisky, though I wouldn't have done if I'd known in time he wasn't having one too. He was what he called a very scanty drinker. Then while he was getting his face back to normal he was asking about the show and I was popping out lies with Sten-gun rapidity. I was most enthusiastic about Merril Holme. Such an experience, as I said, after having seen her only on the screen.

"Merril's always on top of her job," he said, and swivelled round for a moment. "You'd like to meet her?"

There was I, all blushes and deprecation.

"She'd be delighted," he told me. "But I shall have to be rather discourteous, I'm afraid. I have an engagement in a few minutes' time. No, no hurry. I'm sorry I told you, but you know how things are."

We talked and then a certain Fred was called. Fred, I imagined, was his man, parked for the occasion of my call. Fred was given various instructions.

"And see Miss Holme at once, will you? Ask her to drop in when she's ready. I want her to meet a friend."

He turned back towards the dressing-table. Fred caught my eye. He was a short, perky looking chap in the thirties, and what should he do but give me a wink! What that was intended to convey I had no idea. Then I thought I knew. Fred's wink was the equivalent of a street whistle. That quick droop of an eyelid had uttered a paragraph in less than a flash. "And so you're going to meet our Merril. And, boy, are you in luck!"

Wyster was ready to go. My eye had always been surreptitiously on my wrist-watch, and I made it just fifteen minutes since he had entered his room, for he had had little make-up to remove and merely to change back to a lounge suit. The time was three minutes past ten, and the curtain had fallen at a quarter to. Suppose, I said to myself, he were wishing to go to Carr's Hill. Suppose he went by car and took his time. Even then he could make it easily by half-past eleven.

Then Merril Holme came in, and if I hadn't had in mind what I'd seen on the stage and what I'd heard in that room, I'd have thought her the most charming and delightful of women. A how-d'you-do wasn't good enough for me. I had a handshake and a simply dazzling smile.

"You'll excuse me now," Wyster told me.

"Darling, you're not leaving us?"

His smile was grave, but it was still a smile.

"Not exactly leaving you. Mr. Travers knows I've got an appointment."

The three of us went out to the quiet side-street. Wyster said goodbye again and moved off on foot.

"And now what?" I said. "Are you going my way or am I going yours?"

"Which *is* your way?"

"Well," I said, and my smile was something of a titter. "I was actually having the nerve to wish it was your way."

She said nothing but the smile was provocative.

"Supper?" I said. "Or a drink somewhere?"

"That sounds nice," she said, and then frowned. "It's too sweet of you but somehow I don't just feel like it tonight." A frown, a thought, a suggestion.

"Would you think me too dreadful if I just went home? I could find you coffee, or a drink."

"Sounds too good to be true," I said. "I'll call a taxi." And then I, too, remembered something. I had a kind of appointment but now I'd no intention of keeping it. All the same, if she didn't mind waiting just a moment, I thought I ought to telephone.

She waited while I telephoned from inside, and I wondered if she had an inkling that I was calling the Yard.

"It's about Harlan Wyster," I said. "He's just left the theatre and, I think, for his flat. Get a couple of men there and try to contact. Have him under observation all night. You know the address."

I went back and she was still all smiles. A taxi wasn't necessary, she said, and we'd go the homely way by the Piccadilly Line, and her maisonette was not two minutes from the station at the Palmer's Green end.

"Do you know, I feel as if I've known you for an awful long time," she told me, and actually took my arm as we crossed with the traffic lights. "I expect it was the funny way I first saw you, wandering around in the corridors. Had you been right up to the door before?"

From what I told her I hadn't been within the faintest earshot of that scrap of conversation that I'd overheard.

"I'm an awful fool in some things," I said. "I simply have no sense of locality. I expect these glasses of mine have something to do with it, and I'm blind as a bat if I have to take them off."

"But why should you take them off? I think they make you look frightfully distinguished." Then the hand tightened about my arm. "You're awfully good-looking, you know."

"I?" I said. "Good lord, no!"

"That's false modesty," she told me, and my arm had a little squeeze again.

Then we were at the Tube station, and so far I wasn't doing any too badly for the world's worst vamp.

Forty minutes, I made it, from door to door, and we'd waited three minutes for a train. Had we changed at Finsbury Park and there'd been a convenient train there, we could have been at Carr's Hill in about three-quarters of an hour.

She took my arm again as we walked from the station to what she had called her maisonette. It was in Lansing Avenue, and from what I could see of the outside in the early moonlight, I should have called it a charming semi-detached villa, complete with garage and side entrance.

"You run your car?" I said.

"Only on Sundays mostly," she said. "The petrol simply won't run to it. And now there's going to be none. Isn't it too dreadful?"

I commiserated and then we were inside. In less than no time I knew it was a snug little place. Two bedrooms, so I judged, a kitchen, small downstair cloak-room, and a beautiful little lounge.

"A drink?" she said, and indicated a kind of movable cocktail bar in the corner. "Do help yourself. I must just powder my nose."

I had a long whisky and soda. If I was anticipating—or should I have said dreading—her return in something flimsy and transparent, then I was to be wrong, for she was wearing the same powder blue frock she'd had on under her heavy fur coat. But she'd put on some long turquoise earrings and they went well with her blonde hair.

"Drink?" I said, and then as if I had to say it: "You were saying all sorts of pretty things about *my* looks, but—well, you're a damn pretty woman."

She shrugged her shoulders and made an amused grimace.

"What is this? A prelude to seduction?"

"Lady!" I said, as if shocked. "And me a happily married man."

"Really? What an unusual thing. And your wife really understands you?"

"Well," I said, "I wouldn't go so far as that. Besides. . . ."

"Yes?"

"Well, it's only an hour since we met. I resent being thought so crude in my methods."

"There'll be time," she told me, and that might have meant anything. "And now give me a drink. Just a tiny whisky, and heaps of soda."

We said here's how, and she was waving me to the chesterfield. I thought she was joining me but she took a chair.

"Now let's be serious," she said, and sat primly up. "You really did like the show?"

We talked about that and then she was asking what my job was. I told her I was what the Yard calls an unofficial expert, which was really a kind of stooge. That, of course, led to mention of Audrey Grange and I had to admit and with the nicest shade of off-handedness, that I was helping in a humble way.

"Not that it's the kind of thing I take any interest in," I said. "Just a robbery and a brutal murder. No subtlety. No nothing. It's not my line of country at all."

"Perfectly dreadful, though I do feel so sorry for poor Harlan. He's a darling you know, really. We've been friends for years. And poor dear Audrey. Simply lived for her work, you know. Such a tragedy, I think. That's why Harlan's been such a dear. Most men would have left her long ago."

"Really?"

"What was there for him?" She gave a little shrug of the shoulders. "Speak well of the dead they say, but I don't see it. I liked Audrey, mind you. We'd played in pictures together and we were always good enough friends. But that didn't excuse the way she made work the be-all and end-all. She was good, but she wasn't a Bernhardt."

Then she was getting me to tell her all I knew about the murder, as poor Harlan had told her so little. And she'd keep it ever so secret. Heaps of things I must know. I told her perhaps I did and I told her what they were, and that meant some mighty quick adaptation and invention. And then I closed remorselessly down and was looking at my empty glass.

She got me another drink and another tiny one for herself. "The tragedy of Audrey Grange," I said pontifically, "is being an only child. The tragedy for her parents, I mean. Do you happen to be an only child? I was myself."

"I have a brother, but I haven't seen him for quite a time. But about the Merlins, have you met Frank?"

I said I had just caught sight of him.

"I think he's an old darling. Everybody's fond of Frank." Slowly the conversation drew near the borders of strain. I got to my feet at last and said I'd have to be going. Late nights wouldn't buy the baby new shoes.

"You have a baby?"

"A figure of speech," I said. "No family. And my wife's in Scotland, at the moment."

She laughed, just a bit too noisily, and it wasn't that she'd had too much to drink.

"Does that mean we're back where we came in?"

"You mean when you were accusing me of having designs?"

She shrugged that off. It might have been on—if I'd cared.

"Well, I hate going," I said as she went with me to the door.

"Why so tragic? Won't you come and see me again? Or are you expecting a train from Scotland?"

"That wouldn't make any difference to me," I told her belligerently. "But honestly, may I see you again?"

"Why not?"

"Give you a ring?"

"Why not?"

"Or would you rather ring me?"

"If you like."

We were at the door. She made a gesture as if she wanted to whisper something, and I stooped down. One hand of hers must have switched off the light and then both arms were round my neck. Then she had the nerve to push me—me mind you—gently away.

"Too late now," she was whispering. "Hurry up and ring me again soon."

Then the door was open and I was out once more in the chill moonlight.

Across the road I glanced back and then I caught the wave of her hand from a bedroom window. She had gone up there, I thought, to make sure that I was making for the station. And round the corner I wiped my lips with my handkerchief; not from prudery, mind you, for it isn't often one gets a hug from a pretty woman thrown in free in a business like mine. I suppose I just wiped my lips instinctively—a married man's instinct perhaps—and I noticed there was never a trace of lipstick. Honest-to-God and unadulterated, I could tell myself, and then I was trying to work out precisely what it had all meant.

At the station I made straight for the stairs, and, as it turned out, it was lucky I did so. Then I changed my mind and came back to the telephone kiosk.

It was still short of midnight and I thought there might be a chance of catching Wharton at The Croft. The man at that end told me I was just in time. Wharton, in fact, was through the door and on his way down the path, and I could hear the man calling.

"I think I'm on to something, George," I said. "Far too long for the telephone. Will you drop in at my place on your way back, or shall I come to the Yard?"

I had an idea he'd suggest my place, and he did. That was all, and in a minute or two I was in the train. At the flat I rousted round and got some sandwiches and there was beer in the refrigerator. It was a chilly, autumnal night, so I switched on the electric fire, and everything was cosy when George arrived.

There he was then, sandwich in one hand and pencil in the other while he noted down what I had to say, and that, summarised, was this:

    a. "Darling, you'd be mad. Don't say a thing. How could he possibly find out?"

Did the *he* refer to me? Or was the whole reference to something else? (See *c.*)

    b. W's appointment (?) was probably arranged and I had M.H. deliberately thrust on me. It was she who suggested her maisonette.

    c. She questioned me shrewdly from the start, and was anxious to know where I'd been at the time of *a.* She wanted inside information about The Croft affair, and, I think, to know just what the police knew.

    d. She was most friendly. She wanted me to come again when she might be more friendly still.

e. Unimportant perhaps, but she wasn't anxious to talk about her brother. She spoke of W. as a sorely tried man who ought to have left his wife but hadn't.

I gave him an idea of the house itself, and added various timings as I'd worked them out. George seemed quite pleased. He even tried pulling my leg.

"And you left all that to hurry back here? Gone a bit moral suddenly, haven't you?"

"Maybe, George," I said. "But she wasn't quite serious enough. There wasn't even a strip-tease act. I was just being led nicely on and nicely pumped, and what she learned was going to be reported to Wyster. That was his so-called appointment, or so I think, to go home and wait till she rang him. I think she did that in the maisonette when she went to powder her nose. She was out of the room long enough to change everything she had on, and she changed nothing—so far as I could see. Also I'm fairly sure that as soon as I left she rang Wyster again. I'm hoping he went straight along to her place. At that time of night it wouldn't be ten minutes in a car. I had a couple of men trying to pick him up, by the way. We shan't get their report till the morning."

"Not bad work," George said, which was high praise for him. "And what about the woman herself?"

"Hard," I said. "Plenty of charm and sex appeal and that sort of thing, but damned hard underneath. And clever, I'd say, in a cattish, crafty sort of way. And talking of old cats what did you get from Mrs. Ganton?"

George shot a look at me, then took a swig at his beer. Even then he shook a rueful head.

"That woman could bray the head off a wagon load of jackasses. Still," and he shrugged his shoulders, "she'd swear she heard a baby. You can't budge her from that."

"What about the gun?"

"You could just hear a faint something on the road. Any further away—not a sound."

Then he was harking back to myself and Merril Holme. I remembered Fred and his flagrant wink and said there was somebody who might spill quite a lot of things about the lady, and possibly about Wyster.

"That matter of James Holme," I said, "and neither of them wanting to talk about the other. Just what's in it? Could we do anything about the brother?"

"As a matter of fact," George said, and in that quiet voice he adopts when he's having to own up to some slightly shady *fait accompli*, "I thought of that myself. He was hanging round Audrey Grange all right. Used to pop down to the Studios quite frequently and take the lady out in her off spells. Quite common knowledge down there."

Then he was getting up to go.

"This whole case has got itself into the position of a dammed-up river," I told him as we made for the lift. "We're on the thirsty side, and the flaw is what's holding the water back. If only we could find the answer to that flaw!"

"It'll come," George said. "Every fishy thing we find out about Wyster and the Holme woman and the brother, and Merlin, all goes to show I wasn't such a fool as I looked." He stopped in his tracks and whipped round on me. "That Maudie Brown yarn was a pack of lies and I'll bet you a new hat on it."

But there was nothing doing. When I lose I pay, but George has a convenient loss of memory. An hour later I was even more glad I hadn't taken him.

Chapter X
NUMBER THIRTY

I WENT BACK to the room and its fire and I found myself utterly remote from sleep. I didn't feel like a drink; in fact I didn't feel like anything. I saw the evening papers that I hadn't read, and picked one up, but even that wasn't going to hold me. Then as I glanced through it, a name caught my eye. I read the whole paragraph which came from what I call the chatterbox column.

Film fans everywhere will be agog to know who will be cast for the part of Jinny Patman in the film version of Matthew Riche's best-seller *Number Thirty*. Never since the pre-casting weeks of *Gone With the Wind* has there been so much speculation, and everyone is asking who will be the star chosen to take the most important and exacting part that the English screen has ever known. But for the untimely and tragic death of Audrey Grange, there might have been less speculation. Some say there will be a surprise. Israel Kraaf, whom I ran across today in the Grill Room of the Macedonia, still refuses to commit himself. But a little bird tells me that one of the first things Mr. Kraaf did on his arrival was to drop in at the Orpheum, where *Round Square* is still playing to packed houses. Meanwhile speculation goes on. And Mr. Kraaf, be it noted, is due to return to New York in a matter of days.

I let the paper fall to my knees, stretched out my long legs to the fire, and began to think. The part of Jinny Patman was apparently more than a highly desirable plum; it was something that was going to make film history. Audrey Grange was thought by some to have been reasonably sure of that part. Now a tip was being given for Merril Holme.

All that was inherent in the paragraph I'd just read, but hadn't I seen something else somewhere before? I remembered where—in one of the Sunday papers—and how the mention of Merril Holme had been something of a certainty. Maybe that was preliminary and paid-for by publicity designed to sway the decision of Israel Kraaf. And in the middle of that speculation, I remembered something else. In my wall safe was a copy of *Number Thirty*—Audrey Grange's own annotated copy!

My legs shot back and I was out of that chair and making for the safe. And then I did feel like another drink, so I fetched another bottle and got my pipe going, and settled down to a skimming of that tremendously long book.

Another synopsis, you say, and probably shudder. But it has to be done, and it needn't be long. The framework of that book is the important thing, and that, as I've already said, was a series of people living in an apartment house of the cheapest kind in a dingy though not actually squalid part of London. It recalled in some ways *London Belongs to Me*, though that was in my judgment an infinitely finer book.

I'll admit that *Number Thirty* had holding power, and there was skill in the way the characters were presented. A chapter would be devoted to the tenant or tenants of a room or rooms, and in that chapter one would meet, if only casually, another tenant. The following chapter would be devoted to that new character with flashbacks to the first and contact with a third. And so it went on till by the time one had met all the people but one, all of them were fixed firmly in the mind. The one character still not met was Jinny Patman, though to her there had been innumerable references. One knew what the other characters thought of her. Some thought this and some that, but the important thing is that the reader had been brought to a point when he was keenly interested in meeting her himself.

And so to the chapter devoted to Jinny Patman, and I had gone through six chapters of that book before I arrived at her, and that much quick reading had taken me over half an hour. In that chapter, then, I saw her bed-sitting-room and Jinny at her breakfast. She remembered that she hadn't given her cheese ration to Mr. Quale on the floor above, and up she went with it. On the way down she had a quick word with old Mrs. Hankel, with Mrs. Hankel's daughter, Rose, still having her own idea— that Jinny wasn't the day-companion-help she had let people assume she was, but something far more suited to her cheap prettiness. Then—the chapter drawing near its end—Jinny got ready for work, and locked the door and down the stairs she went. A word or two with another tenant or two, and she was making for a bus, and that bus was taken at the Elephant and Castle! Ten minutes later Jinny got off the bus and entered her place of work. It was a pub called The Cat and Mouse. *Jinny was a barmaid!*

* * *

My fingers had gone to my glasses. The book lay on the chair and I was prowling restlessly about the room. I went to the telephone, then turned back. It was half-past two in the morning and George wouldn't thank me for being disturbed when there was nothing immediate he could do. And I still hadn't thought the whole thing out.

A minute or two later my brain had suddenly gone tired. It was late and there had been the strain of reading that book and, however astounding the discovery, it was not enough to jolt me back to full wakefulness. And yet I somehow knew I should not sleep. Naps perhaps, between uneasy tossings, and little more, and a tired mind trying to puzzle out what a fresh one could scarcely cope with. Even the two sleeping tablets that I took, and in a stiff whisky, didn't get me to sleep before another half-hour.

Then the alarm clock went and I was still heavy with sleep and bleary-eyed as I reached across and turned it off. Then I had something which I hate—a cold bath. I soused my head as well and when I'd shaved and dressed I was feeling fine. It was still short of seven o'clock and I rang Wharton at his private address. Jane Wharton said he was having his breakfast.

"Yes?" George said, and rather snappily. "That you, Travers?"

"Yes," I said. "Are you coming straight to the Yard?"

"Why? Got something?"

"Yes," I said. "I've got the answer to that flaw."

"How do you know?" he was firing at once.

"As soon as you get to the Yard, you'll know too," I told him.

Then I rang off and I fixed the bell so that he couldn't ring me back. I knew of old the time it would take him at the quickest to get from his house to the Yard, and it gave me ample time for breakfast. And I made it a good one for I'd a pretty shrewd idea that it might be quite a time before I'd see another meal. Even then I got to the Yard before him and I was in his room when I heard him coming hastily up the last stairs.

"Now what's all this?" he said, and didn't even trouble to hang up his hat.

I gave him that copy of *Number Thirty* and said it was a longish story. I suggested a stenographer to save his notes, and he pushed the buzzer. Then I gave him that synopsis of the first few chapters, and, like the author, I kept the vital paragraph till the very last. Then his eyes opened and his mouth was agape.

"A barmaid," he said. "This Jinny was a barmaid!"

He waved a quick hand for the stenographer to stop. I said he'd better go on. I'd like my own arguments recorded.

"Here's a cutting from last night's paper," I said. "Read it, and read this other one from a Sunday paper, so as to get the full background."

George read them.

"I know what you're at," he said. "But go on."

"The greatest film part for years," I said, "and Audrey Grange had made up her mind she was going to have it. She knew Israel Kraaf, but that wasn't enough. The back-door approach wasn't her way. She wanted that part from merit and she must have known she was the only one who could play it. She was the Jinny build and she could be the Jinny type. That was the part she was studying at The Croft. That's why she read that book at least twice and annotated it carefully. That was the sort of stuff she could use if any convincing was needed with Kraaf.

"But she did more. She didn't want puff paragraphs in chatterbox columns. She wanted something absolutely unanswerable. She wanted to show Kraaf she could play the part. In fact she was going to show him that she *had* played the part—and played it the hard way. Where she got the rudiments of instruction we can find out. Even if we don't, it won't much matter, but she looked out for a favourable advertisement—plenty of them in the papers—and then answered the one that suited her for locality and so on. Its nearness to the Cat and Mouse of the book, shall we say. You'll remember too that she was just a bit out of things when she began the job and claimed it was due to the fact that she hadn't been behind a bar for quite a time, and on account of her marriage. That's why she manipulated the date of that marriage and didn't let Quarren inspect the Certificate.

"The papers were the real Maudie Brown's papers, of course, which is why Mrs. Merlin couldn't find them. I don't know what else there was besides the Certificate, but there may have been an Identity Card and maybe a written reference or two. Whatever there was it was good enough for Quarren. As for disguise—and principally in case anyone who knew her on the screen or off should happen to come into the Seven Bells—she had only to use plenty of make-up and stuff out her bust artistically. I admit that in Bill Ellice's office I noted the incongruity of her slim figure and the prominence of the bust. As for how she did her job, well, we have Quarren's and his customers' word for it.

"As for proof," I went on, timing my words principally for the stenographer, "we have some in the fact that Audrey Grange went to The Croft for three weeks and Maudie was at the Seven Bells for the same three weeks. Audrey was seen on the golf course twice, and each time on a Thursday, which was Maudie's day off. Then Carr's Hill is on the direct route to the Seven Bells part of town, with only one change. Audrey had a choice of ways so as not to call attention to herself, and having to report at as late as ten o'clock gave her plenty of time to use any route she liked. Sometimes she may have varied it by using her car and parking it somewhere handy. Getting home at night was easier still because she wouldn't have to worry about being seen in Hurst Avenue. It'd be too dark for that. As to that arrangement for putting the milk and any possible groceries in the shed, the reason given was that she slept late and wasn't to be disturbed. Actually she'd most likely be away and gone, at least when the groceries came. It might be interesting to see if she paid the milkman and the grocer on Thursdays.

"Now to what was supposed to happen. Audrey was barmaid at the Seven Bells and feeling absolutely safe in her job. She'd given an accommodation address and tested it very early on in case it might be needed at any time. Everything was going smoothly and working up to the time of Kraaf's arrival. That was the real zero hour but certain things had to be done before it. That visit to Bill Ellice's office was a kind of match to fire the train. I'm pretty sure, by the way, that she got that address from an advertisement in her newspaper. In that context, note the times. She left Bill's office at ten o'clock. She pretended to be calling at Liverpool Street when actually on the way to Carr's Hill, and she still had time for golf soon after eleven.

"But first of all, what did she intend to happen? On the Thursday evening she would fake the robbery and go off somewhere in her car and she'd have the car garaged. I want you to notice that there's to be no time lag; everything works smoothly. But she has to call attention to the robbery, so she spins that yarn in Bill's office. I also think that later she intended to ring the police anonymously. But you see the point. By going to Bill Ellice and building up a situation on the three spivs, she was also keeping Maudie Brown anonymous. Bill, as she knew, wouldn't betray a client by telling her affairs to the police.

"I think the robbery should have been discovered on the Friday morning and the disappearance of Audrey Grange with it. There'd be a sensation when it was known that the famous film actress, Audrey Grange, was missing. But Audrey, as Maudie, would be at work at the Seven Bells, and on the Saturday—the date of Kraaf's arrival—she'd ring Holberg. The conversation would go something like this:

H. Audrey! Where are you ringing from? Don't you know what's happened? You're supposed to have disappeared after a robbery at Carr's Hill. Half England is looking for you.

A. You're joking. The bungalow was all right when I left it on Thursday. All I did was go away for a long weekend. Somewhere where I needn't see a paper or listen to the wireless.

H. But don't you realise—

A. Now, Tom, just keep calm. I'll put all that right myself. There's something far more important to do. Has Kraaf arrived? He has? Then you're to bring him tonight to the Seven Bells. That's a pub. . . .

"And so on with an insistence that, however bizarre it seemed, it was vitally important. And when Kraaf did turn up at the Seven Bells, Audrey would do an unmasking act. Maudie Brown would be transformed back to Audrey Grange. It would be in the saloon bar and maybe the Press would have been invited too. And what a sensation! The publicity for Kraaf's picture! And could there be any question of who should play Jinny Patman?"

And there I let out a breath and said I thought that was all. There'd be plenty of time to cross the t's and dot the i's once we'd accepted the main facts.

I read the typed notes, made a slight alteration or two, and everything was ready as a basis for a new start, with the two newspaper clippings as exhibits, and the annotated copy of *Number Thirty*. Then with the notes we got to work hunting for flaws. George said, for instance, that there was something I wanted to have both ways. I'd given evidence and Glass had substantiated it at the golf club, to show that Audrey Grange disliked publicity. Now apparently she had been out for the most hectic publicity.

"I wouldn't call it that, George," I said. "She wasn't out for publicity so much as for proof. She had to drive home the fact that she could *be* a barmaid, which is far more than acting one. But if I've overdrawn it, I take it back."

"The main theory strikes me as true enough," George grunted. "But there's something else. How do you reconcile the Maudie Brown of the Seven Bells with the girl who spun that yarn in Ellice's office?"

"That's easily accounted for," I said. "Maudie in Ellice's office had to put on a badly scared act. Miss Munney actually thought she wasn't all there because she overdid it. And another thing. I never saw Maudie behind the saloon bar. I only took the word of the regulars and watched their reactions to her absence. I mightn't have had any affection or liking for her as they apparently had. I'm not a regular."

"That may be it," George said. "But where does Merlin come in? Why's he bolted?"

"Has he bolted?"

George rang through for the morning's reports. Nothing had been seen of Merlin at 76 Carris Street.

"Then he may be in Scotland after all," I said. "He may be trying to work a pal into the job—private graft, in fact. He may be having a holiday at the expense of that committee, and all the time have someone in London up his sleeve for the job. One thing will have to be done, though. It's got to be done some time or other, and that's to find out if she left a will. If Merlin's down for any considerable amount, it might affect things."

"How do you mean?"

"Well, he might have got himself badly into debt. He may have been helping himself to the funds of that orchestra. Audrey may have put her foot down and refused to help, and he didn't want his wife to know. All conjecture, I admit."

We left it at that. George rang Holberg's office but Holberg hadn't arrived. The secretary said she could find plenty of publicity photographs and stills of Audrey Grange, and George said he'd send at once for a sample. And might Mr. Holberg be warned as soon as he arrived that Mr. Travers was coming to see him on a very urgent matter.

"No point in showing a photograph to the Quarrens," George told me. "If Mrs. Q. goes to the pictures she might recognise her, and the last thing we want is for anything of this to get out prematurely. What I've got in mind is to fake one of the photographs to keep the general look of Audrey Grange and bring the clothes and so on into line with the Maudie of your and Bill Ellice's description. Sort of how Audrey would look when she left The Croft of a morning. She could do any extra touching up in a woman's lavatory. Glass can have one of those composites and try to get her identified at, say, Carr's Hill and Redwood Park."

With that we settled down to things that had to be done: the opening moves in a wholly new campaign. The dam had certainly burst and the water was flowing. The trouble was that it was coming with such a surge that we were almost swept away. Suddenly we had been presented with a whole series of suspects and about each a series of ideas.

"We're only where we wanted to be," Wharton said. "She was killed and then the robbery was faked. Not all faked, though. Enough was actually taken to make it look like the real thing."

Then at once there was a question. Was what was taken a part of the fake? Couldn't it have been taken by someone who wanted the money? Someone whom Audrey Grange had surprised and who had shot because it was—to him at least—a vital thing that she shouldn't be able to tell his name? Then out of that arose another possibility. There was no guarantee that nobody had entered the bungalow during the Friday. Audrey might have been shot and the robbery committed hours later. But would a chance thief, finding her dead, have had the nerve to stay and ransack every room? Wouldn't he have taken the bag, wrist-watch and ring and then bolted?

You see how ideas could crowd in; so many angles that we'd have needed half the Department to have tackled each one. That was why we decided to let theorising rest and try the old elimination method. Wyster, Holme, Merlin and Merril Holme had all given grounds for suspicion, and each would be put through a fine-meshed sieve. Each would have to satisfy us on three points before being finally discarded.

1. Alibi.
2. Lack of motive.
3. Ignorance of Audrey Grange's plans as told to Bill Ellice. That also included ignorance of the fact that she was at The Croft.

On the face of it, the first includes the other two, in the sense that if a person could satisfy us as to his alibi, then innocence followed. But that wasn't quite so. Alibis can be fashioned with devilish ingenuity, as George and I had often known. An alibi may seem perfect, only afterwards to be proved unsound. If, on the other hand, the alibi seemed sound to the limit of our testing, and it could also be reinforced by a satisfying on the other two points, then an elimination of the particular suspect seemed fairly safe. Only *fairly*, mark you. There still remained the question of collusion.

As for the second point, George would be responsible for enquiries into the will. There remained the love or jealousy motive, and, as far as Merril Holme was concerned, the motive of elimination of the rival for the part of Jinny Patman. But other motives might arise as the Case developed.

The third point was, in our judgment, the most immediately important, and it would be the hardest to manipulate from our side of the Case. A suspect had almost to prove his own alibi. A suspect could almost be seen to be without motive. But if a suspect blandly asserted ignorance of Audrey Grange's whereabouts and her scheme, then it would be up to us to disprove the statement, and that was likely to be tough going.

But something was to happen almost at once. I rang down for the report of the men I'd put on Wyster's tail. I read it when it came in and then passed it to George. He was giving what I always call his Coliseum smile—that of the lion who has picked out for himself a specially plump Christian. And no wonder!

Wyster *had* gone to his flat but he was there only a quarter of an hour when he came out again. He walked the few yards to the Tube station and took a train and got off at that same station where Merril Holme and I had got off. And he'd stayed there: not in the actual station but across the road. He had stayed there till I had returned to the station, and then he had gone hurriedly on to the maisonette. There he had let himself in with a key of his own, and there he had stayed for about half an hour. Then he had gone home the way he came.

"The easiest thing in the world to piece together," George said. "Everything was what you said it was. She was a forced card. She got you to the flat and then rang him to say you were there. She worked the old pump handle and let you go when there wasn't any more water. He was watching to see if you were really unofficial as you said you were. He saw you go into the station and down the stairs, and then off he went to hear what she'd found out." Then his lips pursed. "Only one thing wrong with it."

"And what's that?"

"It's too easy." He pursed his lips again. "Something tells me to give that couple a lot more rope. Our policy's to make them both uneasy. Let them have a hint that they're not in the clear."

I said I thought we were safe enough to let the Press have another statement—that dramatic developments might be shortly expected. That ought to put the pair of them in a dither. George thought it over, and agreed. And he'd make arrangements to have the pair followed from then on, even if the trouble there was that they would be in each other's company at the theatre and could do any extra talking over the telephone.

Meanwhile we shifted to James Holme. How he might fit we didn't know, but he was one of my assignments. And I had the most admirable of excuses for seeing him, as you will hear later. He was, in fact, to be lured into thinking himself a co-operator of the police, and all the time we'd be trying to discover just how thick he'd been with Audrey Grange, and a good many things besides.

That brought us at last to Merlin—and he was a problem at once more intricate and more obvious.

"Take Mrs. Merlin's evidence," I said, "and it's good evidence. According to her, Audrey and her step-father never grew up. They had all sorts of secrets that she never knew about. I'll bet it was a secret years ago about Audrey breaking into films, and they only told her when it was a *fait accompli*. It'd be the blandishments of the two of them that reconciled her somewhat to Audrey's career, and maybe to her marriage to an actor. To come to the point, I'm dead sure that Merlin must have known every detail of Audrey's Jinny Patman scheme."

"Then he *has* bolted. He's bolted because he hasn't an alibi."

I didn't know, and we didn't know. Everything was surmise except that curious happening at 76 Carris Street; the fact that Merlin—ostensibly bound for King's Cross or Euston—should have left his taxi at that special spot. George got to his feet.

"About time you saw Holberg. Use your own discretion about what you let out. And what about ringing Holme?"

I waited while he rang Holme at the works. My club was suggested as the rendezvous, and that would give a feeling of the unofficial and friendly. But in the back of Holme's mind would be the wonder why a Superintendent of Scotland Yard had made the appointment instead of Ludovic Travers.

CHAPTER XI
ELIMINATION IS VEXATION

As I WALKED towards Shaftesbury Avenue I was feeling pretty good, and it wasn't the weather that was making things so. Not that it was too bad a morning. It wasn't raining even if it was dull, and it wasn't actually cold though it was far from warm. What it looked like was as if autumn had ended a week ago and now we were prematurely and gradually merging into early winter. And if so, it wasn't too good, for there can be some grand days in early October and this was still September.

I was feeling good because the rubbish had been swept from the Case. We knew more or less where we stood and the problem was clear, if only because we had one dead woman and not two, and one scene only of a crime. I wasn't at all irritated when I had to wait quite a time before Tom Holberg could see me, but it was he who came to the waiting-room and took me along.

"Sit there," he said. "It's comfortable. Cigarette?"

I took one.

"Drink? Or is it too early?"

"No drink," I said. "This is official. Very much so."

"You've—er—"

"That's right," I said. "We've made a discovery. Still in the dark about a lot of things, though, and we'd like you to help."

"Anything," Tom said, and spread his pudgy palms. "Just ask me, Mr. Travers, that's all."

"Well, a question," I said. "You'll probably think I'm a fool not to know the answers. That doesn't matter, and maybe I am. But tell me: just why was Kraaf making that picture over here?"

"Because it's English. Every character is real English. There's only one American in it—Larry O'Shea, the deserter."

"Yes, but wasn't *David Copperfield* English?"

Tom gave a chuckle and his three chins wobbled.

"Not bad for a fool! But that isn't all. There's that 75 per cent tax. He either had to make it here as an English film or make it over there just for the home market. Making it over here he sets off the £25,000 he paid for it against profits. He's got an infinitely cheaper salary list. He'll pay himself out of the English market alone."

"I get you," I said. "He bought before our Government clapped that tax on, and he's taking the safe way out. And now I'll tell you something, and only because we can trust you. All your life you've had to keep things under your hat. But if this ever gets out, there'll be the devil to pay. It *will* get out, but not till we want it to."

There was no point in being too clever with a man like Tom Holberg, so I told him practically all we knew of Audrey Grange's scheme. His eyes never left my face and the cigarette drooped dead in his mouth.

"There we are," I said, "and this is the plain question. Did you know anything about it?"

"Not a word, Mr. Travers; that I'll swear. Mind you, I had suspicions she was up to something, and I told you so."

"She knew when Kraaf was due?"

"She did. I can see now why she asked me."

"Can you tell me when?"

He said he'd have to consult his diary, but in a minute or two he found what he wanted. Friday, August 22nd, had been the date when she'd last called at the office.

"Everything's getting confirmed," I said. "And the part itself—that of Jinny Patman. It was all that important?" He said it was. Naturally he'd wanted it for Audrey and had suggested certain things to her. Her friendship with Kraaf might be exploited, for instance.

"Don't think the worse of us for that, Mr. Travers. I assure you it's something that's regularly done. Not that I'd have done it, if I hadn't been sure she was the only one for the part."

"And what did she say?"

He shrugged his shoulders.

"Told me she'd handle Kraaf. Said I wasn't to work any ropes. I was to do nothing. That's why I told you I guessed she had something up her sleeve. And she was confident. Talked as if the contract was as good as signed."

"Fine," I said, and got to my feet. "You've saved us quite a lot of trouble. Now we all know that Audrey Grange was Maudie Brown. Agreed?"

"Yes," he said slowly, and then he was frowning.

"Thought of something?" I said. "Want to make any reservations?"

"Sit down a minute, Mr. Travers." He was frowning away again. "I'd like to get this off my mind. Something's wrong with that Maudie Brown story. Audrey wouldn't have gone to work the way you said."

That was a bit of a cold douche.

"She'd never have stood for all that publicity," he went on. "She just wasn't made that way. Time after time I'd think out some real nice boost and she always turned it down. The only publicity she was interested in was the pictures themselves, if you follow me."

He said he'd put it another way. I'd seen *Brief Encounter*? Then I'd know that after *Brief Encounter* no cheap publicity was needed for Celia Johnson and Trevor Howard. That was Audrey's argument. A good picture was its own publicity.

"You're not going to tell me she wasn't Maudie after all?"

"She was Maudie all right," he reassured me. "But it wasn't like Audrey to fake a robbery and a disappearance. She'd just have been the barmaid, and she might have asked me to get Kraaf along to the Seven Bells. Maybe I'd have been slipped a note in that saloon bar saying I was to have a word with the barmaid—sort of to explain why Audrey had got us there. Maybe she'd have led Kraaf on and then she'd have let him see that wrist-watch."

He gave himself a little congratulatory nod at the way he'd worked it out. Even to me it sounded good—or was it too much of a film scenario?

"You should know," I told him. "Not that it matters how things might have worked themselves out. But my idea is she'd seen those snippings in the papers and knew Merril Holme—for instance—was a pretty strong rival. That's why she decided to leave no stone unturned, as they say. Act out of character, if you like. But strictly between ourselves, is Merril Holme getting the part?"

Tom's shrug of the shoulders was almost a cringe. Kraaf was choosey. Maybe she would. He wouldn't know.

"Could she play it?"

There was playing, and playing, he said. There was competence and genius. There was something to satisfy a box-office and something to set the entertainment world alight.

That's where we left it. I thanked him profusely and said I'd keep him informed of any developments. He said he didn't want any thanks. His repayment would be helping to get the swine who did it—and not because of the loss of a mighty big commission. Audrey had been more than a client. He'd helped to make her, for instance, and he was venturing to think that she'd regarded him as something far more than an agent.

"Do you know Frank Merlin, her step-father?" I asked him. He smiled.

"Who doesn't? He's very much of a character, is Frank."

This was definitely all. I had fifteen minutes in which to get to my club and I just made it. James Holme was shown into the smoking-room two minutes after I got there.

From the very first second I used everything I had to put him at ease. I gave my very best smile as I shook hands. I took him by the arm and led him to the bar. I got him a drink and I asked him about business. With him I damned the Government, and even then he wasn't perfectly happy. For all the charm there was at the back of his mind the suspicion that I was putting on an act. I even called to a man I knew to join us, and we had a joke or two and a couple more drinks, and he still wasn't altogether what I judged his natural self. Then we went in to lunch.

We chattered aimlessly over some really excellent hors-d'oeuvres and then I knew the time had come to clear the decks.

"Mind if I ask you a question?"

His lips smiled but his eyes didn't.

"You're not worrying about anything? If so, please don't. Mind you," I went on, "I'll admit I had an ulterior motive in asking you to lunch with me today, but it's not one you'd ever guess. To come to the point, this is all very friendly, but it isn't unofficial. We want your help."

"My help?"

"Your help. There's something you can do for us. Perhaps I'd better explain."

The way I put it was this. We'd discovered why Audrey Grange had been at The Croft. What I was telling him was in the strictest confidence—as he was now a collaborator with the police he'd understand that—but she'd been swatting up the part of Jinny Patman in *Number Thirty*, so as to be ready for the film version if she acted that part. What we wanted to know was if she'd done anything else besides read the book and study the character.

"You've read the book?"

He said he had, and he'd liked it enormously. Then he was owning himself mystified as to how he could help. I smiled tolerantly, as if that was easy, and then my face fell. I frowned.

"Let's be serious for a moment," I said, "and personal. This is a murder case. Whether it's a film actress or a common prostitute, it's murder. The hue and cry's out, though you wouldn't know it. The hunt's on, and it won't be off till the murderer's caught. We take no chances. There's nothing we consider too trivial to enquire into. You did a foolish thing, for example. If Audrey Grange was an old friend of yours, why did you try to stop me from seeing her photograph?"

His face flushed and he couldn't get out a word.

"I'm not questioning you," I went on. "All I want to do is set your mind absolutely at rest. You did a foolish thing and it asked for enquiry. We learned that you were often at Denham when Audrey Grange was there, and during rests you'd have a meal together or go out for an hour—"

"I can explain—"

"I don't want you to explain," I told him. "It doesn't need explaining. You were in love with her and she wasn't in love with her husband any longer. That made it fair and above-board. If I were the world's worst prude I couldn't see anything very much wrong in that."

"That's rather decent of you," he said, and was nervously moistening his lips. "All the same I don't see how I can help."

"But you can," I said. "Surely you and Miss Grange must have gone somewhere where there was a barmaid?"

For the first time for a good few minutes he met my eyes.

"As a matter of fact, we did. There's a pub about a mile away, called the Haymakers. Wait a minute now."

The sweet had arrived but it mightn't have been there. He was at the Haymakers, and there was something he was remembering. He told me what it was. I looked at my watch. However fast we made it, we couldn't be at the Haymakers before closing time.

"Is it possible for you to get an afternoon off? Or not turn up again today?"

That was fairly easy, he said, but he'd have to telephone. I said it could stand till after we'd finished our meal, and meanwhile we'd forget everything. So we finished our meal and had our coffee. Then we had a port in the lounge, and it was well on the way to three o'clock when he rang the works. I looked up the cinema programme.

He said he'd rather like to go to a show for a change, so we went to a French film that had been strongly recommended by my favourite critic. Had it been a Wednesday I'd have taken him to *Skip and Jump*, for merely a quarter of an hour with Bobinot would have been worth the money. But he liked the film, and after it we had tea and then went to my flat for a polish. We were going to the Haymakers in my car and he suggested that as I was taking him home, I might have a meal at Finchley. Things had moved since that meeting at the club, but I couldn't accept his invitation.

I liked Holme and the job I was doing wasn't a pretty one. I've said he was a good-looking chap, and of the quiet sort, but he was far from a fool, and as the afternoon had worn on and I had seen him losing most of his uneasiness and seeming to trust me, I felt a bit uncomfortable myself. George would swindle an orphan if it meant solving a murder case and he knew he could get away with it, and there are times when I could do worse. But this wasn't one of them. Holme was a decent sort. He struck one as implicitly straight and the sort of man of whom I could easily make a friend. Everything told me he could have had nothing to do with the actual killing of Audrey Grange. But I had to be more than sure. Intuitions are no good to the records. I had to question and if necessary I had to trick, and, as I said, I didn't like it.

We had a good journey down and the old Bentley was running as well as ever, and I was regretting that I hadn't sold her when prices were sky high. At half-past seven we drew up at the pub: one of those pubs that seem to be nowhere and yet are the centre of everywhere. It was at a cross-roads for one thing and beautifully placed in a clump of fine old trees, and though its Tudor was Edwardian, it had a mellowed look about it. Three cars were outside the saloon bar.

"You don't like the job," I said to Holme, for I'd had a quick glimpse of his face.

"I'll be all right," he said. "I'm like most other people. I don't like ghosts."

I knew what he meant. Probably he'd never been there except in the company of Audrey Grange. But we made our way into the bar, and a fine airy room it was. A couple of men and their girls were playing darts, and three men were drinking and yarning in a corner. The barmaid was reading the evening paper. She was a pretty girl with little make-up, and her face was all smiles as she caught sight of Holme.

"Well I never!" she said. "We haven't seen you for quite a time, Jimmy. How are you?"

"Can't grumble, Molly. This is Mr. Travers."

I gave Molly a how-d'you-do and asked Holme what he'd have. Molly got two beers, and I could see her giving Holme an anxious look or two. There was something she wanted to say, and at last she brought herself to say it.

"Wasn't it dreadful about Miss Grange? It so upset me, I cried my eyes out. And her coming in here as she did."

"Yes," Holme said quietly. "A pretty hellish business. It knocked me all of a heap, too."

"I'll bet it did," she said. "You knew her Mr. . . . ?"

"Travers," I told her. "Yes, Molly, I knew her. Only on the screen, though."

"Wasn't she wonderful?" Her eyes rolled ecstatically. "And after knowing her, too. Never a bit of silly pride when she came in here, had she, Jimmy?"

"Never a bit," he said, and there was his cue. "Remember when she got you to show her how to handle the bar?"

"Oh yes," she said, as if it were a shared, delicious secret. "Something else I can tell you, too. She came on one day when you weren't here and got me to show her again. How to work everything and—well, you know. How to be a proper barmaid. Reckoned she might want it for a film one day."

She remembered something else and her eyes opened wide. "Oh, and something else." Then her face fell. "Of course it never happened but it'd have been a real scream if it had." Her voice lowered. "She wanted to get me to let her take my place here one night when I was off. She was going to make herself up so that no one would know her, but I said we'd have to see Mr. Sanson about it. I daren't do it without."

"What was her idea?" I wanted to know.

"Doing it for a bet. That's what she said. I thought she wanted to do it once and get the hang of it, and then do it again when some friends of hers were coming in, and win the bet. Of course they wouldn't know; I mean if they hadn't been in here before."

"A damn good joke," I said, and couldn't help wondering what Molly would think if ever the truth got out. But Holme's face was almost grim. Molly shook her head at me, and then her hand went out and she was patting his arm.

"Cheer up, Jimmy."

"I'm all right, Molly."

"I know you are," she said. "You thought a lot of her, didn't you?"

"Didn't all of us?" He nodded to himself and smiled. "She was a good sort, Molly. One of the best."

"I see she's being buried tomorrow. Cremated, or something." She shook her head. "Don't let's talk about it any more. It gives me the miserables."

"Who began it?" he asked her with the same quiet smile. She patted his arm again, and then in came more customers, and we sheered away to a couple of stools at the other end of the bar. I had a beer with him and it was only eight o'clock when he was suggesting we should go. I said it would suit me, so we said goodbye to Molly as we passed, and out we went. The young moon was well up the evening sky, and it almost looked as if the weather was on the change.

I drove quite slowly for me but we didn't do more than talk trivialities, and then the time came when I had to start the ball really rolling again.

"Well," I said. "You've had your first go at working for the police. And a fine job you've made of it. Everything links up with what we need."

"You think it'll help to find the ones who did it?"

"I don't think—I'm fairly sure. A nice girl, Molly. And a good witness."

He said Molly was a nice girl.

"Witnesses aren't all the same," I went on. "You'll soon find that out if we ask you to do another job for us. The worst kind are those that don't trust the police. They're not what *you'd* regard as witnesses, of course, but suspects. People we think might have been mixed up in something; not necessarily guilty in themselves, but afraid of giving something else away. We question them and we know they're holding back. We tell 'em again that everything's strictly confidential and never a word's going to get out, and even then they hang back. Then we have a bit of luck perhaps and we bring them in again and tell them what we've found out about them. Then we try to show how foolish they've been and advise them to come clean. Still in confidence of course. Then they hedge again or lie, and so it goes on. Not that we don't ultimately get at the truth. And I don't mind telling you then that some of them are mighty sorry. There's no pledge of secrecy when we have to find out things for ourselves. Into the witness box they have to go. Everything that could have been confidential is everyone's knowledge."

"Yes," he said, and seemed to be thinking it over. I didn't attempt a look at him. I didn't mind how much time he took to come to a decision, so long as he told us what he knew. For there *was* something that he knew. I was somehow dead sure of that.

But I was not to hear it that night, though when I left him I was even more sure. And the reason was that he hesitated when he got out of the car. It was on the tip of his tongue to ask me to come in and have a drink. Over that drink he might have talked, but it was a drink I didn't have. All he said was that I'd given him a grand day—and his face belied even that—and some time soon I must have lunch with him somewhere in town.

George was in his room and he'd had a far busier day than I. Things had quietened down when I got there and he didn't hurry me over my report. And he looked pleased that we now had the unquestionable proof that Audrey Grange had been Maudie Brown. He had found something of confirmation himself.

The photograph job had been a rush one but a good one. Bill Ellice had actually been brought along to lend a hand, and when Bill saw a pretty good resemblance to Maudie, George went to the Seven Bells, and during closing time Quarren said it was Maudie all right, but not a good one of her. Mrs. Quarren said with a sniff that it was her. When asked if Maudie had been fond of make-up she had called her a painted hussy.

Glass had had some luck too, and he was still on the job. The photograph had been recognised, if none too confidently, at Carr's Hill. Even if the photograph hadn't been shown at all, there'd have been some useful evidence, for a woman of Glass's verbal description had occasionally gone to town by the 8.58. But only during the three weeks in question. Much the same thing had happened at Redwood Park.

I wanted to know about the will, and George showed me his own summary. It was quite a small estate compared with what it might have been if she had lived only a year or two longer. Heavy taxation had reduced a really big income to the wholly unspectacular, and the slump had heavily depreciated the realisable value of investments. Expenses must have been fairly heavy and she had paid half those of the flat, whether actually there or not and had always been generous to her parents. The estate, in fact, might not amount to more than seven thousand pounds, plus car and jewellery and oddments.

Wyster was left the car and nothing else. Mrs. Merlin had the jewellery—except the diamond ring, which went to Wyster— and personal belongings, and a thousand pounds. Merlin had five thousand pounds, but in trust, the income only to be paid. Reversion was to the Actor's Orphanage. There were minor bequests including a hundred pounds to 'my very dear friend James Holme' with which to buy something in remembrance. The bank was the executor and the bank and the solicitors were the trustees. Since the estate might not now meet all the charges, legacies would have to be scaled down.

"What's the date of the will?" I asked George, for he hadn't written it down.

He gave me a look and I guessed something was coming.

"When do you think?"

"Don't know. I'm asking you."

"And I'm telling you," he said. "Just over a month ago."

My eyes popped a bit.

"Had there been a previous will?"

There had and its provisions had been very different except in the case of Merlin. The estate had been expected then to realise much more. Wyster had had two thousand and car and jewellery, except any two pieces that Mrs. Merlin might select. Mrs. Merlin had also had two thousand. Holme had had his hundred.

"I don't see much difference," I told George, "except the money to Wyster."

"Turn over the page," he told me. "In the original will, drawn up about eighteen months ago, there wasn't a mention of your lady friend. See what she gets now."

There it was—*to Merril Beatrice Holme my annotated copy of Number Thirty, with my love.*

My fingers were at my glasses, and I didn't quite know why. Then I had to smile.

"Thank God for a bit of cattishness, George. She was human after all."

"Maybe," George said. "You tell me what you read into it."

"Well," I said, "it's rather in the line of Shakespeare's bequest of a second-best bed. She was dead sure she'd get that Jinny Patman part and she knew Merril would be doing her damnedest to get it, too. All the same she was so sure that she was doing some crowing in advance."

"Yes?"

"She obviously hated Merril."

"And why?"

"I've told you," I said. "But wait a minute though. Suppose she'd become aware that Wyster was carrying on with the lady. Wouldn't that add an extra piquance to the bequest?"

George merely told me I'd taken the devil of a time to arrive at the obvious.

"Holme apparently wasn't cutting any ice with her," he went on. "She thought a lot of him and that was about all. Merlin's got a motive, though—if he knew what was in that will."

"Nothing from Carris Street?"

George said he'd called the men off. And he was suggesting that in the morning I should go to the cremation. I might slip into the chapel for the service and see if Merlin turned up after all.

"Has his wife heard anything from him?"

Not a thing, George said. He'd rung her up specially. And she hadn't been able to find Maudie's papers.

"Just what I told you," he said. What *he* told *me*, mind you. But there's never any point in pointing out such lapses to George, and we began settling arrangements for the morning.

Chapter XII
FAINT YET PURSUING

I HAD A MAN with me in the back seat of the unobtrusive police car. I'd also done something to myself, for the last thing I wanted was to be recognised, even by Holberg or Wyster. The sight of me might have given all sorts of people all sorts of ideas.

Disguise may be thought to have gone out with Lecoq: it smacks of boys playing at Red Indians. Wharton never has to do it because he has underlings—myself included—to do that sort of detecting for him. I didn't tell him what I was doing, but I flattered myself that he'd have passed me and never known who I was. Even with my height it wasn't all that difficult, for I could have a middle-aged stoop. Also I had on less obvious glasses, and my hair was artistically greyed. A badger moustache was over my clipped military one and I had plumpers to slip in my cheeks at the last moment.

There seemed to be thousands of the curious outside the crematorium premises, and in the grounds I never saw so many mourners or so many flowers. Representatives of heaven knew what were there besides the family and friends and near acquaintances. I sidled into the chapel at almost the rear of everybody and my man and I had to stand at the back. It was a special service, choral but simple, but I had to risk the newly acquired stoop and crane round people and over heads. Soon I spotted Holberg. Then I found Wyster, in the front pew, and next to him was Mrs. Merlin. And there, at the side of her, was none other than Merlin himself!

After that there was no point in my staying. Only the family would be present at the actual cremation and as the service neared its end, I sidled gently and respectfully out. But my man had had his instructions and there was nothing for me to do. So I went to my flat by bus, got back to Ludovic Travers again, put away my topper and morning clothes, ordered a service lunch, and settled down to wait. News ought to be coming at any moment, and it came when I was only halfway through the leisured meal.

"Parks ringing, sir. He's at Greenwood Street."

"Who else is there?"

"Three or four people, sir. All I could identify was that Mr. Wyster."

"Carry on," I told him. "I'll have a man along to relieve you."

I got hold of Wharton and left it to him. Then I settled down to waiting again. It was not till half-past two that more news came through.

"Jimson speaking, sir." Jimson was the relief man. "Merlin has just gone off in someone else's car. Parks is tailing them."

I told him to enlarge, and this is apparently what happened. Two men left, and I judged them to be the solicitor and possibly his clerk. Then Wyster left and just behind him someone I guessed from his description to be Holberg. Merlin was with him and he got into Holberg's car. The car drove off. Mrs. Merlin didn't come to the door. Merlin had no luggage.

Those were the facts and I had to be patient till Parks rang me. That was just before three o'clock.

"I've lost Merlin, sir. The traffic lights beat us."

He went on to explain. I told him to report back to Jimson and tell Jimson to send anything direct to the Yard. Then I went along to the Yard myself. George was jabbing at once at the buzzer, and in two minutes I was through to Holberg.

"Travers speaking," I said. "You were at the Merlin house after the cremation this morning?"

"I was," he said. "Quite a lot to explain to the solicitor and the family."

"Did you come back to your office alone?"

"As a matter of fact I didn't," he said. "I gave Merlin a lift to King's Cross. He was going back to Scotland on business."

I thanked him and said I'd explain later. Meanwhile it was confidential and official.

In a couple of minutes George was rushing men to King's Cross to pick up Merlin's trail. I was to go to Greenwood Street and see Mrs. Merlin. She mightn't be in a state to see anybody but somehow or other I was to contrive to have a word. And that again was a job I didn't like.

It was she who came to the door and she even seemed pleased to see me.

"I wouldn't dream of troubling you, Mrs. Merlin," I began, "but we wanted a word with your husband. Will you tell him I shan't keep him a minute?"

She was showing me into the room and telling me regretfully how I was no more than an hour late.

"He felt he had to come down all that way," she said. "He just couldn't bear to be away and not see the very last of our dear one. And now he's had to hurry back."

"He didn't complete his business then?"

"No," she said. "He didn't after all like the man he had in mind, and tomorrow he's seeing another. My husband, you know, is a very good judge. And conscientious. He wouldn't be satisfied with anything but the best."

"I can quite believe it," I said, and then let out a breath. "Still, it's a pity I missed him. Perhaps I can see him when he comes back."

"Is it anything I can do?"

I said that unfortunately it wasn't. Then I was thanking her and getting up to go.

"Won't you stay and have a cup of tea? I'm just making one for myself."

I said I couldn't. Then I said just a cup of tea and nothing else, and she hurried off to make it. The kettle had apparently been on the boil, for she was back in under five minutes.

"You must try one of these cakes," she said, "I made them myself." She smiled deprecatingly. "My husband says I'm the best cake maker he knows, but of course he's biased."

I was to tell her he was biased with every justification. I had two of the cakes and two cups of tea, and I had to stay on like that because she had been telling me guardedly about the will.

"Have you read a book called *Number Thirty*?" she was suddenly asking me.

I said truthfully that I hadn't, but I'd heard of it.

"My husband hadn't either," she said, and then she was realising that she'd said too much, and was changing the subject to Tom Holberg and how nice he always was. And she said how wonderful it had been that morning to see all the important people who'd been at the crematorium and all the marvellous flowers. Then I really had to go, and she waved to me from the door as if I was an old friend.

I left Jimson there just on the odd chance and hurried back to the Yard. As I told George, there was nothing I'd learned. On the face of it everything was in order as regards Merlin. Except perhaps that it was curious that he'd found in Scotland a second string to his bow.

"My idea is, he's keeping out of our way," George said. "He doesn't want to be questioned. Why, I don't know. But it must be something to do with what happened at Carr's Hill."

I reminded him that Merlin had gone to Scotland—if gone he had—as soon as he'd learned from Wyster that we might be coming to ask him about Maudie. If he was scared at all, it was of enquiries into Maudie. And how could we fit that in with the fact that Audrey was Maudie?

"Plenty of time for that," George told me impatiently. "That'll straighten itself out when we get hold of him. If that isn't soon I'll have out the hue and cry. Anything else did you find out?"

I said there wasn't, except that Mrs. Merlin had been puzzled about that mention in the will of the bequest of *Number Thirty* to Merril Holme. She'd asked her husband if he'd heard of the book and he'd probably said he hadn't. And he'd also looked as if he had. His wife ought by this time to know well enough when he was prevaricating. At any rate, she had asked me about the book, and had changed the subject very quickly when I'd said I hadn't read it.

"And now what?" I said.

"Enquiries into Wyster's movements on that Thursday night," he said. "At his garage for instance, to see at what time he took out his car—if he went by car—and when he brought it back."

"He told us he went out in his car," I said. "I admit that doesn't mean anything."

I got out my notes and quoted almost the words. He'd said he'd gone straight from the theatre to his flat, and what he'd then done was confidential—that is, his own business and not ours. He'd then spent the night with friends.

At the time we'd thought that Wyster was a man who naturally and as a free citizen of our so-called democracy, resented any enquiry into affairs that were lawful and private, but now his remarks were acquiring a wholly new significance. Then we'd known he hadn't killed his wife; now we had an open but suspicious mind. Then he'd been nothing but the husband of the dead woman and a somewhat distinguished actor who had come voluntarily to help the police. Now he was a suspect with a motive, and the onus was on him to substantiate an alibi.

To go back then to what he had said on that Saturday morning at The Croft. Wharton put it like this.

"We jockeyed him into a position where he either had to refuse to tell us where he was on the Thursday night or else simply tell us. No need for complications. Now what should he have done? Merely said he had gone from the theatre to his flat and then spent the night with friends. That's all. Under the circumstances we shouldn't have asked for more, and he must have known it. Yet he started to bring in complications. This was confidential and he wasn't going to tell us that. And why did he take up that attitude? Because although he'd almost a perfect control of himself, the control wasn't a hundred per cent perfect. We'd put him in a cleft stick. He had to tell us something, and he hadn't been expecting us to do anything of the sort. That's why he said too much, and I'll bet a fiver he's already regretting it. I'll also bet that wherever he was that night, he's taken steps to cover it up. He may even have fabricated a perfectly sound alibi."

"Then why not ask him to make a further statement?" I said.

"Because we want to get a certain amount of truth to set against what he's going to tell us. Then if we know he's telling us a lie, we've got a lever. No hurry, no panic. We're not doing so bad so far. All we want is his timings for that night, as shown by his car."

I said I'd rather like to do that job myself, and I didn't add that I had at least one other idea.

"Why not?" George said. "I've got plenty to do here and I might go out later on. Don't know that I won't go to the Orpheum. I'd like to run my rule over that Merril woman."

That idea of mine was just a bit vague and it wasn't much clearer by the time I set out for Wyster's flat, and that was at half-past six when I knew he'd be on his way to the theatre. What I thought, in fact, was that he might have gone out in his car that night as the result of a telephone message. It was a Thursday night, remember, and he'd already played at a matinée. Surely if anything had been arranged beforehand, it would have been for a night when he was likely to be feeling less tired.

I'd also had two other ideas and one of them had been checked. Maybe Audrey Grange had done some telephoning on that Thursday night, since secrecy as to her whereabouts—she was leaving The Croft practically at once—need no longer be strictly observed. But that proved a dead end as I'd rather feared. Her calls for the Greater London area would be dialled direct and automatically registered, and there was no means of telling on what day or at what hour they'd been sent. Toll calls didn't interest me at the moment.

Then I'd thought it might be a good idea to have a look through the room or rooms at the flat, and that I discarded because I hadn't the least notion what I'd be looking for. And she'd have taken with her to The Croft everything really personal—letters, for instance. The fact that she might have been suspicious of the relationship between her husband and Merril Holme—as shown by the new will—was also an indication that she mightn't have trusted Wyster sufficiently to have left all the drawers unlocked.

There was no trouble in finding the flats for it was a huge and palatial block built between the wars. The office wasn't at all obtrusive as some are, but was at the end of a short passage leading off the main entrance hall, and at the end of the same passage was the telephone exchange. I found the manager in. He was a man of my own age but plump, sleek and almost dapper, and his cheeks had a pink cherubic bloom and all the lustre of a recent shave. He looked most unhappy when I showed him my credentials. That there should be a crook among his exclusive clientele was a horrifying thought. Then he seemed to cheer up. Maybe he was thinking my business was to do with the staff.

We went into his private room and he was so anxious that he didn't even offer me a cigarette. I cautioned him—and even more strictly than usual—and said I wanted information about telephone calls. That surprised him. He wanted to know what calls. Incoming calls weren't checked—there was no reason why they should be. Outgoing calls definitely were since the Laurel Mansions Exchange was just like any other exchange.

You should have seen his face when I said it was the calls sent out by Wyster that I wanted to check, and for that Thursday night. You could see his brain putting two and two together and making it five, and with it was an incredibility that a notability like Wyster should be suffering the contamination of the police.

"Mr. Wyster!"

"Look," I said. "Yours is not to reason why, Mr. . . . . ?"

"Ammon."

"All we want from you, Mr. Ammon, is co-operation and in absolute secrecy. I ask the questions and you give the answers."

His shake of the head was quite belligerent.

"I'm sorry, Mr. Travers, I'm a person of trust. The whole—er—fabric of this—er—concern would be shaken if it was expected that I was divulging the—er—private affairs of—"

I cut in with the reminder that that was up to him. He'd been assured of secrecy so how could there be suspicion? But if he'd rather go along to the Yard or appear at the reopened inquest and give public evidence, then—and I shrugged my shoulders for the rest.

In a couple of seconds he was asking exactly what I wanted to know, and I repeated that it was the calls Wyster had made between ten-thirty, say on the Thursday night, and midnight the same night. He asked me if I'd be so good as to wait, and it was only then that he produced a box of cigarettes. It was five minutes before he was back. Wyster had sent out no calls whatever on that night, and that he was prepared to guarantee. I turned on the charm.

"You see?" I said. "All we have to have is a check-up for purely official purposes. Everything in order as we thought it would be. And now the incoming calls."

"But that's impossible. I've already explained."

I didn't quote Nelson. All I said was that we might have a try at it. For instance, could he get hold of the operator who'd been on duty at those times on that Thursday night. He said reluctantly that he could.

"You bring her in here," I said. "Don't tell her what she's wanted for and don't say a word when she gets here. Leave me to do the talking. No need to be alarmed. I shall use tact."

He told me almost despairingly that he was sure I would. And this time he was away only three minutes. A pleasant-looking girl wearing glasses was with him. I gave her my best smile and my hand, and asked her name.

"Nothing to be alarmed about, Miss Poland. I'm a special inspector from the telephone department. We have a suspicion that attempts have been made to listen in to the private conversations of your clientele. That's all I can tell you, and you must regard this as absolutely confidential. If a single hint gets out, then there might be trouble. But you don't look that kind of person."

She assured me she wasn't.

"Mr. Ammon here is giving us every help," I said, "and we're trying to trace incoming calls for last Thursday night between ten and midnight." I frowned at Ammon. "What was the name of that actor, wasn't it, we said we might try? Wyster, that was it. If Mr. Wyster had any incoming calls. Now then, Miss Poland, can you help us? We know you've no official record but is there anything you remember?"

"Thursday night," she said, and was tapping her chin with her fingertips. Then the frown went.

"There *was* something," she said. "Let me see now. When was it? I know. About a quarter-past eleven. A call came and Mr. Wyster wasn't in. I said, 'Sorry, madam, but there's no reply'."

"A lady's voice, then. And that's all?"

"Well, I did wonder if it had anything to do with a call he had earlier. About half an hour earlier. That was from a lady, too."

"This is just the kind of thing we want," I told Ammon. "The same lady, was it?"

"No, not the same lady."

That was definitely all she remembered about calls for Wyster. I said we might have to question her later about calls on other nights for other clients, but meanwhile we were most grateful.

"But just one thing," I went on, and again with what I hope was a ravishing smile. "Any particular reason why you should have remembered anything to do with Mr. Wyster?"

She smiled, too. Maybe it was because he was a famous actor. And because Audrey Grange was his wife.

"Yes," I said. "A sad business that. And so you're a Wyster fan?"

She said rather shyly that she wouldn't say that, but naturally she was interested in his living at Laurel Mansions. And she'd seen him in *Round Square*.

So much for that. Even Ammon had to agree that everything had gone smoothly enough. And he was pretty relieved, too, when I said that was all. I didn't ask him where Wyster garaged his car. That information I got when I was outside, and from one of the flat owners, though I didn't mention Wyster's name.

But there was something far more important that I had realised as soon as I'd set foot in the main hall with its central lift and twin stairways, and it was this. Occupants of those flats had the maximum amount of privacy with regard to their comings and goings. Had the office been where, say, the lift was, then each entrance or leaving might have been under the eyes of the clerk on duty. But the office had been off the hall, and a prominent notice had merely said, with an arrow indication—OFFICE AND ENQUIRIES. Wyster, for example, could have gone out at a time that couldn't be checked and returned in the same way. The only possible check would be through a liftman or by the evidence of some other tenant who had seen him go or come.

For the moment that wasn't worrying me. I went on to Haley Street and there was an enormous garage apparently chock-a-block with cars. Two brothers owned it and I saw the one who was doing duty. I told him I was enquiring into a job that had been done in a pre-war Martlet the previous Thursday night. The man concerned had got away, and we had only the house-owner's word that the car was really what he said it was.

"We've only got one here," he said, "and that belongs to a Mr. Wyster of Laurel Mansions."

"Really?"

"No use to you," he told me. "Mr. Wyster's the well-known actor. He didn't pull the job."

I smiled ruefully. In fact it wasn't a bad replica of Wharton's other Coliseum smile—the one where the lion has missed his first snap at the fat Christian.

"That's no good then," I said. "I might take the number for our records."

He took me to his office and gave me the number.

"Any chance," I said, "of any unauthorised person taking this particular car out last Thursday night?"

"Never a hope," he said, and then was looking at one of his books. "Everyone of our clients is known to the staff. Besides, Mr. Wyster had the car out himself that night."

His finger indicated the entry. Wyster had left with the car at 10.45 and the car had been brought in again at 11.30 the following morning. That settled that, as I said. But I did have to warn him to keep under his hat what we'd been talking about. People were touchy, I said, and we didn't want that Mr. Wyster kicking up a fuss. He might even think we were accusing him of something.

I walked back to the Tube station and dropped into a nearby pub for a drink, and over my tankard I began assessing the value of what I'd learned. Miss Poland's evidence was vague in its timings but the garage had brought those timings into line. Soon after half-past ten on that Thursday night Wyster had had a call, and almost certainly as a result of it, he had gone to his garage and at 10.45 had taken out his car. Some time later—say half an hour—he had had another call, and the caller had been told there was no reply. That second call might have been from any-body who knew two things—that he was likely to be in and that as an actor he would keep latish hours. But the calls had been from two different women, and my guess was that the first call had come from Merril Holme.

The fact that the car wasn't returned till the following morning didn't matter in the least. It was no proof whatever that Wyster had spent the night out, for the man I'd asked about the garage had told me what my own eyes had told me—that plenty of people left their cars in the car park of the Mansions. But the Thursday had been a glorious day and the Friday had dawned wet. That was why Wyster had taken his car back to the garage when he'd breakfasted and dressed, and that would be fairly late. Nor was it easy to check when Wyster had returned to Laurel Mansions. One couldn't question every tenant in a vast place like that. Some time later we might have to, but for the moment it didn't seem to matter.

But the depressing thing was that I'd learned nothing that actually belied what Wyster himself had told us. He *had* gone straight from the theatre to his flat. He *had* taken his car and gone out. That was what I couldn't help saying ruefully to George when I made my report.

George had been to the theatre and I guessed he'd enjoyed himself, though he was trying to make out it had been only another job to end a heavy day. George is the sort who'd be strong on domestic drama.

"And what'd you think of Merril?"

"A fine looking woman," he said. "Clever too."

"In any particular way?"

He instanced the cooing of a dove in Act 1, and the frustrated infuriated termagant of Act 2 and so back to the penitent and yet opportunist wife of Act 1. And he'd noticed the real woman—

as he thought—who'd smiled and bowed and been apparently overwhelmed by the friendliness of the audience. I didn't say that actresses—like actors—could always put on an act. George hates eating his own words.

"You didn't go behind the scenes?" I asked.

"If I had I wouldn't be here," he told me, and the leer was a reminder of my night with the lady. "My wife isn't away in Scotland."

"Mine's due back at any day now," I told him, "so if you want to follow up that invitation, I'd rather it was soon."

"I don't know," he said, and his face sobered. "To tell you the truth, I'm rather up a gum-tree. What I don't want to do is tackle Wyster too soon. Now if you'd collected anything useful tonight, we might have made a start on him."

"Even I can't do the impossible," I told him for his look had had both pain and reproach. "But why not take a chance? Tell him the robbery business was bogus. You needn't tell him more, except that the situation's changed. Ask him point-blank for his alibi."

All he would say was that he'd sleep on it. The best thing for both of us was to get a good night's rest, and if I reported at ten in the morning, it'd be soon enough. I went home wondering what was up his sleeve.

Chapter XIII
GETTING TO GRIPS

THE NEXT MORNING brought a letter from my wife. She was returning the following day and if possible I was to meet the 11.50 at King's Cross. The morning brought something else—a change in the weather. The sky was clear and there was a new warmth in the air. The Weather Report said that we might expect a few days fine and warm.

George was in his room when I got to the Yard and there seemed little doing. He said he'd had no new ideas and I said—

perhaps more truthfully—that I had none either. I did raise a question which we'd discussed before. Now, in view of the previous evening's discoveries, there seemed something strange about the theft of Audrey Grange's car. If Wyster went to Carr's Hill he went in his own car, and how then could he remove the other car.

"If the Holme woman was with him, he or she might have driven the other car," Wharton said. "And look where the car was found. Not half a mile from Laurel Mansions."

We were back where we'd left off before. I said it wouldn't have been a murder like that: not another Thompson and Bywaters affair. Wyster and Merril Holme just weren't that type.

"Then there's that baby business," I said. "That's never been cleared up. It's beginning to get on my nerves."

I expected him to damn the baby and maybe he would have damned it if the buzzer hadn't gone.

"Right," he said. "Bring him up."

Then he was donning his antiquated spectacles, and in a couple of minutes I knew what he'd had up his sleeve the previous night. Who should be ushered in but Wyster.

Wharton was all over him—apologies for dragging him out at such an hour, placing a chair and almost dusting the seat, and spreading lavish thanks in advance. Wyster seemed reasonably at ease. If there was an uneasiness it was at Wharton's effusiveness which was just a bit too marked.

We settled in our seats and George did the peering act over his spectacle tops.

"Some remarkable news for you, Mr. Wyster," he said, "and we thought you'd like to have it at first hand." For all that peering business he was looking quite magisterial. "I've got a typed summary here. Perhaps you'll allow me to read it."

What he read was the proof that Audrey Grange had been Maudie Brown. I was watching Wyster and I was prepared to swear that never in my life had I seen a man so genuinely surprised. He was bewildered. He could hardly keep from bursting in with questions.

"There we are," Wharton said, laying the typed sheets aside. "Does that surprise you, Mr. Wyster?"

"It does more than that," Wyster said. "If you hadn't assured me it was absolute fact, I'd have said it was bunkum. Sheer fantastic bunkum."

"You didn't think your wife was capable of such a thing?"

I didn't see what at that immediate moment he was driving at, but the question seemed to pull Wyster up with a jerk.

"I wonder," he said, and then thought some more. "Yes, you may be right. Perhaps it's the sort of thing she might have done."

"Well, there it is," Wharton said, and took the spectacles off and laid them aside. He leaned forward across the desk, fingers clasped.

"Do you realise the full implications of what I've read?"

Wyster was afraid he didn't.

"You don't?" There was an edge to his tone. "Then I'll tell you. Your wife's story—Maudie Brown's story—hadn't a word of truth in it. There wasn't a robbery, Mr. Wyster. Your wife was murdered and the robbery was a fake to give a false idea of what happened. Now do you see the implications?"

"Yes," Wyster said, and his eyes were beyond Wharton and somewhere across the room.

"Someone killed her," Wharton said, and his fist thumped the desk. "A cold-blooded, calculated murder. Every single person, however remotely connected, is now a suspect. It's up to everyone to show cause of innocence. We're standing for no hoity-toity business. We're going to ask questions and we want the truth. Those that are innocent won't be afraid of telling that truth, and God help those who don't."

His voice had had a Churchillian crescendo. Then it fell again and almost to the inaudible.

"The fools we have to question. We assure them of secrecy and still they keep things back. We beg them; we plead with them, but no. Then they're brought to a coroner's court or a court of justice. Perjury's a curious thing: a different thing. They tell the truth or take the consequences. What they might have told us in confidence is hot news for the Press. They thought they were being clever. Saving their reputations." He grunted. "When they've told the truth in court they've got no reputations to save."

He leaned back and let out a breath.

"Forgive me. I'm afraid I let myself go. Still that's how it stands. But you're not that kind of fool. You're a man of the world and a man of intelligence. You'll give us straight answers to what we'd like to know. For instance, did you tell a living soul that you knew your wife was at that bungalow?"

I'd expected a demand for an alibi. This was much more subtle.

"Why should I?" Wyster said, and his eyes had narrowed. "Who could it possibly interest?"

"Well, your mother-in-law."

"I rarely see her," Wyster said, "or speak over the telephone, in fact I can say here and now that I never mentioned the matter to a soul."

"Nevertheless someone knew," Wharton said. "Your wife wasn't killed by chance. But we'll take it as read. It wasn't through you that the murderer learned of your wife's whereabouts. And now another question in quite a different context, and I should warn you that it's to be a matter of the strictest confidence. It's about a James or Jimmy Holme. We've made enquiries and we're of the opinion that he was in love with your wife. Did you know anything about it?"

Wyster fidgeted on his hard seat. The question was sudden, and difficult.

"I agree," Wharton told him largely. "Our time's our own. Think it over, then tell us the truth."

"The truth is that I had no personal knowledge," Wyster said. "People—mischief makers and those who like a cheap sneer at you—did mention it to me at various times. Within the last six months is perhaps the truth. I was told he was often down at Denham, for instance."

"And what did you think?"

Wyster waved an indifferent hand.

"My wife was only my wife in name. Why should I worry? Besides, I didn't believe she'd fall for any man, whatever he thought about her. I've told you already and I'm ready to swear to it in any court whatever. The one thing my wife lived for was her work. And—" he gave a dry smile—"I'll tell you before you ask it. I wasn't worrying about either her reputation or my own. I regarded them both as absolutely safe, and in spite of tittle-tattle."

Wharton turned to me. That, he said, was the kind of answer we liked. Straight from the shoulder and be damned to the consequences.

"But roughly in the same context," he said, and donned the spectacles again. "You happen to be playing with Holme's sister. I gave myself the pleasure of seeing you last night, not that that's here nor there. But we have to make all sorts of enquiries. In fact a good many people would be astonished if they knew just how much we knew. And we had the impression that there wasn't good feeling between Miss Holme and her brother. Do you know anything about that?"

Wyster looked puzzled.

"I don't. I mean, why should I know the—"

"Exactly!" cut in George. "Why should you? We just thought you might happen to know. She might have been indignant, for instance, because he was seeing quite a lot of your wife. They were good friends, your wife and Miss Holme?"

"I wouldn't say that," Wyster said dubiously. "I think, as a matter of fact, they were just a bit allergic to each other."

Wharton was getting to his feet and going across to the safe.

"I know," he said. "Like the packets of a seidletz powder. All right apart but pretty fizzy when they get together. Ever seen a gun like this, by the way?"

Wyster took the Lautrec and he was frowning as he examined it.

"I can't say that I have. I know very little about guns. Never owned one in my life."

"This is the kind of bullet," Wharton said, and showed him one. "But of course you wouldn't have seen that either." He took his time putting the gun away. Wyster fidgeted again on his seat. Then Wharton came slowly back and again the spectacles were taken off.

"I think that's about all," he said, "except one thing. We shall have to be told the whole of your movements for that night from the time you left the theatre."

"But I've already told you."

"Oh, no," Wharton said, and reached for a sheet of notes. "You told us you'd gone out in your car and spent the night with friends. Which might have been perfectly correct. You came straight to your flat from the theatre, that's quite true. Not long afterwards you had a telephone call from a lady. We'd like you to tell us what lady."

Wyster said he didn't even remember the call.

"Come, come," Wharton told him ironically. "You don't remember the only telephone call you had on the night your wife was killed?"

"Sorry, but I don't."

Wharton shrugged his shoulders.

"Then it wasn't as a result of that call you went out?"

"How could it be?"

"Then why did you go out? You'd had a matinée, and a pretty long day."

"I suppose I happened to feel like it."

"That's reasonable. And where exactly did you go?"

Wyster's eyes narrowed, then he shook his head.

"Sorry, but I can't tell you that."

"You can't?" Wharton looked at me as if he couldn't believe his ears. "But why not?"

"Simply because I can't. If you like, I regard it as a personal matter."

"He regards it as a personal matter," Wharton told me. "The death of his wife isn't a personal matter. Getting the one who killed her isn't a personal matter."

"I didn't kill her," Wyster told him calmly. "There's no need for me to swear it or to get hysterical or anything like that. I didn't kill her. I know I didn't kill her and I'm the one to know. If you think that's a lie, then go ahead and prove it. I've no fear."

Wharton began again. He tried a new angle; he cajoled and finally he almost threatened. Wyster was immovable. I've told you that part of his in *Round Square* might have been written for him, and there he was, just like his Henry Hallitt in Act 2, having what he regarded as his principles and refusing to budge from them. Wharton couldn't shake him. At last there was nothing to be done, and Wharton recognised the fact. He shrugged his shoulders and got to his feet.

"Very well, Mr. Wyster, that's all—for the time being. If there're any consequences, you must take them."

"I wonder if I might ask a question," I said, and even my few extra inches of height were somehow putting Wyster at a disadvantage. "It's a ridiculous question, but I'd like you to humour me and tell me what you think."

His eyes were on mine and he was wondering what was coming.

"Say it's a dream," I said. "A dark night and one's approaching a house. There's never a light and the house looks deserted. Everywhere's deadly quiet. Then suddenly there's a sound. A weird sound. A plaintive sound, like the whimpering of a baby. Have you ever had a dream like that?". In spite of himself his lips had parted and then they were clamped together again. By the time I'd asked the question, he could shake his head.

"Afraid not," he said. "And if this is some kind of psychological test, I'm sorry I haven't been able to help you." His eyes shifted to Wharton, and as if to ignore me. Wharton ushered him towards the door and the two went out together.

"Well, what now?" I asked George as he came in again. "Make him talk, if it's the last thing we do," he told me grimly.

"That question about a baby shook him," I said. "For a moment it got him clean in the wind. He gave a start. He just couldn't help himself."

"He was there that night?"

"Yes," I said. "I'm dead sure he was. I'll bet any money in the world that he heard that crying baby." Then I could only shrug my shoulders. "Proving it is quite a different thing."

George glanced up at the clock.

"Expecting anybody else?"

"Yes," he said. "The Holme woman. I've timed it so that they can't meet and compare notes. I wouldn't be surprised if she's waiting now, though that won't do her any harm. I suppose it was she who made that telephone call?"

"Probably," I said. "Though I don't see why that should have sent him to Carr's Hill."

The buzzer went.

"This'll be her," George said.

But it wasn't. It was a call for me. And from Holme. He'd rung my private number and there'd been no reply, so he chanced ringing the Yard.

"Well, here I am," I said. "And what's your trouble?"

"None really," he said, in that quiet, diffident voice of his. "I know it's rather soon after yesterday but I wondered if you'd care to lunch with me. Very short notice and all that."

"I think I'd love to. But why not go to my club?"

"But this is on me."

"So it can be," I told him. "I merely suggested it because we can be reasonably sure of the food."

So that was settled.

"Something on his mind," I told George. "Sounded like a man who's been dodging the dentist and at last screws up his courage."

George didn't look too optimistic as he pressed the buzzer and asked about Miss Holme. She'd just arrived, he was told, and at once he was prinking himself in the glass and getting ready for the morning's second act. Then out he went, just like a conductor who leaves the platform to bring on the prima donna from the wings. I could hear the chatter of gay voices as they neared. Then I was on my feet and all ready to turn on the tap of charm.

"You know Travers?" Wharton said.

"Of course! We're old friends."

She made a wicked little moue at me and I grinned feebly. She was looking extraordinarily charming, I thought, and superbly dressed, even to my male eyes. The black costume was beautifully cut and the hat was the halo kind that formed a kind of lofty frame for the face and made it curiously madonna-like. There was a touch of red in it, and on the lapels of the coat, and again in the small earrings, and even in the expensive handbag she had tucked beneath her arm.

"This is more than a favour," Wharton was saying. "May I give you a cushion? These seats are none too comfortable. A cigarette? That's fine."

The preliminaries came to an end and on went the spectacles, and there was the kindly old gentleman who couldn't conceivably harm a fly.

"Too bad of us," he said, "but we've just got to have your help. But let me read you something," and he gave a premonitory smile. "It's going to surprise you."

So Merril Holme listened to the story of Maudie Brown. And she too was surprised. More than once she looked across at me as if to ask if it were true. That was the question she put to Wharton as soon as he'd finished.

"Every word's true," he said. "You didn't think she was capable of it?"

"Well," she said, and seemed to be appealing to me, "I don't know quite what made me say it. The whole thing was a surprise, it's like something out of a book."

"In a way it *was* out of a book."

"Yes," she said, and gave a little frown. "I suppose it was. And looking at it like that, I'd say she was quite capable of it. Where work was concerned she was absolutely ruthless. Never spared herself, if you know what I mean."

"Like Habbakuk," I suggested. *"Capable de tout."*

She smiled.

"I wouldn't quite say that, but she was wrapped up in her work. Nothing else mattered." There was a little pout. "If she thought that barmaid act would get her the part of Jinny

Patman—well, she'd do what she did. And after all it was a bit of a scream."

"I suppose it was," I said. "An awfully big adventure, shall we say."

"You, of course, had not the faintest idea she was living at The Croft?" asked Wharton.

"Not the least. To tell the truth I hadn't the faintest interest in her at all. Why should I have?" Maybe she saw the quick look in his eye and anticipated the question. "I admit that I would have liked the part of Jinny Patman myself. After all, it's my job too, but that wouldn't make me interested in Audrey."

"You weren't close friends."

"Haven't I said so?" That had been a bit too tart and she gave an apologetic smile. "You're not going to think the worse of me if I say this, but in some ways she was very much of a cat."

"We know quite a lot," Wharton assured her, and quite genially. "We've seen her will."

Her face flushed at that and the lips were viciously tight.

"Not a nice thing to do," Wharton said kindly. "Still, that's the sort of thing that happens. My own view mind you, is that she hadn't the faintest intention of dying, and don't take that as a joke. What I mean is that she had every reason to think she'd live to a good old age till long after Jinny Patman had been forgotten. That clause in the will merely gave her a sort of cattish pleasure. It'd have been eliminated when she made a new will."

"I know," she said, "but it's maddening all the same."

"Forget it," Wharton said paternally. "But now something else."

The tone was discursive and mildly off-hand.

"Mr. Wyster was good enough to drop in this morning and lend us a hand, and there was a question to which he'd forgotten the answer. Perhaps you can help us. He had a telephone call to his flat that Thursday night at about half-past ten. You didn't make the call?"

"I?" she said. "But I'd been with him all night at the theatre! Why should I want to telephone him?"

"That's what we said," Wharton told her with a look at me. "I told Travers it was silly to ask you. Still, that's settled."

Then he was making play with a look at his notes.

"Oh yes," he said. "A rather personal matter. And don't forget Miss Holme, that every word that's uttered here is in the very strictest confidence. It's about that brother of yours. We happened to be told that he was—what shall we say—smitten with Mrs. Wyster. Had you heard anything of the sort?"

She didn't know what to make of that and Wharton was peering intently over his spectacle tops, which didn't help.

"Well, I had," she said, "and I didn't like it."

Then she was looking surprised and almost rounding on me.

"Why, I told Mr. Travers all about it!"

She'd told me nothing of the sort. She'd certainly mentioned the relationship between Wyster and his wife, but her brother had never come into it.

"So you did," I said, and hoped I looked as if I'd just remembered. "That's right. You thought it was a dirty trick after the way Wyster had been loyal to his wife."

"I did. And I still think so."

"And very gallant of you if I may say so," Wharton told her. "And may I apologise for Mr. Travers's lapse of memory. And, of course, he didn't know that I was asking the question."

He gave a kind of bow and another apologetic smile and then was getting to his feet.

"Well, that seems to be about all."

He had flashed a look at me. I wondered why, and then took a chance.

"It isn't a very nice thing to have to do," I said, "but we really ought to ask Miss Holme for her whereabouts that night. We'll have to have it for the records."

"Damn the records!" Wharton said, and was beginning a new apology.

"I often say far more than damn myself," Merril told him charmingly. "What was it you wanted?"

Explanations and more apologies. But she made no bones whatever about giving her alibi. We didn't tell her that it wasn't an alibi at all.

"You don't know what one feels like on a Thursday night," she told us amusedly. "All I want to do when I get home is to make myself a cup of tea. I just creep into bed and sleep and sleep and sleep."

"Which is what you did that night."

"It certainly was."

"And often what I feel like doing myself," Wharton added with a sigh.

He was moving towards the door. I cut in again.

"You interested in all that psychology business, Miss Holme? You know, the sort of thing they do in the Services nowadays. Asking silly questions and making heaven knows what out of the answers."

"I don't know that I am," she said, "but it must be rather fun."

"A pity," I said. "And you don't believe in telling fortunes from dreams?" Then I gave a sigh too as I offered my cigarette case. "I had an awfully funny dream the night before last and I've asked one or two people to explain it. I just thought you might be the psychic type, if that's what they call it. . . ."

And so on till she was asking for my dream. I varied it slightly from the version I'd given Wyster, for a second telling profited from the haste of the first. I expanded it, for instance, and so worked up to a far more effective climax.

"A weird sound. A sort of blood-curdling sound. It absolutely froze me where I stood. And then I knew what it was."

"Yes?" she said, lips parted and eyes intently on mine.

The whimper of a baby!

For some reason her tongue was suddenly moistening her lips. Then she laughed, and to me there was something synthetic in that laugh.

"But how priceless! Do go on."

I shrugged my shoulders.

"I can't. That's where I woke up."

She laughed again, a delicious little chuckle of a laugh. Then she was suddenly serious.

"You're married aren't you?"

"Yes," I said, and not too heartily.

"Then—if I may be indelicate—is your wife expecting a baby?"

"Not to my knowledge," I said. "And I ought to know."

And then Wharton was cutting in. Miss Holme was a busy woman and I ought to know better than waste her time with all sorts of twaddle. And so to the smiles and handshakes, and the faint scent of the leather glove still on my hand when she'd gone. And Wharton with her, of course, the conductor leading off the prima donna. And it was a good five minutes before he was back.

"Well, what did you make of her?" he was firing at me at once.

"If you mean the baby stunt, then I don't know," I said. "It seemed to startle her but it might have been quite legitimate surprise at the unexpected dénouement. It was a different surprise from Wyster's."

"She's a tougher character than Wyster," George said, and then was damning the whole race of actresses. To her that morning had been merely the playing of an unstudied scene, and she had made a first-class job of it.

"But listen to this," he said. "I was surprised she'd come by Tube and not by car. She said she was spending the afternoon in town in any case—not going home again, so to speak—and she wasn't driving her car nowadays. Had a narrow escape one Sunday from a bloke cutting in and it shook her so much that she lost her nerve for driving. That's why she's reconciled to the loss of her basic petrol. What I want to know is why she told me all that herself—about the car, I mean. She'd only got to say she was staying in town or she hadn't anywhere handy to park the car."

I said it was certainly suspicious. What she'd been doing, apparently, was going out of her way to impress on his mind that she didn't have her car out on that vital night. Which again was wholly unnecessary.

"You didn't ask either her or Wyster about that second telephone call on the Thursday night," I said. "Any particular reason?"

"Ask no questions and you'll hear no lies," he told me. "No use asking too many questions in any case."

Then he was glancing up at the clock and saying I shouldn't have any too much time to get ready for that lunch with Holme.

"Something I rather wanted you to do," he said. "Still, the afternoon will do just as well. I'll let Holberg know you're coming."

"What do we want from Holberg?"

"Anything he's got about the Holme woman's past," he said. "We don't know a thing about her really. Better get it confidentially from Holberg than direct from her own agent—if she has one."

I said I'd see what I could do. I did add from the door that in spite of an occasional glimpse of what I might call not quite the perfect lady, she hadn't graduated from the gutter, the reason for which brilliant piece of deduction being that she'd understood my immaculate French.

Chapter XIV
HOLME—AND A BABY

HOLME WAS NOT the same man who'd spent best part of a day with me, but though I'm a pretty old hand at the kind of game I was playing, I didn't quite know wherein the difference lay. He was friendly, but the friendliness wasn't too natural. It had for him a certain strain. His manner was quiet; almost too quiet considering we'd had that day together. I hoped he had something on his mind and that with tactful handling he'd get it off. More than once I've been told that I'm the sort of chap who inspires confidences. I don't altogether believe that. I do believe that one of Wharton's japes is nearer the mark—that I hear and can tell an infinite number of lies because I look so little of a liar myself.

We'd got to the port stage and were in a corner of the lounge and almost by ourselves. What talk there was around us was decorous, and if you know my club you'll be only too aware of that. All the symptoms told me that Holme had something on the tip of his tongue, and at last I thought it was up to me to lend a helping hand.

"I wonder if I might make a guess?"

"A guess?"

"Yes. At what's in your mind. Would I be right, for instance, if I thought there was something you wanted to tell me and you were wondering if I'd believe it?"

He had the last drink of his port and was taking out his cigarette case. The cigarette was slowly tapped before he spoke.

"I don't know how you knew it, but you're right."

I may have hinted that he had charming manners, but the cigarette case went back into his pocket. I lighted one of my own.

"I'm going to sound very much of a fool," was how he began.

"That's nothing unusual," I told him. "When I think back to some of the things I've done in my time, I wince."

"Yes," he said, eyes on his cigarette. And then suddenly: "How old do you think I am?"

"Oh, getting on for forty?"

"Thirty-nine," he said. "And till I met Audrey I'd never been in love with a woman in my life. That's what's making it difficult."

"How's it make it difficult?"

"Well—-just because. I mean, I'm not a sort of callow youth. I'm a business man and used to the rough-and-tumble of things. You can't imagine a man like me being a kind of Romeo."

"Don't you believe it," I told him. "I was nearly as old as you when I married and I had it most damnable badly at the time. I might have been nineteen, not a staid thirty-six."

"I'm glad you said that," he said, "but there's something else too. I didn't make up my mind to talk to you just because of what you'd done about my car."

Things were getting confused. I'd no idea what he was talking about and I said so. Then I knew Wharton had been up to his tricks. Or had George merely forgotten to tell me?

"They told me next door that a man had been making enquiries about my car being out that night," Holme went on. "They'd told him in quite good faith that they'd heard it come back after midnight. Then they wondered what'd been behind it, and they spoke to me."

I assured him that I'd known never a thing.

"But you *were* out that night in your car?"

"Yes," he said. "I was at Carr's Hill."

This was his story, and in my words, not his. He had seen Audrey Grange that morning on the golf course and had kept his partner waiting while he spoke to her. He upbraided her with having left him for a month with never a letter or call. She gave work as an excuse and he said he'd rung up Denham and everywhere he could think of—even her mother.

She said she'd be going back to normal life in a day or so, and she promised to lunch with him the following week. She also said she'd have a delightful surprise for him.

"You're going to get a divorce!" he said.

It wasn't that, she said, and then he'd had to hurry on, with a reminder that she'd promised to ring him later and fix up that meeting. Then he finished his round but just as he got back to the club-house she had finished her lunch, for she had done the last half first. He just caught sight of her with her bag on her shoulder crossing the car park and then making for the direction of the station. He watched her and she turned right which was up Hurst Avenue. That made him wonder, and he followed her, keeping out of sight in the shelter of the tall boundary hedge. That was how he came to see her go into The Croft. He waited for a time and saw her open the lounge windows, and somehow he knew she was living in that bungalow.

After lunch he went back to the works—he had been playing with his accountant—and he spent a wretched afternoon and evening. After dinner he got out his car and went to a cinema but the picture was poor and it was about a quarter to ten when he came out, and before the end of the show. Then he had an overwhelming desire to go to Carr's Hill; not, as he said, that he'd see her but merely to see perhaps the light in a window.

There was of course, and deep down, the mad hope that he might see her, and there was also, as he frankly owned, a torturing jealousy and the fear that some other man might be with her at The Croft.

Late as it was he set off, and the journey shouldn't have taken more than twenty minutes at the most. Then he had a puncture and had to change his wheel. All his tyres were wearing thin and he hated to risk the drive on. Then he saw an all-night garage—he gave me the address—and had the puncture repaired. And then, even later though it was, he knew he had to go to Carr's Hill or he'd never sleep. So he went, and as near as he could remember, it was just after half-past eleven when he got there.

He had come into Hurst Avenue from the Redwood Park end, and as he neared the top of the rise he switched off his head-lights. Then at the very top of the rise he just discerned a car ahead, and parked by the verge beyond where he thought the bungalow must be. That was again a moment of jealousy. Off went his side-lights and he stayed where he was in the car. Five minutes and the other car drove off though he never saw the driver get in. It must have been facing north for it disappeared in the darkness in the direction of the golf course.

He waited another few minutes then got out of his car. The road was wider where he was and he let the car run backwards downhill and then reversed. Then he made his way on the grass verge to the bungalow. Everything was dark. He moved on to the garage drive and went cautiously along it. The doors were open and there was no car there. There was only one thing to think—that it had been Audrey's car and she had gone off in it. And that was when he heard again the curious noise. He had heard it before and it made his flesh creep.

"The cry of a whimpering baby!"

His eyes bulged.

"My God! how did you know?"

"Never mind that," I said. "Go on with your story."

"It sounded like a baby," he said, "and then I was wondering what a baby could be doing out there. I had a torch in the car and I'd got it in my pocket, and there was a path between the garage and the house so I went to explore. And what do you think it was? A Siamese cat!"

"Good God!" I said, and my face must have gone a bit red. "So that's what it was."

"I saw it," he said. "I sort of snapped my fingers for it to come to me but it went off through the bushes. Then I heard it further away."

"Yes," I said. "My sister had a Siamese cat. That's just the damn noise they make. If it hadn't been for Mabel Ganton, maybe I'd have guessed it."

"Mabel Ganton?"

"Just a woman whose bungalow we enquired at. She swore blind it was a baby. But go on. What happened next?"

Nothing had happened. He had waited a few minutes with the hope that Audrey might return, and then he let his car run down the hill, switched on his side-lights and drove home. The next night he thought of going back, and didn't. On the Saturday he had made up his mind to go back, even if she had left the bungalow as their talk on the golf course had rather suggested. Then he read the news in the evening paper.

"But why didn't you come to the police?" I was asking him.

"Well, I was rather stunned," he said. "And somehow I didn't want her name mixed up with mine. I didn't want to start any scandal. You see I hadn't been able to work things out. I still thought the car I saw might have belonged to some other man. Then you came to Finchley."

I told him his story was terrific. Just what we needed to get the whole thing tied up—provided he'd go along to the Yard and make his statement official. As far as was humanly possible everything should be in confidence. In fact I didn't see any reason why his name should be mentioned at all. He didn't care a lot for the idea, and that wasn't unnatural. Then I got him to my way of thinking.

He didn't say much in the taxi and it's only a five minute trip in any case. Now the burst of excitement had gone, I was feeling less optimistic. His story, as I was beginning to realise, was helpful and confirmatory enough, but it wasn't the vital and clinching thing for which we were looking. And at the back of my mind was always something else, the fear that I had been the dupe and he the clever one: that the whole thing was a brilliant adaptation of what had really happened that night. But two heads are better than one, even if they're sheep's heads, as my old nurse used to say. George was farther away from Holme than I was and his might be the more reliable summing up.

George was in and I took Holme straight up to his room. There I left him looking far more at home than I'd thought, for George had turned on the charm, and when George sets out to be genial and pleasant, he can deceive the very elect. I had told the taxi to wait, and it took me to Shaftesbury Avenue.

A client was just leaving as I arrived and I went straight into Holberg's office. I told him we were giving him a lot of trouble and couldn't be expected to do that sort of thing at his expense. He must keep an account of things and be ready to send in a bill. He whipped round on me at that.

"A bill?" he said. "To help find a dirty murderer? You've got me all wrong. Holberg's the name. I was Audrey Grange's agent. I don't want your money."

I pacified him. I told him he was the good fellow he was, not that that perhaps cut any ice, and we got down to the job. His job, I mean. Wharton had rung him pretty early and he'd been making surreptitious enquiries and adding them to what he knew himself, and that was pretty well enough. A man doesn't do his job for forty years without becoming something of a walking *Who's Who*.

The Holme history was simple. The parents had gone down in the *Lusitania* and the two children had been brought up by two different uncles and aunts. James had gone to the uncle who then ran the small but thriving business that had become the big works it now was. Merril had gone to the Fletchings.

"You remember old Dave Fletching?" Tom said. "Used to own the old Belvoir Music-Hall? Quite a character, he was. He was Mrs. Holme's brother. One of the sporting, racing type and when he died pretty suddenly, his affairs were in quite a tangle. About enough for the widow to live on and no more."

"How old was Merril then?" I said.

"Can't say," he said, "but she'd just left school. Quite a good school, I believe. The old man was lavish enough with his money. She'd a hankering for the stage. She actually ran away—so I'm told—and tried to join a show at Brighton. Then she got a regular job with a summer show, the old Red Robins. You know the Red Robins. Old Dick Atherton used to run it. Three or four shows and changing round during the season."

I said I thought I'd seen one of them at Torquay.

"That's right," Tom said. "Merril was a sort of general utility. Sang a snappy song or two, and took a hand in sketches, and did an impression or two. You know the kind of thing. Soubrette stuff. Then she met Tom Olney and married him. That was when she was twenty."

"Was that Olney the playwright?"

"He did write a play or two," Tom said, and shrugged his shoulders. "*Middle Distance* was his and that wasn't bad. Free-lance stuff was his general line—scenarios, sketches, books of words and that sort of thing. It was he who got Merril on the stage. A small part in a show called *Widows Mightn't*. And at the Orpheum, by the way."

"And then, as they say, she never looked back."

"That's it. She has talent, mind you. And she's a damn pretty woman. A bit tough perhaps, but old Dave Fletching was a rough and ready customer himself, in spite of his money. You knew she divorced Olney?"

I said I'd heard it somewhere.

"All sorts of yarns going about," he said. "Everybody thought it was a rigged-up affair."

"She was a tail-swisher?"

"I wouldn't say that," Tom said. "The general idea seems to be that Olney was rather in the way. Then she was friendly with Carl Bletz for a time, and that's how she broke into films—so they say."

And that was all that he could tell me. He didn't place much reliance on tittle-tattle about her and Wyster. That sort of thing always got around when two people placed as she and Wyster were, were principals in the same play.

Before I thanked him I had to make the position perfectly clear. Merril Holme was mixed up in the case, but that didn't make her in any way a suspect, and Holberg must get that right into his head. I didn't need to tell him how she was involved in things, but it was just as well that he shouldn't jump to conclusions. That might prejudice any further enquiries we asked him to make, and inadvertently he might let something slip.

That was that. I told him my wife was due back the next morning and got him to promise to come round soon for a meal and a yarn. Then I went back to the Yard. Holme was still with Wharton so I went out to a tea-shop. When I got back Holme had just gone.

"Not a bad chap, Holme," I said. "Didn't you think so?"

If George ever enters heaven's gates it will be with his hands in his pockets for fear someone should snatch his wallet. And he'll probably give Peter a quick once-over too.

"Had to winkle everything out of him with a pin," he said. "Not that that isn't better than the gabblers."

"But his story. What about that?"

"Sounds reasonable. So did some other yarns we've heard in our time."

He wasn't mentioning the Siamese cat, and maybe because he was as much up to the ears in that oversight as I was. What he wanted to know was where Holme's story got us—assuming it was true. I said I'd like to read his statement to see if it differed from the one he gave me.

It did, but only in one small detail. He had found the garage gates open, and that had been why he had walked in. When he had come out he had instinctively shut the gates, a natural enough proceeding considering he had gates of his own. But he hadn't bolted them. He remembered that when he got back to his car and had thought of opening them again in case Audrey should come back. Then he thought that if she did come back, she would find the gates shut and would have to get out of the car, and that would give him a chance to speak to her.

"She was definitely dead and the car had gone by half-past eleven," I said. "Ousten was pretty well on the mark. But our problem is who was in the other car? One car's eliminated, and that's something."

"Holme's alibi still isn't an alibi," George said. "He's not eliminated by a long chalk. We can put him by for a bit on a nice handy shelf and concentrate elsewhere, but he's the devil of a long way off being eliminated."

"What's his motive?" I wanted to know. "If he killed her it wasn't without a reason."

"Theorising won't get us anywhere," he told me with a snort. "Not that I can't do a bit of it myself. Unrequited love, for instance. If he couldn't have her, no-one else should. And what about this? He's there in that bungalow and Wyster catches him there. There's a row and a gun's pulled out and Audrey gets shot by mistake. Nobody's fault but the two panic. Then they fake a burglary and beat it." He gave a grunt and waved a contemptuous hand. "I can theorise as well as the next one, but where's it get us?"

I might have said that as theories both were in the class of the super-dud. What I did ask was whom he was going to concentrate on. He looked at me as if I'd never heard the names of Wyster and Merril Holme and Merlin.

"Nothing from Carris Street?"

"Nothing at all," he told me. "I got in touch with the lessor and he tells me there isn't a tenant who has been there less than three months. How could Merlin have had an office there three months ago? That'd have meant he had everything planned three months ago. And that's lunacy."

He gave that curious sparrow-like tilt of the head. Something was coming.

"By the way, I didn't get a chance to tell you because the full reports didn't get in till this afternoon. But what do you think of this? Every Division was asked to make urgent enquiries and there's no such thing as a big new amateur orchestra in existence. The whole thing's bunkum!"

Somehow I wasn't surprised, and I said so.

"What I've been wondering is this," I said. "I think it's a certainty he was wise to that barmaid scheme. Why shouldn't he have spent his evenings or part of them, in the Seven Bells, keeping an eye on Audrey? And seeing her to the station after closing time. That might explain the orchestra yarn he spun his wife."

Then I thought of something else. I'd thought of it before and now I got it off my chest.

"And another thing, talking of the Seven Bells. Quarren had a crush on his barmaid. Why shouldn't he have followed her home one night? Why shouldn't it have been his car Holme saw?"

"He doesn't drive a car," he told me. "I thought that one out myself. But Merlin drives a car. He used to have one up to just pre-war, then he sold it."

"And what about that hue and cry for him?"

"I'm giving him just another twenty-four hours," George said. "Up till then he can rest in peace. Meanwhile we're concentrating on Wyster and the Holme woman. Another little bit of news since I saw you last. I had her tailed from here and you can guess where she went. To have lunch with Wyster. A quiet little place in Chelsea. He was waiting for her when she got there."

"What about that chap Fred I mentioned as likely?"

"He's being worked on this very afternoon. Sergeant Crolly's struck up an acquaintance with him. Crolly's a good man. He'll pump him dry."

I asked what he wanted me to do, and all he could say was that at the moment there was nothing. Glass would be working on a cold scent, trying to get something more on the other car after Holme's extremely dim description. The best thing I could do was to get back home and if anything happened he'd ring. If not I might report in the morning. There might be time for me to meet the Euston train and, if not, then something could be arranged.

Then at the very door he made a remark.

"Damn funny business about that Siamese cat? You know anything about them?"

I said I'd seen them, and that was quite a good side-track. "That Ganton woman," George said. "Next time I'm that way I'll give myself the pleasure of a call."

I said I'd like to be with him. But what about the cat?

"We rang Glass and he knew about it all the time," George said disgustedly. "Belonged to the wife of the secretary of the golf club. It just strayed for the night—that's all."

I still wished I could be there when he called on Mabel Ganton.

I didn't go straight home and because an idea came to me. What I did was ring Bill Ellice instead. He was in and I said I'd be along as soon as I could make it.

Before I say what happened, let me do a little explaining. You perhaps patronise the dogs or the races or have a good seat at a cricket or football match. It's a kind of hobby interest and it costs you money, and it's money you don't grudge. My interests don't happen to lie that way, but I don't grudge money on what hobbies I have. And my job is one of them. That's why I made no bones about giving Bill an assignment.

I told him all about Merlin and I laid heavy emphasis on that Carris Street episode. Bill has a fine detecting brain and I wanted to hear what he made of it all.

"It seems unanswerable," he said. "He didn't say, 'Set me down at Carris Street'. He said, 'Set me down at 76, Carris Street'. The number itself has simply *got* to have some significance."

"And yet not a single lessee has been there for less than three months!"

"I don't see how that affects it," Bill said. "Who says he hired an office? Why shouldn't he have a pal of some sort there who's putting him up?"

"Then there's a job for you," I said. "For my private account. Find out who's putting him up."

Bill shrugged his shoulders. He was up to the eyes and couldn't spare a man. I said it would be a twenty-four hour job at the most. Hallows could do it in the time.

"Well, I'll do it for you," Bill said, "but I'm damned if I would for anyone else. He's working on a pilfering job at one of the big wholesalers. Perhaps I could call him off."

I said the sooner the better. If Merlin was dug in there, it'd be at night when he crawled out. That was how we left it and when I'd written a Merlin description I went back to the flat. It was a quarter to six when I got there. The telephone rang at five minutes to.

"That you, Travers?" George was saying.

"Yes," I said.

"Nip along here quick. A certain lady wants to see me *confidentially* at a quarter-past six—on her way to the theatre."

"I'll be there," I said, and I was.

Outside the flat I ran clean into a taxi and I was at the Yard with five minutes to spare. George was in such a state of expectancy that his very voice was hushed. You'd have thought he was talking confidences over the telephone.

"She rang me just before I rang you. Wanted to know if I could see her most confidentially for just a minute or two. I said that was what I was here for."

"What'd she sound like?"

"Hushed and tragic," George said, and was waving his hands about as if that might help. "Something's happened, you bet your life. And as a result of that little lunch and confab at Chelsea."

"If it's all that confidential, ought she to see me here?"

"Just what I was thinking," George said. "You'd better nip into the Holy of Holies."

That's the little lavatory and cloak-room that leads off from the main room. There's an elegant fanlight over the door and by standing on the lavatory seat one can get a good view of what's going on, and every word is audible. I'd used that room a good few times before. And almost as soon as we'd decided on it, the buzzer went. George picked up the receiver, gave a grunt, and then tipped me the wink.

"Show her up," I heard him say as I went through the side door.

I mounted my rostrum and prepared for the show. I saw George go out to do his leading-on act and I held my breath as he ushered Merril in.

Chapter XV
DEADLOCK

Tragic and mournful was how Wharton had summed her up, and that's what she now seemed. The clothes she was wearing were dark, and the fur round her neck was dark, and there was a kind of widow's veil on her hat. Her voice, usually a vivacious sort of soprano, was a kind of slow contralto.

"I'm so sorry to have bothered you," she was saying as Wharton ushered her in. "I wouldn't have done it if it hadn't seemed an absolute necessity."

Wharton, with every good intention, was placing her chair where she would face my door and that was to ruin my view, for she had only to lift her eyes to the fanlight and catch perhaps a quick glimpse of me.

"There's never any sense in harbouring worries," Wharton was telling her. "Tell me what they are and I'll see what I can do."

"You're sure it will be strictly confidential?"

"I can't go so far as that." His tone was grave. "That'd be asking for a blank cheque. You'll have to trust me to use my judgment."

"It's going to be difficult." She paused. "I hardly know where to begin."

Wharton was saying nothing.

"It's about Harlan—Mr. Wyster. I think you're going to arrest him."

"Yes?"

"Well, you mustn't. It'd be a mistake. An awful mistake."

Wharton gave a grunt.

"Well, we don't want to make mistakes," he told her quietly. "But perhaps you'll explain."

"Will you tell me something? . . . When she was killed?"

"When?" said Wharton slowly. "I thought it was fairly general knowledge that she was killed between, say, eleven o'clock and midnight."

"Then he *couldn't* have done it!"

"That's excellent." Was there a faint irony? "But just why couldn't he have done it?"

There was a pause. Then she was saying, and in a voice that to me was almost inaudible, that she couldn't tell him.

"You can't tell me?"

There was another silence and then a movement. I had to risk a look, and there was Wharton on his feet.

"If that's so, Miss Holme, why on earth did you come here? Surely a woman of your intelligence must know that I couldn't accept a bare statement like that."

"But I assure you it's true."

"Look," he said patiently. "Whatever you tell me will be confidential as far as I can make it. Either you trust me or you don't. If you don't, then we'll bid each other a very good evening. If you do, then what are you afraid of?"

There was a long pause. I stole another look and there she was, eyes downcast and fingers nervously twiddling.

"Very well," she said, and her tone had a sudden resolution. "He was with me. I did make that telephone call. I was feeling wretched and tired and I knew I shouldn't sleep. So I rang him and asked him to come."

"And he came?"

"Yes. He came at once."

"And he stayed till when?"

"Does that matter? . . . Surely I've told you enough."

I could imagine Wharton's shrug of the shoulders.

"Put it another way then. He was with you till after midnight?"

"Yes."

"You'd swear to that?"

"If I had to—yes."

"And you'd sign a simple statement? The statement, by the way, wouldn't be made public unless we discovered there was something wrong with it. It'd be something like this. . . ."

"But of course."

"Excellent," he said. I heard the buzzer and he was asking for a stenographer to be sent in. Then apparently she was scared of the stenographer. He seemed a breach of the promise of confidence. Wharton was reassuring her and then the stenographer came in.

Wharton said a few words of the statement, asked her if that was satisfactory, repeated it to the stenographer, embodying any amendments, and so it went on. Out went the stenographer with instructions to bring the usual typed copies.

"Now, Miss Holme, I have to be serious," Wharton said. "I'm old enough to be your father. If it interests you, I've a daughter of about your own age."

I guessed the spectacles were on and he was peering paternally over their tops, but I daren't risk a look.

"What you're going to sign is a witnessed statement. It's a serious statement because murder's a serious matter. You realise all that?"

"Yes." The voice again was almost inaudible.

"By the way, does Mr. Wyster know what you're doing?"

"Well—no. I mean I told him I would but he wouldn't believe me. He wouldn't take me seriously. He thought I was just bluffing."

"I see."

I heard the shift of his chair as the typed copies were coming in.

"You might remain, sergeant, and witness the signature," Wharton said. "Will you read that, Miss Holme, and make absolutely sure it's exactly what you want to state?"

I saw her go to the desk and take the chair Wharton placed for her. He was leaning over her as she signed. A couple of minutes and that ordeal was over.

"Well," he said briskly, "that little matter's concluded. All the same I'd still like you to tell me what you were telling me when we were interrupted. Mr. Wyster thought you were bluffing?"

"That's right," she said, and the voice had something of its old alertness. "As soon as he told me you'd been questioning him, I was terrified. I didn't want my name brought in. Then I changed my mind. I could see he was worried to death and I knew I was wrong. Then I got frightened. I sort of felt he was going to be arrested. That's why I came."

"Very gallant of him." Now there seemed a definite irony. "And very gallant of you too. All the same it's a pity you both saw fit to bolster the position up with lies. You see I don't mince words."

"I know," she said, and there was a little catch in her voice. "I'm ashamed of myself. Dreadfully ashamed. But you can't blame him really. He was only protecting my good name."

"Of course," he said. "You realise, by the way, that I shall have to hear what he now has to say?"

"That won't matter," she said. "I think he'll be very angry, but—well, he'll know I did it for the best. And he can't deny it now."

There was a movement in the room and I had another look.

"That seems to be everything," he was saying, and they were moving towards the door. "I'll see that a car takes you to the theatre."

I heard just that much and then the door closed. A minute or two's wait and I got down from my perch and I was ready for Wharton when he came back. He merely made a motion for silence and was picking up the receiver. I guessed he'd asked downstairs for Wyster at the theatre and was now expecting his man on the line. Then he was stirring in his seat.

"That you, Mr. Wyster? This is Superintendent Wharton speaking from New Scotland Yard. Miss Holme has just been here and made a statement about your movements on a certain night. . . . That surprises you? . . . Well, there it is. You're busy and I'm busy. Get her to tell you all about it. . . . That's it. But just a minute. I'd like to see you in your room immediately after the show. . . . Alone, yes. . . . That's right. I'll bring a similar state-ment with me. . . . Right. Good-bye."

He hung up and leaned back in his chair, and he was giving me a grim nod or two.

"A nasty business," I said.

"It stinks!" He spat the words out, and then he was on his feet, and in a minute he was prowling about the room.

"If it's perjury," I said lamely, "then there's something mighty serious behind it."

"Of course there is. It's perjury and collusion, and we know it. But how're we going to prove it? We're up a gum tree. We're back where we started."

He came round to his desk, picked up the signed statement, and I thought for a moment he was going to rip it in pieces. Then he got up again and was locking it in his safe. It was just that perhaps that cooled him down a bit. A minute or two and we were trying to calculate just where we now stood.

And that, as George had said, was on much the same spot from which we had started. Wyster and Holme were ready to swear in any court whatever that they had been in each other's company for at least the vital period of that night. A jury would naturally assume that they had spent the whole of that night in each other's company, but that was no help. Wyster was a man of considerable standing and his sworn word would be believed.

But in our judgment, Wyster and Holme were sure enough that no case would come into any court. How could a case be brought in face of such statements? And with every day that passed, the two could make their position even more secure. There'd be conferences between them and the addition of all sorts of little confirmatory facts. Each would become word per-fect in the final story. As for ourselves and in view of merely the two statements, we should be mad to approach the Director of Public Prosecutions with even a hint of a case against either Wyster or Holme.

"The devil of it is, too," I said, "that everyone knew Audrey Grange was wrapped up in her work and she and her husband were just about friends and no more. He'd no reason to kill her.

If she wouldn't divorce him—so that he could marry Merril, for instance—why should that matter much? He could have lived with Merril if he wished. The theatre isn't the B.B.C. You don't get fired for immorality."

"There's motive enough," Wharton said. "She wanted that Jinny Patman part so badly that somehow she got Wyster worked up sufficiently to do her in."

He got to his feet, then sat down again.

"That reminds me. This is Crolly's report of his afternoon with Fred."

It was a verbose affair: a kind of currant duff with mighty few currants. All that seemed of any good to us was one remark which Crolly had given verbally.

"All over him she was," Fred had said. "I don't reckon he was so keen, though. But her! Always popping in and out of his room. Darling this and darling that. Of course that don't amount to much, but it was the way she said it."

But, as Wharton said, it still didn't help. In fact, there was only one thing for it. Somehow we had to break that alibi. And there was only one hope—to get a line on that second car that had just been glimpsed by Holme at Carr's Hill. Prove that that was Wyster's, and above all that Wyster was in it, and the end was in sight. But Holme couldn't help us. He did remember he'd seen something like a faint shadow when the someone got into the car, and that was as far as he could go. And it wasn't far enough. He'd not the faintest idea of the make of the car and only the vaguest idea that it was fairly large. But the dim light and the looming up of a shadow—and that was all that second car was to him—would have given an impression of greater size if—and the *if* was a big one—the car was Wyster's small-sized Martlet ten.

But there was no point in our fuddling our wits with talk that got us nowhere, and there are times when sleep is better than prayer, whatever the muezzins may tell to the faithful.

George said it might be better if he saw Wyster at the theatre and I might as well get back home. In the morning I could ring him early and if there was still nothing doing then I could get along to Euston to meet Bernice.

It had been a grand day, that Thursday, and there had been times when I had been uncomfortably warm. The Friday looked like being just such another day, though there was an autumnal mist. That was at seven o'clock, the time at which I had set my alarm clock. That was rather early for me, but I had plenty to do.

Ours is a service flat which means that one can get meals in the ground floor restaurant, or have them sent up, and that a kind of peripatetic chambermaid—if asked for—goes like a whirlwind through one's rooms and gives them a semblance of tidiness. That was what Bernice had regretfully left me to, for normally we never see a chambermaid. Like most women of this worse-than-war epoch, Bernice does the housework herself. But that's why I was up early. I was going to begin where the chambermaid ended, and an orgy of cleaning would leave the flat spotless. I had told Bernice I should be all right, and the flat would be all right, and I was out to prove it.

Then while I was having breakfast, the telephone went. I thought it was Wharton, but it wasn't. It was Bill Ellice.

"Thought you might like to know how that job of yours is going," he said. "Hallows thinks he's on to something."

"Really?"

"Late last night a man came in. Hallows stayed till one o'clock and he was still there. He'd seen the same man go out, by the way, and he'd thought he was just about the build of our man. Naturally he couldn't follow him. What he's proposing to do now is follow him when he comes out again. I'm running round a relief. How the hell I'm going to manage it I don't know."

"Look, Bill," I said, "would it ease your mind if I sent a couple of men to take over where Hallows left off? Hallows could tell them all he knows."

"It certainly would," Bill said. "I hate to let you down, but—"

I cut in hastily. No letting down at all and I was only too grateful for what he'd already done. So that was fixed up and then I remembered something I wanted to ask.

"Which of the premises is Hallows suspicious of?"

"The British and Empire Educational Press on the first floor," Bill said. "That's where this chap came from and where he probably still is."

I rang the Yard at once and fixed things up. Wharton wasn't there and I was rather relieved, for I was realising that I'd had rather a narrow escape. Suppose Merlin was run to earth. How could I explain to Wharton how I had got on his tracks? If Wharton had called off our own men, then I'd be making something of a fool of him by owning that I'd mistrusted his judgment—or rather the competence and handling of our men—and had privately employed Ellice. And then as I was ending my much disturbed meal, Wharton rang.

Wyster had signed a statement, he said. He too had been apologetic and highly ashamed of himself.

"Anything for me to do?" I wanted to know.

Nothing at the moment, he said. He was going to Carr's Hill with some additional men to try to get something about that second car. He might even be seeing James Holme again. When he wanted me he'd let me know.

"Something I ought to report, George," I said. "I had an overwhelming sort of hunch about Merlin still being somewhere in that building. You weren't in, so I sent a couple of men there again—just as a chance."

He gave a grunt and that was all. Then he was asking me to remember him to Bernice, and maybe he'd drop in later in the day. Then he rang off. I let out a breath of relief as I replaced my receiver.

Then I got to work on the flat. Don't think these domestic details are unimportant. I can assure you they're not. And in less than no time I was emptying ash-trays and stowing away private papers and correspondence. Dirty garments went into the linen basket and a suit or two I'd been wearing was taken from chairs or the floor and stuffed into drawers or the wardrobe. Then Lightning—as we call that chambermaid—came in, and I read my paper. When she'd gone I cleaned out some more corners, did some dusting and at half-past ten I could look upon my work and tell myself that behold it was very good. Then I rang down for some flowers and arranged them in a vase in the lounge. Then I got some grime from my person, had a final polish, and went to get my car.

The mist had gone and it was a grand morning. Before the day was out, the temperature was to touch the eighties, but it was gloriously sunny and still fresh and cool as I waited for the train. It was fairly on time and the luggage was in and we were on the way home by half-past twelve. I had told Bernice I was on the Audrey Grange job with Wharton, but we didn't talk about it a lot. She never pesters with questions, and maybe because she knows that with patience she'll know the final answers sooner than the next one. Wharton trusts her implicitly too; in fact he's far more indiscreet than I am.

We got home. Bernice did some personal tidying and I ordered two lunches. Then she was telling me how spotless I'd kept the flat and wondering how on earth I'd done it.

"Toiling, rejoicing, sorrowing," I said. "Here a little and there a little. And you honestly think I haven't done too bad?"

She thought it was marvellous and the flowers simply lovely. But all that was before she found out! And if she hadn't found out, then we might have been much longer in solving that Case.

In the afternoon she did her unpacking and I sat over a book, ready to lend a hand if required. Then by way of celebration I took her out to tea and after that we sat in the Park and watched a gang of urchins playing their own brand of highly contentious football. Then the first faint chill was in the air and we went back home. Ten minutes after we got there the telephone went. It was from one of the men at 76 Carris Street.

"That you, sir? He's gone out and Holt is on his tail. We don't know if it's him but we're taking a chance."

That was that. The evening papers came and I had a look at one of them. At a quarter to seven the telephone went again.

"Travers speaking."

"This is Holt, sir. I followed our man up and he went in the stage door of the Palliceum. I'm ringing from there now."

"Get back to the stage door and stay there," I told him. "I'll be along at once."

But I wasn't, for I stood there polishing my glasses.

It was fantastic, and yet I didn't know. Then I made up my mind.

"Sorry, darling, but I've got to go out. It's a job of work and I may be a bit late. Not later than ten, though, with any luck."

The nights were a bit chilly, so I grabbed an overcoat and made for the lift. Then I had the devil of a wait for a taxi and it was nearly half-past seven when I got to the Palliceum. Holt was there and I told him to stay. If our man happened to come out, he was to follow him. Then I flashed my Card at the door and went in search of Newton Crole. He was up to his ears in the job.

"Can't spare you a minute," he said. "If you want a seat, help yourself."

"I don't," I said. "I want to see Bobinot."

His eyes bulged.

"Don't tell me he's been up to something!"

"Lord, no," I said. "We think he knows someone who might give us some information—that's all. What I want is a word with him in his room."

"He's on in fifteen minutes," he told me. "Can't you wait till after his act?"

"What happens after his act?"

"He has some dinner brought in from outside and has it in his room. Then he makes an appearance in the finale. That's at nine thirty-five."

I said that'd suit me down to the ground and meanwhile I'd have a look at the show. He told me which way to take, and then he even took me himself and handed me over to an attendant. Then he had a last word before he scurried away. I was to mind how I handled Bobinot. He was damnably temperamental.

I was shown to a seat at the back of the pit stalls. A pillar obscured my view, which was probably why it wasn't sold, but it suited me well enough for it was at the end of a row.

One of the spectacular scenes was on and then at last came Bobinot.

Everything was as I had seen it that Sunday at the Charity Show, and only in very small details did the business vary. To me it was something vastly different, for over it hung the shadow of a murder. So heavy did that shadow hang that never once did I laugh. Around me there were shrieks of laughter, but most of the time my eyes were closed and I was still trying to think. Then came the finale of the act and a terrific burst of applause. Bobinot came on again and again, and then the roar died away and there was a hush. Then came the stirring as the curtain fell on the interval. The lights went up. I made for the attendant who'd showed me to my seat.

"When did this show first come on?" I asked her, and she said it was early in June.

That was all, and I went on through and round. I waited for best part of ten minutes when the curtain was rising again. Then I caught sight of a boy and asked for Bobinot's room. He gave me a scared look, and I told him I'd seen Mr. Crole about it and I had an appointment. He asked for my name and he didn't get the right one. Then he took me as far as the door. When he'd gone I waited for a moment before I gave a knock. Then I didn't knock for I caught sight of an attendant coming with a tray. So I walked on instead and round the end of the corridor. The attendant came out and I went back. A moment, and I knocked.

"*Entrez!*"

I entered. Bobinot, still in his full rig-out, was seated at a side-table on which was the large dinner tray. He looked up and his hands were motionless; held as it were in full air. Then he spoke. It was a squeaky sort of voice.

"You wish, what is it?"

"You are M'sieur Bobinot?"

"I am Bobinot." He gestured, palms upward. "I am busy. Cannot I eat my dinner! You want, what is it?"

I gave him my warrant card. He looked at it, held it at arm's length, then grimaced as he handed it back.

"To me it is nothing. Later, perhaps, I see you when I have finished my dinner."

"I am sorry," I said, "but I must see you now."

"Must? But it is I who say must. You must go. I must eat my dinner. Afterwards, perhaps, you come back."

I smiled. The comedy had been played.

"Why go on fooling," I told him. "I'm Ludovic Travers, and you know it. You're Frank Merlin, and I know it. So now let's talk."

The gesture had been halted. The hands were falling. One more look at me and Bobinot was a punctured toy balloon.

CHAPTER XVI
IN AT THE KILL

MERLIN HAD BROKEN DOWN and had not been able to utter a word. I slipped out and found Crole again, and I asked him if it was absolutely essential that Bobinot should appear in that finale. He had valuable information for us and he and I ought to go at once. He thought for a bit and said it might be managed.

"If I said no, you'd flash that card of yours and take him," he told me, and I said it was hardly as crude as that. Then I thanked him and hurried back to Bobinot's room. He had dried his eyes and taken off his wig, and the bulbous nose, and now he was having a wash in the corner basin. I told him to leave his dinner. We'd go out and have a meal and a talk elsewhere. But he insisted on going out in the black wig and moustache that changed him, as far as the theatre was concerned, from Merlin to Bobinot. As soon as we were in a taxi I told him to put them in his pocket. Where we were going, nobody would mind if he was Montgomery or George Robey. Holt, by the way, had been sent back to collect his partner in Garris Street and I told him I shouldn't need a report.

We went to a little place in Soho where Bernice and I often went. We had a preliminary drink and Merlin was beginning to be less deflated, though still subdued. I still won't tell how I knew exactly what I knew. When the meal came he said he had no appetite but I literally made him eat, and I noticed he wasn't so shy about the wine. Slowly and after a deal of prodding, I got the whole thing out of him.

It had been Audrey's idea.

"I've got a scheme, daddy. Why should you go on being dependent on mother's money? Why not make some of your own? A lot of your own?"

Then she had broached the scheme, which had its origin in the famous act of Grock, and yet was to be no plagiarism.

"I *had* been a concert pianist in my young days," Merlin said, and drew himself up with the first show of his old cock-sureness. "I was once the soloist in the Mendelssohn No. 1 in G Minor at the old Queen's Hall. That's what she reminded me about. I thought it was going to be something of the same sort and when she told me what it was, I was horrified. You didn't know her, did you?"

I said I'd never seen her except on the screen.

"It was no use," he said. "She had a way with her and you couldn't resist her. She'd had that back-cloth painted and she started teaching me the act. I hated it to the very marrow. I was ashamed. I knew it was a horrible come-down. Then I began to get interested. I even began to contribute ideas of my own, and I may tell you, my dear sir, that I've had experience. For three months we worked hard; every single minute she could spare from her work. Then the time came for a try-out for an agency and she actually hired the old Memorial Hall one afternoon at Camberwell."

He gave a dry, reminiscent smile.

"I was scared. I, who'd played in front of thousands and conducted some of the best provincial orchestras, was scared. But I got away with it. The act was booked and we tried it up North. Audrey worked that too when we were supposed to be on a holiday. It went over big and we got the booking for the Palliceum show."

"She booked that office in Carris Street?"

"Arranged the whole thing, my dear sir. I used to use it as a half-way dressing-room. It's only a few yards from the theatre. Then of course we had to fabricate that story about an amateur orchestra. Beware of lies, my dear sir. The poet is still true about the tangled web. Or don't you know the quotation?"

I hurriedly said I did. And I was asking him why he'd thought it necessary to hide himself away in Carris Street. He looked a bit sheepish.

"It was on account of your wife?" I said. "You were afraid the police would ask you for an alibi or something like that and the whole story would come out?"

"That was it," he said. It would have shocked his wife beyond bearance if she had learned the truth. And Audrey, who had promised optimistically to put everything right, was no longer there. So he had bolted, so to speak, and hoped that in a short time the murderer would be found and there'd be no fear of the police troubling him. He'd slipped away after the reading of the will because of the afternoon's matinée.

"And wasn't there another reason why you didn't want the truth to get out about Bobinot?" I said with a meaning smile. "You hadn't been talking just a bit too largely about your prospects among your old acquaintances? To put it vulgarly, spreading your weight around?"

There was another slight deflation, but I didn't labour the point. And if there were oddments about himself and his act that he hadn't told me, they could wait till a more convenient time. I wanted to hear just how much he knew of that barmaid scheme. And, as I thought, he knew everything.

He had been as keen as she on her getting that Jinny Patman part. They even had a fanciful idea of her going to Hollywood and he to the States with his act, though ostensibly to be a kind of guardian-chaperone.

"You give me your version of what she was supposed to do," I said, and now he was off the subject of himself, he was voluble enough.

Everything followed the pattern we had traced. He had had a private inspection of the Seven Bells and had looked in once or twice in his free time when she was there. All there was to the scheme was a synchronisation with Kraaf's arrival. Kraaf was to be induced to go to the Seven Bells and Audrey would unmask as we thought. And also at The Croft she'd have been making her own study of the part.

That was when I warned him that what I was going to tell him was in the strictest confidence, and then he was hearing the story of how she came to Bill Ellice's office and fabricated a tale about a robbery at The Croft. Then she was going to fake that robbery and disappear, and profit from the resultant publicity.

"Did you know anything about that?" I asked him.

He swore that he'd known never a word. And it wasn't like Audrey not to have told him. Not that she hadn't an inventive mind. Look how she'd invented that act of his—not that he hadn't contributed something himself.

"Leave it," I said, "and look at it this way. It's the crux of the whole murder. Her story was a fabricated one. She wasn't murdered by spivs or toughs. She was murdered by someone who wanted her murdered or thought he was forced to shoot. *But*—and I want you to remember that *but*—there *was* a fake robbery at The Croft. Therefore someone must have been wise to her scheme. Someone knew what she was going to do, and that someone profited by it to commit murder and then fake the robbery. *Did you know?*"

"But I've told you I didn't know!" His voice had risen and I had to hush him down. "I'd swear I didn't know."

"Then do you know anyone who'd be likely to know?"

He didn't.

"What about her husband?"

He reminded me that she'd even kept The Croft a secret from him. He himself had been her only confidant for months. I didn't tell him that Wyster had learned about The Croft at the last moment through June Harboard.

And that's where things petered out. Our meal was finished and over the coffee I ventured to give him some advice.

"I want you to take this in the right way," I said. "You're an older man than I and you may think me unpardonably presumptuous, but why not tell your wife the whole truth? Tell her Bobinot was Audrey's scheme and yours. What's it matter what so-called friends and acquaintances think? I'll wager a good many would like to be in Bobinot's shoes. And if you want any moral support, let me know and I'll come along and lend a hand in smoothing things down with your wife. I have an idea she'd listen to me."

He was all resolution at once. That very night he'd go home and make a clean breast. The moment he could get his bag from Carris Street.

"You go back to Carris Street and sleep there for the last time and think things over," I said. "And when you do talk to your wife, take a stand on Bobinot. He's a national possession. It'd be criminal to do away with Bobinot."

"You think so?" he said, and his eyes lighted.

"I'm sure of it," I told him. "So is everyone who's seen the act. It's the greatest thing since Grock. In some ways it even beats Grock. And there's more to it than that. You owe it as a duty to Audrey."

"Yes," he said, and was quiet for a minute. A lip was beginning to quiver and I hustled him to his feet. The world, I said, was going to be a good place from then on. The bill was paid and we went out to find a taxi. It took him to Carris Street where we said good night, and he wrung my hand so hard that I could still feel the grip when I got out at my flat.

It was just short of eleven o'clock and I walked into a scene of domesticity and drowsy peace. The electric fire was on and Bernice had one easy chair and George had the other. She was knitting and he had a bottle of beer and his pipe. He said he'd dropped in on the off chance at about ten and had kept Bernice company till I saw fit to return.

He tried to pull my leg about the state the flat must have been in when she walked into it, but there wasn't a joke to be got out of it, so warmly was I defended and praised. Then we were left to ourselves, for she was tired after the long train journey.

"Bernice is too good for you," George said. "Never a word as to where you'd been and never a thing about being away half the night. Where *have* you been, by the way?"

As soon as I told him, he was pricking up his ears. That Bobinot business hadn't meant to him what it had meant to me, for he had never seen the act, and he was only mildly interested in what I might call the unmasking of Merlin. What he was interested in was just what Merlin knew about Maudie Brown. I told him everything I'd gleaned and it's an understatement to say that he was disappointed.

"Merlin's eliminated, and that's something," I said.

It might have been, but it wasn't enough.

"You hit the nail on the head," he said, "when you told him what the crux of the matter was. Someone *must* have known about that plan for a fake robbery and disappearance. Now if he'd known it, he might have blabbed. He's a talker, you say, and still doesn't mind a drink. Wyster might have given him a few drinks and loosened his tongue." His eyes popped a bit. "Why shouldn't that be it! Wyster got him talking and Merlin was too tight to remember it afterwards."

"No harm in seeing Merlin again," I said. "But you're the one who'd better do it this time. But if there's nothing to it, then what?"

He could only shrug his shoulders. If Merlin hadn't known and hadn't blabbed, then who on earth could have known that Maudie Brown was going to fake that robbery and disappearance. Audrey herself could never conceivably have told a soul.

Then we said tomorrow was another day and maybe something might turn up even if nothing had happened at the Carr's Hill end and nothing whatever had been picked up about that second car. As for the morning, it promised a day of standing by for both of us. If Wyster's alibi could be broken at all, it was only through that second car. Even the Palmer's Green end had failed us. Wyster had said and Merril Holme had corroborated, that he had gone straight from his flat to her maisonette. But her garage lay well back from the road and we could find no one who had seen the car parked in the driveway outside it. Wyster had admitted to Wharton that he had stayed at the maisonette all night and had left at about nine the next morning. But that end wasn't of consequence. We didn't need evidence to tell us when the car had gone away; what we wanted, and urgently, was to know just when it arrived.

George went home and I went to bed, and I slept as well as ever I've slept in my life. In fact I was still asleep when Bernice roused me for the early morning cup of tea. I hadn't even heard her making it.

"Well, here we are back to normal again," I remarked sententiously as I sipped the scalding tea. "Living alone's no life for any man."

"That reminds me," she said. "You know, darling, I'd never let you down in front of George Wharton, but what on earth have you been doing with your clothes? I went through them while you were out last night. There was one suit that actually looked as if you slept in it."

"Must have been those damn fairies," I said. The fairies are the excuse for every untoward happening in our household.

"The fairies didn't crease that best tussore suit," she said. "It was so bad that I pressed it at once myself. You'll find it in the wardrobe."

I said that was very nice of her. And now it was pressed, it might as well be packed away from the moths.

"But aren't you going to wear it? Look what a lovely day it's going to be. It's easily your nicest suit and you always look so well in it."

"Butchered to make a Travers' holiday," I said, and then added quickly that maybe it would be hot again, and I might as well put it on.

"There was a sheet of note-paper in the inside pocket," she said, "but I left it there. It looked as if you'd begun to write me a letter and hadn't had the time to finish it."

And then the tone subtly changed. The question had just the faintest brittle edge. If you're a married man you'll know what I mean.

"There were the queerest marks all over it. They couldn't have been lipstick?"

"My God!" I said, and was suddenly getting out of bed. "It's that letter I was writing in Bill Ellice's office!"

I, told her as much as I dared but what was worrying me was how I was going to explain to Wharton. Of all the dolt-headed fools I was the worst. There we'd been, hunting the Seven Bells for a finger-print of Maudie Brown's and all the time I'd probably had one in that pocket.

I did put on that suit and after a leisurely breakfast I went along to the Yard. Wharton was there, and busy doing very little, and when he'd finished telephoning to Glass I gave him that unfinished letter. I explained the circumstances and said airily that I didn't suppose there'd be a Maudie print on it. If there did happen to be one, then it might be useful as a sort of final clinching for the records.

Neither of us had any ideas and after an hour I left. It was a Saturday, and Merlin would have a matinée.

"Get this Case off your mind for a bit," I told him. "Perhaps we've both been living too close to it and that's why we're getting stale on ideas. Go and see Bobinot and drop in on Merlin after the show."

He didn't seem too keen, though that was probably a pose. I said if he didn't like Bobinot's act I'd stand him the best dinner in town.

"That isn't saying much," he told me. "Still, I may drop in. There might be something in what you say."

I went home and, while Bernice cleaned out the corners that I'd missed, got down to some arrears of private business. It was about an hour later when the telephone went.

"That you, Travers?" Wharton's voice was urgent.

"Yes," I said.

"Get along here quick! Something's turned up."

"Right," I said, and before I could ask a single question, he'd rung off.

I rang Bernice at midday to say I shouldn't be in till the evening meal, and then George and I went on with our rehearsal. In the afternoon I had a stroll in the Park to get my mind off things, and I went out to tea. Just before five o'clock I was back at the Yard. Wharton was there and everything was set. Wyster and Merril Holme arrived together and we kept them waiting for a minute or two. Merlin and Holberg were not due till six o'clock. James Holme was standing by and mightn't be wanted, but we'd ring him as soon as we knew.

"Well, let's get it over," George said, and pressed the buzzer. I took a modest seat in the corner as became a subordinate.

George laid his spectacle case nice and handy, and moved a paper or two within easy reach. He looked perfectly unperturbed. My heart was beginning to race a bit as it always does when we get to the climax of a Case.

Wyster and Merril Holme were being ushered in. Wharton got to his feet. There were apologies but this time there was no effusion. There wasn't a handshake and he merely indicated the two chairs. Merril and Wyster were looking rather like two boys with guilty consciences who've been summoned to the Head's room and are wondering just how much he knows.

"I hope I shan't keep you very long," Wharton said. "It was too bad of us to eat into your scanty time between the two shows. Still, it had to be done."

Neither said a thing. In fact there was nothing to say.

"It's probable," Wharton went on, "that you'll think we've been wasting your time. All I ask you to believe is that we have our motives for most things."

On went the spectacles and he was picking up a sheet of paper.

"We go to work sometimes in a curious way," he said. "For instance, we often work out what might be called a hypothetical case against nobody in particular. We ask that person to do us the favour of coming along and listening to that case, and picking all the holes in it he possibly can. That seems pretty curious to you, I expect, but it's the holes we're after. They're the things that give us ideas—new ideas."

He had another look at the sheet of notes.

"For instance, we've asked you two kind people to do much the same thing this afternoon. Neither of you had a thing to do with the murder of Mrs. Wyster, so you can't possibly take this the wrong way." The fatherly smile was turned on me. "Now who's the one to be tried out first?"

"Well, ladies first," I said gallantly. "That's a sound rule."

"Well, if Miss Holme agrees?"

Merril had been frowning and no wonder. That verbiage of Wharton's had been a hotchpotch of the soothing, the disturbing and the bewildering. Now she gave a rather tepid smile.

"That's fine," Wharton said heartily. "We'll pretend then that Miss Holme has done certain things, and it's up to her—and to Mr. Wyster, of course—to point out the flaws and raise objections. Be as rude as you like and as blunt as you like."

A playful peer over the spectacle tops and he was having another quick look at his notes.

"At just before eleven o'clock on a certain Thursday night," he began, "the lady we'll call Audrey Grange was murdered. She was killed, and someone killed her. Let's imagine that Miss Holme killed her—"

"Why?" asked Wyster, and his tone already had an edge.

"For two imaginary reasons," Wharton told him calmly. "Because she was determined to have the part of Jinny Patman herself—"

"But that's silly!"

Wharton's eyebrows lifted humorously.

"There you are," he said to me. "I told you Miss Holme would get the hang of things. But why is it silly?"

"As if anyone would murder anyone for a reason like that!"

"Well, there's still another reason. Because you also wanted to marry her husband."

"Isn't that rather bad taste?"

Wharton looked hurt. He looked at me and he looked at her. "But surely this cuts both ways. You can be as rude—shall I say— to us as you like. Then why can't we be a bit rude to you? As for bad taste—well, for the life of me I can't see it. Wouldn't it have been in far worse taste if I'd reminded you that Mr. Wyster spent at least one whole night at your house?"

"You're surely not implying—"

"It's what a jury or a divorce court judge would think," cut in Wharton. "I'm no moralist, but to call marriage bad taste and ignore the other thing—well, it doesn't make sense. But leave it. Let's come to how we imagine it might have been done."

"I don't like this," Wyster suddenly said. "There's something unreal about it."

"The hypothetical is often unreal," Wharton told him. "It isn't unreal, though, to imagine that Miss Holme *might* have gone straight from the theatre to Carr's Hill by Tube and train and have been there before eleven."

"But why?"

She was looking ruffled and just a bit scared. She gave a quick look at Wyster but her eyes went straight through me.

"All sorts of excuses," Wharton said airily. "You'd been spending the evening with friends nearby and you'd only just heard she was there and you just had to drop in, late as it was."

"That's absurd." She gave a little toss of the head. "Besides, I wasn't aware she was at Carr's Hill."

"Wyster, there, *might* have told you," Wharton reminded her. "He knew. But it's a good point. Let's go on to how she might have been killed. You two didn't like each other a lot. There might have been words. You might have thought she was going to attack you. She might have threatened you with a gun, and you struggled and the gun went off and shot her. Those things *might* have happened."

"But they didn't."

"But why didn't they?"

"This is ridiculous!" She was appealing to Wyster again. "They didn't happen because I wasn't there. I was at home, and I've proved it."

"That's the kind of answer I like," Wharton told us amiably. "But let's get on to something else. Suppose you did kill her in some way? Why should you then fake a robbery?"

"That's simple," Wyster said, and his lip curled. "Anyone in a situation like that would have tried to divert suspicion. A burglary was the obvious thing."

"Excellent!" Wharton told him. "But if that is so, how do we reconcile it with the fact that Audrey Grange had announced—well before she was murdered—that her house was going to be burgled and her car and jewellery taken? I refer, of course, to the statement she made in the office of that detective agency. You're both familiar with that. I read it to you myself, and assured you it was true."

Wyster threw up his hands in a gesture of bewilderment. Merril shrugged her shoulders—then thought of something.

"She might have told somebody about it herself. Why not her step-father?"

She was looking round at Wyster. He gave a little gesture of agreement.

"A capital point," Wharton told me. "You might make a note of it."

More play with his notes, and then the glasses came off. He rubbed his eyes with a synthetic weariness.

"It would be absurd, of course, to imagine that Miss Holme knew that Audrey Grange was Maudie Brown. Still being strictly hypothetical, I suppose neither of you could suggest a link?"

Wyster could only shrug his shoulders again.

"What do you mean by a link?" Merril asked.

"Well, something to prove that the still hypothetical Merril Holme did actually know that Audrey Grange was Maudie Brown."

"You certainly ask some queer questions," she told him, and ventured on another smile. "The whole thing still seems absurd. I hope that doesn't sound too rude."

"Not a bit of it," Wharton assured her.

Then he was turning to me.

"Another idea we did have. You know more about this than I do, Travers. Just show Miss Holme, will you?"

"It's nothing, really," I said as I went to the desk. "But would you mind coming here just for a moment, Miss Holme? You recognise this as the statement you made about your whereabouts on that Thursday night?"

Wharton handed it to her and she took it. She frowned, then there was a little titter with her smile.

"But, of course."

"It's the actual document you signed?"

"Of course it is."

"That's amazing," I said, and pointed to that spoilt letter of mine that lay by Wharton's hand. "When Maudie Brown was in Ellice's office, she handled that sheet of paper. It lay on the table by her bag. It has her finger-prints on it. And they're the same as those on that statement. *In fact they're both yours!* In other words it was you who impersonated Maudie Brown."

Wharton was on his feet. Merril's hand went forward to the table and her face was suddenly a deathly white. She was trying desperately to keep a hold on herself. Then she swayed, and before I could get to her she pitched sideways. There was a thud—it was almost a crack—as her head struck the edge of Wharton's desk.

CHAPTER XVII
EPILOGUE

THIS IS our case against Merril Holme as we prepared it for the D.P.P. I am writing this, by the way, some days after what happened that late afternoon in Wharton's room, but nothing has been done about a possible trial, and this is why. That blow on the head ruptured blood vessels leading to the brain. There was cerebral haemorrhage, in other words, and partial paralysis affecting one side of the body. The doctors still think there's just a chance of an almost complete recovery, but at the moment she's a pretty bad risk.

Here then are synopses of the evidence, but only of what you've not hitherto heard. Everything not strictly relevant has been omitted and the synopses themselves are the barest bones.

STATEMENTS, etc.

(a) *Statement by Harlan Wyster.*

I *had* told Merril Holme where my wife was. On that Thursday night it was not Merril, as I stated, but my wife—or so I then thought—who rang me and asked me to come at once to Carr's Hill. Her voice was very low and urgent, and I went there at once in my car. I arrived to find her car gone and the house absolutely dark. June Harboard had sent me a spare key to the bungalow, thinking Audrey might need it, but when I thought of looking inside and felt in my pocket for the key, I couldn't find it. Naturally I didn't think the door was open. What I thought was that she'd changed her mind, so I went back home. I did think I heard another car while I was there but I thought it had turned into one of the bungalows the other side of the rise. While I was there I did hear a sound like a whimpering baby and I confess that it gave me the creeps.

I didn't go straight home but decided to talk it over with Merril. She had no explanations but she did induce me to stay the night. A day or so later I found that key to the bungalow and in one of the pockets where I'd looked, and it made me wonder. There was also the matter of why the gate to Merril's garage had been open that night so that I could drive straight in. She said it was because she'd have rung me up in any case and asked me to come as she was feeling lonely.

When the news of the murder was told me, I at once had suspicions, but by that time I was too deeply involved myself. Merril had begged me not to mention that I had been with her since it might injure her reputation. Then gradually I felt as if I was being caught up in a web of lies, and when Merril suggested that faking of the times as an alibi, it seemed the best way out and I was only too ready to agree.

Enquiries about detective agencies had been Wharton's idea. Merril had had to know exactly what Audrey was doing at The Croft, and in order to be able to carry out that impersonation in Ellice's office, she must have studied Maudie Brown. So we tried every agency that advertised and Wharton made short work of the plea of professional secrecy as an excuse for not giving information about a client.

(b) *Statement by Levit and Waterham, Enquiry Agents.*

A lady, whom we cannot positively identify as the original of the photograph shown to us, came here and said she had seen our advertisement in a certain Sunday paper and would we watch and report on the movements of a certain Mrs. Wyster of The Croft, Carr's Hill. We furnished a very full report to the address given and received payment in cash.

The Mrs. Wyster turned out to be a barmaid at the Seven Bells, Witney Street, and we kept her under observation both there and at Carr's Hill for a period of ten days, when the client called and settled her account.

(It should be added that the client's address was an accommodation one, and that information about Maudie Brown included the morning visits to Porelli's.)

(c) *Statement by James Everhard Holme* (Before he was aware that his sister was implicated).

The reason for the coolness between my sister and myself was a suggestion she made to me about Audrey, and which I strongly resented. She put it to me in the most cynical way that if I compromised Audrey, Wyster would divorce her and I could marry her. Knowing Merril as I did, I suspected an ulterior motive—that she was making a pawn of me in a damnably dirty way, so that she herself could marry Wyster.

(d) *Statement by Arthur Kidford, Manager of Red Robins, Ltd.* Merril Holme was a member of our No. 1 Company for three years and played Torquay, Weston-super-Mare and Ilfracombe. Her impersonations were particularly good and she had a repertoire of about ten stage and screen stars, all women. She also had one of a Cockney servant.

VARIOUS EXHIBITS including the annotated copy of *Number Thirty,* and the identical finger-prints of Merril Holme and Maudie Brown. It was lucky for us, by the way, that Merril had taken off a glove when she had signed that statement.

In view of all the above we come to—

THE CASE AGAINST MERRIL HOLME

Put very briefly, that case was this. When she knew Audrey Grange was Maudie Brown, she knew the reason. As for motives for the killing, they were mainly two—beyond a general hatred. Killing her would give a chance of the Jinny Patman part to herself, and that part would have meant a chance of world fame and something of a fortune. It would also give her the chance to marry Wyster, with whom she was absolutely infatuated.

Using a disguise that made her an older woman perhaps—a big bust and a temporary darkening of the blonde hair, for instance—she certainly went to the Seven Bells and saw Audrey-Maudie for herself. In conjunction with the agency report, she made a study of her, and so evolved her scheme. That Thursday being Maudie's day off, Audrey would be at Carr's Hill, and so it wasn't too hard to plan so that Maudie should never be seen again. Hence the visit to Ellice's office and the story. That story would cover the subsequent killing and robbery. Neither Travers nor Ellice had ever seen the real Maudie, and neither would ever see her, and so far there was no real risk. Travers never saw the slightest resemblance between the made-up Maudie and Merril Holme. In Travers' company Merril took care to make up hardly at all. Then her hair was blonde and her bosom comparatively flat, and she wore hats to heighten her face.

The actual killing is surmise, but if she had gone to Carr's Hill that night and her courage had failed her, then no real harm would have been done, except that Maudie might have been questioned by myself or Ellice when she turned up as usual at the Seven Bells, and then there would have been a mystery indeed. But all one can surmise about the killing is that Merril hoped to find Audrey asleep. But she wasn't. When Merril quietly let herself in with Wyster's key, Audrey heard a sound. Then Merril had to shoot, for she had no ready excuse to explain her presence. Then she faked the robbery as foreshadowed, took the car and jewellery and bag and later left the car at Highbury. What happened to the other things we don't know, but likely spots for hiding them are being searched. Then after leaving the car she took the Tube or a bus home, and was there when Wyster arrived.

Meanwhile she had made things awkward for him. She had rung him as his wife and sent him to Carr's Hill. Maybe she had intended to leave the front door locked so that he couldn't have entered the house if he had tried except through a window. But she forgot it in her desperate hurry. Or she mayn't have worried if he did find the body. She knew him for something of a coward, and that he'd probably be afraid of admitting that he'd been near the bungalow that night. But she also rang the flats subsequent to the murder, so as to make sure that if the police did make enquiries they'd discover that he had been out.

Later she begged him not to say a word because of where he had actually spent the night. She took command, in fact. She let him get almost to a state of panic and then extricated him by an apparent sacrifice of her reputation. After that, as she almost certainly calculated, he could do no less than marry her. In fact he'd have had to marry her. And remember that his alibi was also her own.

Those, as I have said, are the barest bones of the case. When we looked back, as you can look back, we found a score of pieces of evidence that we now scarcely needed in view of the damning comprehensiveness of those fingerprints. Wharton, and he ought by this time to be a good enough judge, was sure we had enough to secure a conviction, and we're hoping to have even more. I mean, of course, if Merril Holme ever comes up for trial. A few minutes ago George rang for the latest news and that news was that her condition was much the same. For my part I think that even if she gets back the use of her body, with a slight paralysis remaining and that twisted face, then that'll be a worse hell than any she'd be likely to find after a hanging, and that sort of recovery is all the most optimistic of the doctors hope for—if hope's the right word.

And so that's about all—except Merlin. Maybe you'd like to hear more about Merlin.

Wharton didn't go to see him on that Saturday night as you may well imagine, but he did go a night or two ago, and he grudgingly admitted the next morning that I wouldn't have to stand him that dinner. But he did have to have a kind of sideways kick at me.

"I thought you said that wife of his was dead against him being connected with anything to do with the stage. A bit wide of the mark, weren't you?"

"How do you mean?" I said.

"Well, he's living at home, isn't he? Isn't that where we took his statement? And didn't he say in front of his wife it was getting on for time to go to the theatre?"

I didn't tell him that I'd seen Mrs. Merlin long before that, for what she and I, and then she and I and Merlin, had talked about is nobody's business.

"Dammit, George!" I said. "You of all people ought to know it's a woman's prerogative to change her mind. If the truth were known, that's one of women's main attractions."

"Being a bit plausible, aren't you?" he told me. "You're not the only one who makes mistakes, you know."

I gave a grunt that might have been his own.

"All right then, George," I said. "I made a mistake and I hope it won't be my last. But talking of mistakes reminds me of something. When are we going to pay that threatened visit of yours to Mabel Ganton?"

THE END

www.ingramcontent.com/pod-product-compliance
Lightning Source LLC
Chambersburg PA
CBHW031014190726
48286CB00003BA/833